King   Monkey's   Hedophilia

Negel Narcolep

About the Book

Possessed by the spirits of himself, Jove Nobody disintegrates into constituent parts whose incarnations squabble among themselves just as before. Perverse Hedophilia likewise wages war unseen against uncharted Atlantis and its principled horde of landlocked desert fish who fight with naught but grit for lack of material wealth: a double edged boggy muck that blinds the common Hedo to the war they do not even know to be fighting.

Thud, thud, thud, you agents of Neurotypicles, and the thing that comes knocking is you! Individuation waxes easy to the individual what for two is an eternal cahoots of bloody murder and the screaming of it. That is to say, more than one is two plus bedlam and the thin line between. Lo! Will there ever come a leader to unite the cosmos that hates itself? Bah, but King Monkey has buggered off elsewhere and only his dollar remains!

Dear Reader, taste words on the page and give consciousness unto them; experience just as Jove Nobody the futility of wrestling with identity and the world spirit.

ISBN: 978-1-969241-00-0

Prologue

Muttered from the Universal Mind Palace

Amid the desolation of the Arena, there is aught but a spark, a kindling nigh bright as the midnight moon in the vast expanse of space. And huddled around the effigy — at the top of which lies the skull of a goat transfused to that of a man's — are, perhaps, an individual of multidimensional consciousness and his many aspects, all of whom watch the flames careen upward, granting tentative life to the recently deceased corpse, but fizzling at the eye sockets sparkling brighter than whence alive, and reaching no farther, lest they challenge the sun itself. Pray tell, what quantity of half-desiccated skulls need reach the heavens and how long would the fire of salvation burn, provided the effort not topple in futility and rain literal death on the world in fiery armageddon, snuffing the lives of stragglers late to the pyre but due all the same? In search of an answer to this dreadful query, consider the following conjecture:

Monkeys are said to think quickly on their feet, for there they possess prehensile toes and may thus count them for the purpose of arithmetic. Far removed from nature and the very world of Katsikoskoni, in this proverbial pyre does humanidkind (humid humans of the id) acquit thinking and balance. Had they learned to walk atop both hands they could, perchance, avert such crises, but such a concept is far too nuanced for the modern clubfoot thinker and bootstrap fetishist, let alone he of the ass bound by agricultural sedentarism and its forthcoming machinations: the modern office swivel chair; 'tis a daft invention of many wheels and nary an intended destination save where it sits, akin to the fudgel-curmudgeon it serves and his many toes, both dead in function and due for fire, O blasphemers all. And if toes may die, if not gradually consumed by necrosis, how too does the liver die? What of the lungs and heart, the brain? How may it be fatally struck, cleansed in fire, and struck again?

What lives in the brain? It is a well-known fact

men are beholden to the congenital aggressive impulsive disorder, abbreviated AID and common among lizards and monkeys, both. Women, alas, suffer from clinical hysteria, and while some may consider this diagnosis antiquated and defunct, it has simply been refurbished to Karenism among practitioners in the West: Karen, from the ancient root Aikaterine, meaning pure. This suggests such is the way we are (and) meant to be, and any attempt to sway from this fundamental fact of life culminates in impurity and a certain death of the mind, wherein this "impurity" is due for cleansing and fire. And in this sun-scorched desert, where near all succumb to heat, only the alleged schizophrenic and his alleged cohort of alleged individuals survive the onslaught of externalities, which, to each, a different perspective is required. Quiet is not calm. Calm is the welcome death.

Do you see the significance of this? Under the modern framework, we expect people-folk to succumb to brief periods of psychosis when, in fact, we psychomaniacs often endure prolonged periods of docility. Blind self-preservation encourages this inhibition, which is dreadfully dull. Be reckless, suicidal, even. But I do not blame some of you for thinking otherwise; denialism is denihilism. Go amble, you blighters. I will be here, rambling, and the pyre will burn however long you need, forever trapped in the annals of time — so did it happen and so will it always have been, like a fossil on the page approximating the story as it might have been. The remaining ideators may stay. Or perhaps it is the amblers that would hear this. How lucky am I not to hear your prospective disagreements and lamentations. In turn, you endure mine. What joy. Suffer the injustice without recourse, for justice is, at worst, a rhetorical replacement for order. The law people really pulled a masterful hoodwink. But alas, like a driftwood colonizer spore who thought himself indigenous to the place he found himself but later discovered otherwise, we lose nothing in the epiphany of predetermination. Let ring the great "Meh!" Just as a freely willful convict might face justice for his wrongdoing, the cog will come under the hammer of order, even if it has a family of coglings. Meh! Let us separate out from church and state into church and church of the dollar! Meh!

But lo! There is yet another predilection, Aeroscorpion's: on whose outstretched wings of rippling and cascading silk carry a burden, a grief, for if he knew he would not find his comrade, he would fly the barrens ever still, if only to quell the voices and remain as one, a foolish ordeal. On the horizon the pyre burns, releasing the huffs of eons of innocents until recently calcified in an array of brambles, their ashes soon to reinfest the reaches of Katsikoskoni like a cancer or sporous fungus. The great amalgam is inevitable, for at the base of this fire is long-lost Jove, a man of light-dark complexion with a penchant for some, if not all, things thing-like — or not. Meh!

Aeroscorpion spans his wings and beats at the earth, homing slowly on the revelers as moth to flame, and takes stock of the humanid and his many asinine personae, settling for whichever one smells the most familiar, one of blood and unkempt crevices, impulse and anger, the lot. Leathery wing flaps curl into a loaf beside friend, Aeroscorpion's beady face staring longingly at the time lost within sun-damaged wrinkles and hazy eyes.

Jove strokes gently from scalp to spine and tail, eliciting a purr most akin to that of a house cat, or any cat, really. To Aeroscorpion is offered on weathered hands a morsel of indeterminate birth, a fish of sorts, from the hearty kebab of Jove. The winged one, head crooked and outstretched, inspects the smell before sweeping tongue across the breadth, timidly at first but with increasing eagerness, ultimately committing fish to teeth and gullet, sated. Meat carries a memory, and this one was a fish, its carcass in the sand over yonder dune. Aeroscorpion divines little more, like a necrotic eyeball not fully connected to the brain, or else he'd see the lot, its life, its story.

That is to say, Aeroscorpion did not know of fish because he remembered it but because he had been fish; and in tasting / smelling / observing it, Aeroscorpion psychically took fish into himself. As but a single dimension and node, he could only hope to achieve a fraction of the perspective of his comrade. He sat there reminiscing of this fellow he consumed, hoping to understand more of its origin, almost in prayer. The bonfire smells of smoky coal. Embers flicker and fade into the surrounding dark, and some plummet onto standers-by and scorch the skin, a therapeutic soothing on weathered flesh like a fiery suture on the open wound of the soul.

Taken aback, Aeroscorpion stares longingly at Jove as if to ask where he'd been and what happened in his own absence. Jove stays a moment, idle and expressionless, his gaze piercing the aerial Atlantean's flappy blubber. It is as if, in this moment, he dissociated from his very body, ascended far away, leaving but a breathing husk, a seldom blinking corpse akin to that of a squashed yet twitching spider, or perhaps this was always so; perhaps Jove's lifelong animation was but a coincidental twitching, moving, speaking, and willing of a corpse long deceased operating on the last of frayed wires. Two hands, belonging to one of Jove's aspects, spasm forward toward

Aeroscorpion, clamping ahold of the curvature of his carapace, slimy yet calloused in places. The humanid's neck wrings violently to attach mouth to mouth and spews heftily into his compatriot a forceful transfer and reliving of the following memories:

I

Book of Jove

I am prey to a great melancholy ill defined by even learned men: I count each wretched day. It is now morning of the thirteenth day of the tenth month (of the year 1950 of our king, or O.K.). Yes, I do count them all, mundane as they are. I'm not quite sure what I'm counting down to . . . up to? Whatever it is, I have a feeling something will come of it and only then will I know what it is. Or it could be I'm waiting for all the days of existence itself to elapse so finally and ultimately that I might never exist again. Hopeful, I know, but I fear not even death is final; it's a dreadful feeling to have in the bustle of Hedophilia, its shining, humbling towers that, in their hubris, atomize even the stars above.

Partisans, artisans, or whatever they call themselves nowadays dance a busy nonsense, an erratic moving of the legs from one place to the other; where the fuck are you going, the thought-thinking parlor to think thoughts? Un-sodding-likely. Of course, I'm not the only humanid that thinks — it would be conceited to think as much — but it's especially hard to imagine that's what they do when they bustle like crazed fish in a sea of their wallow, a smog of the mind that compels the common Hedo to emasculate themselves under thumb of the hand that grants them sip from a puddle of mortgages and good livin'. Oh, but what if I go to the streets? Here I am, and it is not so bad that it is the worst.

And as I preponder the weight of my sorrow, I notice the sky before me clouded by the dome of the Playhouse, a novel attraction that had not been there before — may as well pry. I mean to pay the fare and, try as I may, remain undetected to the naked eye of the clerk, who seems more the pensive than bustling type. I stare her down and think to myself this isn't worth the bother, for she is an enlightened soul and best left to her musings. I find on the counter a disparate copy of *The Playbook* and am well on my way. Thank you, O kindred one.

Thud, thud, thud, thud, thud!

It appears the opening act concluded with great applause. At everyone's lap is a bashing slab for bashing their skulls into. I was never fond of the practice. The cheer dies down with a thud, thud, thud. And so I seat myself; on center stage is this vile creature, and I mean it. This is the ugliest man-thing I've seen in my life. He is clean shaven, wears a suit, and keeps a ten-mile smile, the one that means to sell you something and later, behind closed doors, betrays you with bitter jabs to his family, like a dog eager to fetch and return juicy gossip. (Don't think I can't hear it, you puppet!) And this man, having brought to my doorstep the karma of millions of salespeople, will feel shock when I share with him my disgust for his kind. Only then, after my brief neuroticism, do I notice the strings from the ceiling puppeteering this man to dance. Serves you right. May as well be a woman with that shaven face of yours. I would heckle you if I wasn't so bloody cultured; I am indeed so cultured that I am of a different race — the antigen to your progenitor culture of hustling, bustling, justling, and smiling — and you the racist, for I am so far removed from the order of things that I might be an animal or alien, least of all a humanid.

Disturbed by a noise, I gauge my surroundings as to its origins. Be ye friend or be ye foe? Lo, raggedy peasant actors ascend a tower built into the wall where some attendees look on with great liegely interest. With their farm tools, they make a show of brutally murdering the puppeteer out of view. Perhaps the common Hedo has only the wherewithal to revolt in the sanctity of his imagination. Hm!

The mannequin man slumps below, his face made firmly accustomed with the ground on whose surface many a dusty boot has tread its heel. The suited man-thing rises slowly, bewilderedly, and, taking stock of his surroundings like a hazy-eyed newborn calf, dances the same dance as if that's what he would've done anyway regardless of the strings. 'Tis the nature of the puppet to serve and be docile, it seems.

This showing is painfully proletariat, but this is what passes for entertainment. Hell, I begrudge the boogers too and almost as much as the common Hedo for faithfully serving their masters — and maybe that's the point — but this is cheap, free, even. To investigate the purpose of things, I crack open *The Playbook*, but it is blank, or at least it might've been before I noticed a jumbled glaze of nonsense. I reckon this is part and parcel the experience. A sordid-looking fellow with freakishly pallid eyes takes note and draws uncomfortably close to me. There is a grating silence between the rustling of his bustling to my side and his next words that could bring anyone to murderous rage; out with it or off with you! (Yes, I see your cogs turning and you're not as clever as you think you're going to be.) The sickly fellow spoke thus, "This bloke's a sinner!" He stood there with peeping eyes that strained.

Interest sparks in the crowd of automatons as they come around to the spectacle of my misfortune, never mind a man had been murdered, albeit behind a curtain of plausible deniability and disbelief. Can you not see, O countrymen, that your neurons have fired astray?

A farmer in red flannel seizes *The Playbook*, reads it, and seems to have a thought: "This here feller is a sodomite and a gay, for shame," and shakes his head meaningfully. A snaky, long-necked individual with a suspicious mug also takes issue: "Methinks I see blood and murder. Phee! Couldn't be me." A rotund woman with pouty lips and an upturned nose in her shaggy coat sneers down at *The Playbook*, gasps womanishly and faints, dying.

What do they see that I don't? Are these commoners so wise in the ways of things that I am wrong in my perceptions and they are right? Why can't I simply intuit what they do from the page? I do not think I quite understand. And as I ponder the meaning of things, I am carried away. I see from my sideways glance the man yet dances; I know I am to face the judgment of King Monkey. Woe unto me!

Thud thud thud.

Dragged by the collar through muddy streets, I am brought before the courthouse that sits on the tallest hill around which is built a grand staircase; it is never the patricians who are seen climbing these stairs. Perhaps they live and grow fat on the hill in disgust of the common men who slither beneath them. Or it might be they sneak out at night for fear of being seen descending from anything, and before dawn climb again so they do not see and are thus not humbled by the great house imposing down on them. It is said when the sun shines on the golden dome, it burns away the pride of men; it is unfortunate they are composed of nothing else. Of course, few buildings, unlike the Playhouse, are still domed in this era of postmodernity. What should antiquity want with me today, I wonder?

The marble doors heave open with great distress; this too is an act and I am more annoyed than disconcerted by the conviction with which these inanimate objects play their parts, and that is nothing to say of the suit-wearing panel that looks at me with that sneering, narcissistic, cluster-B gleam in their eyes that reminds of the pallid man and perhaps every high-ranking disciple of King Monkey. "Where is your suit?" asks the particularly offended-looking one. Suit up, monkeys, with your monolith of culture that is black, drab, and common. I do not own one, but do not say as much, for this is not a game I wish to play — this choice I made before my coming here, a principled if unhealthy decision, to reject wholesale the influence of Hedophilia. Indeed, I hate suits in part because of the people who wear them: bureaucrats and money men — men of the money, insatiable canid humpers — who are in direct dichotomy to the whites of noble doctors and lab technicians; the former live to win and the latter to learn, not unless all play the politics of their king in disguise! Oh, how I curse the progenitors and fornicators of King Monkey's power-knowledge structures! (What do I know of sociology? Nothing that I know, which is to say if someone came along who was knowledgeable in such matters might they understand that which I do not know I do. Mumbling again, curses.) King Monkey . . . no, me: Jove Nobody! Nobody forbid I take on the countenance of a suit for my own!

At the center is an erratically shifting individual with a mole-like but indeterminate spec beside the lip that exudes a courtly demeanor; this is a child and judge-priest of the Great Organized Book Club. Or he may as well have been, in the grand cosmological sense of the development of a species, just such a child to think we can impose anything on anyone for any reason. Or perhaps I am the child for thinking this, for who am I, ever the hypocrite, to judge the ones who judge? And if not a hypocrite, mayhaps I am the vessel for a number of perspectives such that every nominal "hypocrisy" comes from a different place and is therefore no hypocrisy at all, but a conflict of the selves, to each owed a dusty corner of the mind.

In any case, this holder of office needs no qualifications, save that he be sufficiently judgmental. In the event he does not hold up to scrutiny, the loudest juror ousts and replaces him. Everyone is in silent agreement today. Well, I suppose they might all be children, the way they squabble for things to fill their pockets like mischievous squirrels. Heaven forbid I should one day sell anything to anyone and, in doing so, join their ranks. Oh, how I loathe to be of the same material plane, drawing from the same reservoir of axioms, nature's salty wellspring. Bah! I am muttering again, it seems.

The farmer had some time ago delivered *The Playbook* to the judge-priest who, in turn, passed it to the panel: "The club at present finds this reading material an affront to all things just, and you stink badly. Shame on you, mud-skin. You might even pass for an Ashkenigga in these parts." The jurors each express a muted surprise at the book, never mind the judge-priest, who continues, "Not the sharpest tool nor the palest Negro on the plantation neither." Misplacing his gavel, Judge-Priest Hedoberger slams *The Playbook* on the judicial altar. "Jove Nobody, you stand accused of somehow offending King Monkey, but his will is merciful and it is through him I speak. Repent, mister!" He grins malevolently; a nigh impenetrable, suffocating aura of superiority separates him from the attending rabble, and they, participating in the illusion, turn their noses down from him for fear they might be taken for thumbs.

I occupy a moment to remind myself that I am motivated neither by the carrot nor the stick, that I am an anomaly to myself. I am blessed only with the patience to wait out the performance. So be it, let us entertain the prospect in which I find myself beleaguered. In the game of rock-paper-sense, good sense beats the prior sense on paper, the written law, which, in turn, is carved into the stone that cracks the skull housing common sense. Disarmed of one, I am without legal counsel, so I raise a finger in meek objection although I might later regret not thinking to strangle someone with it.

"Oh, now hold on a moment! Won't someone provide this man a lawyer?"

"Can I do it?" cries one of the jurors with glee.

"Aw, shucks! I can't not do my job. It took a lot of humility to get me to swear on anything before taking office. Have at it!"

He hops to my side before presenting his swaying anus to the ceiling, supported only by his neck, remaining in this position for so long as I lay eyes on him, and until otherwise stated. He must have thought to console me: "Don't worry. I come from a land of snippy comebacks and exploitative practices. I will honor my lifeblood."

"What say you in your defense?" proclaims Hedoberger in the tradition of his people.

The man at my side begins, "If this is the land of opportunity, then we, the people, are the opportunities to be taken advantage of by other opportunists."

"Sound reasoning. Yes, I follow, I follow! Go on."

"Would you like to reconsider our expropriation of the products of the common man, that he might so much as subsist, even exist, in the perfumed shadow of the noble souls that are great and smart and such?"

To this, Hedoberger's features spread slowly into a flabbergasted, even disgusted countenance. "I didn't swear on the monkey dollar for you to undermine this democratic people's social circle. No," he mutters with a soft, disappointed dismissiveness, as if the reason why he'd disagreed was obvious to everyone in the room. The room nods in return.

"Aha, so let us bargain! How about a bribe? Would you like a bribe?" The lawyer vaults forth with every flip of his person and presents his anus to the judge-priest, who reaches into his pocket and dismisses him. The jurors plug their ears as he goes to and fro, returning as he was before, buttocks pointed to the ceiling at my side.

"Let's hope this works. A dirty fiver is all I'm worth." His bottom did not come down still.

The room sits silent with anticipation. Humidity wells in the center, the lowest point where I stand. It seems to radiate something fierce, I the center of the controversy. Then from nowhere, perhaps reminded by the heat or else inspired by it, the judge-priest's face flushes red with a great fury. "Contemptuous! Contemptuous devil! Seize him! The sentence is life!"

In your hubris you think to sentence me to life, but the honor is King Monkey's. It's not like I was living it up anyway — shows me what you know. Do you mean to give me a new one? (I am not particularly quick witted; I had this thought some time after my judgment and rewrote the canon of my mind; I am not so conceited to have imagined actually saying it, only thinking it.)

I suspect I am a paranoid individual. Just as a schizoid might evolve into the schizophrenic, I may one day perhaps sprout hallucinations from the unkempt places of my mind and live among them as equals. They will call me mad, or at least I think they will. They who? Whoever! Especially in the event an alien is reading my thoughts or I'm in some simulation for a supernatural being's amusement — or else my suffering might be for nothing — know this! I expected nothing less of the book club. I am so unbothered by this sequence of events in the same way I might not hold a grudge against the witless forces of nature that might endanger my life in any other way. I would not plead with the winds their dismantling of my home, nor the flood the drowning of my person, and neither would I beg of the Hedo to cease his involvement in my affairs. Of course, I'd never say it aloud, but I am proud and superstitious enough to relay this thought to the universe in the event someone out there would've thought me a fool otherwise. I occasionally take such precautions. And if I am a greater fool for having thought it, so be it. Gape at me with your peepers if you must, you foreign perverts. (And this is not exclusive to the telling of a story so much as a consideration for any sapient, non-omniscient life-form, I think to add.)

Oh, but of course I'm bothered! Not two seconds after the issuing of a command to calm my body does it redouble its anger. Does it, the fool, know better than I? Woe to me who thought to reason with myself, that I am angrier for it than if I surrendered to rage immediately. I would regret to give these Hedoes the satisfaction of anything; it is my one solace I do not show any such grievance on my face for them to guffaw at.

"Send him away!" The judge-priest enacts wrath upon the dusty altar, bashing his face into it like a gavel. The panel harrumphs in agreement and, producing their bashing slabs, make thuds. Their mouths froth with the lizard's gravy. I reckon a goblin is running 'round and he's scrambling everyone's eggs.

Squalls follow from a murder of crows but are overtaken by a more cacophonous grouping of bloodlustful Hedoes who think themselves the heroes who'd won a victory over a dastardly criminal — I could not be bothered to understand the significance. I am shown from the book club by the way I came; various thrown foodstuffs from either side of the grand staircase mean to ceremoniously induct me to my new life, a common courtesy. The sheep bleat their boos unlike the honorable goat who might shriek them. Once the proceedings are finished and done with, the

Hedoes will go home to their families and put on acts of decency, oblivious to the reality of things, and perhaps gab among themselves a superficial and unflattering recollection of events while their spouses dream of infidelity, the nerve of the lot of them!

Carved into the hillside are the chronicles of our people; I take a moment to distract myself and reflect upon things on my descent, which would otherwise be a drudge of rumination. My attention is brought to one of the earlier carvings, the legend of the valiant and outnumbered Autismos who fell to Neurotypicles and his horde in the first year O.K. where began the Troubles and the inception of all things: It is said King Monkey championed Neurotypicles to keep order in the first kingdom, and so he gathered an order of fellows to keep the peace. And in their vigilance, they'd noticed Autismos, who was loitering in the field.

"You there!" proclaimed Neurotypicles. "What business have ye on the king's land?"

"Nothing in particular," he answered.

This sent Neurotypicles into a rage, and he called on his fellows to encircle Autismos, but Autismos smote them with powerful Gypsy magic so they would disintegrate and depart the mortal realm. Neurotypicles grew fearful and it was written on his face so everyone could see — he was an exhibitionist in that way — but did not falter for he had magic of his own. Neurotypicles conjured from the soil a horde of bees that banded together in the form of a bear. The disciples of Neurotypicles had been galvanized! The fighting was long but honorable Autismos lay slain. Picked apart by bugs, his flesh would feed the future.

Returning to King Monkey, Neurotypicles found the throne empty and, presuming his king abdicated, seized it for himself. Thus began the Troubles in the absence of King Monkey, who'd reigned for a year and ascended to a higher plane or perhaps wandered off. Some accounts claim he still rules as king in Hedophilia — who knows, really? Later holy men would claim to have communed with him, but with every year that passes, the accounts lose a certain mystique and (counterintuitively) credibility, leading us farther astray from the king, or even closer. We're certainly not where we started, though. Some contemporaries claim the decline in credibility correlates to the production of armchairs, rocketed since the advent of the industrial revolution. I lament that, in spite of the king's ephemeral nature, each and every high-ranking Hedo makes a show of answering to him as if he rules the country. I, myself, could not name the sovereign that rules Hedophilia, and this weighs on my mind somewhat.

Whoever these Hedoes serve, I tire that they scribble into the margins of their books a smug, uncontested nonsense for the benefit of their masters who dribble on them a meager pittance scarcely worth the bother. Perhaps they are not so proud as shameless and permissive, or else they might ask for more, and the proudest among them nothing at all.

Nevertheless, every so often, predictably enraged Neurotypicles finds exhausted Autismos in a field, a cave, or some desolate frontier and reenacts this famous battle, a perpetual struggle of culture and counterculture (and the clinicization of this abjection) as one yields to the other, as some theologians choose to interpret it.

As I reach the bottom, I see an odd fellow stands at the road, his person onset with a slew of congenital debilitations and their signs: for instance, a slack jaw, small forehead, round face, heavy breathing, sagging trousers, unkempt fingernails, drab clothes, dark complexion (a racism of the time), and an overall uncouth disposition. In fact, upon further inspection, we might also find eyes so large the whites completely envelop the iris, hard to determine the color. The obtuse, mangy chauffeur dog awaits me — and it does indeed have the phrenology of a lapdog because of the ridge on its forehead. I of course refer to the chassis of metal that unthinkingly obeys the will of men. If the motor carriage were a man, he would have all these congenital defects I described. The actual man beside it is not as unflattering, but the defects somewhat apply to him also, albeit to a lesser extent. Like man, like dog, or some bother!

It is a small mercy that he is curt and does not make a show of things. "In ye go," he insists. I still suspect he feels entitled, in the cosmic dance of the universe, to direct the course of action of the sorry spectacle before him for failure to uphold the contract to which not so many agree but acknowledge involuntarily and enforce in a twisted mass psychosis. Tacit, I think they call it. Sod it all.

Three mid-heat yokels clamber atop one another and finish the chauffeur's thought. "In you go, pop a squat, don't let go until you drop." There is fun to be had past the halfway line of the blood sport arena, life.

I dare to ask, "Is it far?"

Nobody cares to answer, but I interject on their behalf to preserve what semblance of dignity I think I might have: "Farther than you've ever been."

I lumber toward the attached car; it is a gilded cage like I'd see in a circus attached to this open-air, vulgarly bright-green buggy. "Is this punishment too extreme, I mean?"

I pull myself upright. "Humiliating, maybe. And

you let them do it to you."

"To what end?" I clamber up on the dirty cushion and edge near the bars closest to the buggy, separating criminal from evildoer. "You tell me."

The chaff looks to me, his captive. "Piss if I know. Hic."

I jolt like I'd seen the ghastly apparition of a man — which is to say I realized I was talking to myself but didn't think to be embarrassed until someone properly noticed, and I do not mean the misers gaping at me with their peepers. I damn near regret slandering his countenance in the bungle of my mind; ugly folk tend to be bitter about it and he is kind . . . kinder even, a low bar. I, myself, am of a middling attractiveness when I don't possess a mirror to prove me wrong — I am a narcissist at times, yes. (And it is a good thing I keep one such mirror in the vanity of my mind palace at times like these.)

He continues, "No harm in talkin' an' we've got a ways to go. You look like 'ou've seen a ghost." He slaps his belly. "I reckon 'ey're gaunt an' spindly, though."

"What do you know about them?"

"Reckon I've seen a movie once, somethin' to do with ghosts. Don't suppose 'ou'll be turnin' me inta one. Har har," he bellows. "I ain't one fer complainin'. Pale complexion oughts t' help with 'em business opportunities." He swirls his pinky fancifully.

"I could, but why bother? The common Hedo spends a lot of man hours on this nonsense. It's a matter of time before the noble yellows overtake the uppity whites just as the whites have overtaken the leisurely browns, the very same who shunned the greys if the stories are believed."

"Nae, friend. Ne'er mind the skin. 'Tis a racism of the soul! Whites can be Negroes insofer as they's black o' 'eart." He spits as he revs the engine and aways from the Great Organized Book Club.

"I myself have found it odd the darker fellows have appropriated the word for its original use and not in reference to their oppressors who would, undoubtedly, take issue . . ."

"Ain't a' been the first time I'd a' called 'em th' like, meself. Reckon them fellers'd hate it most!"

"Precisely, my good man!"

"Bah! I ain't ne'er seen a white. Bah hah hah! Now's you got me talkin', are ye one of 'em race haters?"

"A misanthrope at times, maybe."

"'At there public conscience ain't yet 'quated the two, but I'm sure it'll catch on. An' so lowly are fish to 'umanids that they ain't part o' the racism conversation. An' whattas it mean, sub'umanid?

Sure, animals ain't 'umanid, nor 'neath 'em neither. Eguh!" (Ego, I think he meant to say.)

"It takes a baseline level of intelligence to be this insufferable."

"Damn humanids." He spits.

"If say you so, so say I."

"Perhappenstance."

"What was that, you pompous fool? What if someone heard you?"

"I'll say whate'er I damn well please howe'er it comes out. If'n'eir pretense o' ma' pretense bothers 'em such, 'haps 'ey oughtta take 'eir monkey colloquialisms elseplace, 'ferably among themselves."

"Not us, for we are a pair of like-minded individuals," I say wryly.

"Like mind, ye say? Nae! At cannae be!"

"I reckon we're of like body and fractured mind; separated only by the faintest threads of air, we are but one at odds with ourselves, for you are complicit in my death for driving, as I am for existing in the shadow of Neurotypicles, as we all are for perpetuating a universe that lets us die."

The chauffeur keeps one hand on the wheel. "Gimme yer 'and. I'd 'old it."

I embrace his fingers with mine through the bars of the paddy wagon; it means to be that intimate.

"Now ye an' I are one body, interlocked. But yer right insofar as ye aren't, for if I agree wit ye, ye will be wrong an' our minds will be fractured ne'er longer." He pauses a moment to ponder. "'Haps I caen agree wit ye fer a different reason from ye an' remain fractured in 'at regard? Yes, 'at'll work. Why'dya believe'n such?"

"Why, it seems rather empirical, don't you think?"

"An' whattaya know o' empiricism, Doctor Scientist? What be ye preoccupation?"

"I have a job, but I am not preoccupied with it, nor can I properly say I identify with it strongly enough to so much as bother saying what it is. I could very well be homeless too. I don't remember nor want to."

"Quaint, but I dunnae ask fer a career, fair associate. Me, I am preoccupied with breathing, in an' out, sometimes held, other times stopped, at which point I oughta be occupied by peace. I ask again, what occupies ye?"

"Were you hoping I was an expert on myself? Poppycock, you tosser!"

"Meanin'?"

"I do jack all."

"Nothin'?"

"Everything, all trades."

"Slippery fella, 'ppears y'are."

"For instance, the inevitable stopping of my breath weighs somewhat on my noggin, I say."

This fellow a number of years my senior, as I thought would inevitably be the case, hits me with the experience angle: "'Ave ye tested this hypothesis?"

"You may know more, you coot, but I know better on account of my noggin."

"'Ave ye?"

"No. I fumble about at the intuitive stage. I have not tried dying, and do not doubt if an elder rose from the grave they would not hesitate to inform me they know better of such matters."

"Ne'er mind that complex ya got there . . . So how caen ye say beyond reasonable doubt ye will inevitably stop breathin'?"

"Others have tested it."

"Be thar published findings on th' topic?'

"I can't quite check from here."

"Well I 'ave, an' ye know wot I found? 'Orse piss. Mayhap the happenstance of 'eir stance be it ain't so profitable, or gets 'em laughed outta 'eir quaint 'stitutions. I ain't willin' t' conclude any darn thing 'til I see enough of you's croak an' pass on. 'At's what I'm 'ere fer. 'At's why I'm taking you up the road t' the place Hedoes send all capital o-ffenders. An' 'at's why I agree with ye, but where ye think yer gonna to die, I'm willin' to make the hyp-o-thetical a-ssumption ye ain't, all a'while holding yer hand so as t' remain one o' body. I will not let go, no sir, not 'till you an' I go a throttlin' towards our supposed deaths together." His last word hangs in the air.

A spark of unconsciousness pangs at me. My hand slips as my head rebounds off the bars of the cage, crackling the sound of thunder consigning bolt to tree and lighting it afire, a signature of the Feistian variety and bargain struck, as if.

I pass into that place of bliss for but a moment. On my waking, little seems to have changed save that my hand now free does not keep the warmth. Had the man before me been a sage or a hallucination? And if that latter thing, was I talking only to myself? Is the man before me still but a working-class puppet, an idiot in the service of assholes not so much in high places as on high horses eking an opulent living scarcely better than principled poverty? Screw you and the horse you rode in on!

The vision recedes, which is not to say I had not gone blind altogether, but that I still might see the world around me as before, plainly and without the introspection of hallucination, but who is not to say I haven't been hallucinating a reality all this time? Was I the chauffeur? Who are you and I, really? Is there a oneness of King Monkey present in us all? Bah! I'm a narcissist. Translation: I'm better than you monkeys, and the day I lose is the day I pretend it didn't happen. And should I be embarrassed for thinking these thoughts? Could I come to regret them, or forever be burdened by the nonsense of my very existence? How often should I loan out the burden on external circumstances before I combust of shame from the accruing interest, defaulting with the staking of my soul? Credit is a devilish thing, so I hear, and the heat is particularly bothersome.

I dissociate for a time.

***

Tomato paste blends with cold sweat, a waste. Sat in blistering agony, Jove needs not wipe the hellfire ingredients from his sockets, only savor the variety of life and reflect aloud, "I never thought to ask. Where are we going?"

The chauffeur answers after a time as if he didn't quite hear and, replaying the event in his head, realized what the convict had asked and that the question was posed to him: "Heh. Them Hedoes 'emselves nary know wher'st ye'll go; they's be too preoccupied with'n'eir families an' bein' good an' honest folk t' care. I's like t' think 'I have a family' be th' new jus' 'followin' orders.' I's loathe t' think wot 'ey'll say 'n th' nex' century: may'aps ain't like I 'ave free will' or 'das jus' me nature.' Well, ne'er you mind. They's figure y'all're loonies an' oughta be locked up tighter than me belly 'neath me belt. Das 'nough fer me." The driver speaks the same dialect as before — a premonition? Or did indeed the vision come to pass?

"So you don't?"

"Nae!"

"How else do you know where you're going?"

And whether from rage or sunburn, he is a beet red not the muddled brown of earlier. The driver wholly halts the vehicle to accommodate his tirade, displacing Jove in the process, and retaliates with incoherent gibberish, blood gushing from his heat-stricken cranium to pores that cry of red: for every burst vessel an insult on someone's mother. Fathomably, the cage means to protect the detainee. A gradual, arrogant steam churns into a personal rain cloud that brings a torrent of tears. "Onemsiz, my son, gone to the Arena over yonder. Evil eye spit on ye!" An odd moisture fumes from his nostrils and envelops the carriage behind; it is oddly cool and refreshing, and if Jove had not kept his fascinum amulet — a curious phallic trinket and safeguard against one such eye of evil — said fumes would not fail to suffocate.

A days-long silence ensues on deaf ears and the chauffeur is left to his internal, maniacal ravings; practice for the future? In that time it can at least be deduced his name is Turkey.

Sweltering under the harsh sun brings out quite the suntan, and had Jove been on holiday, he'd've turned off the oven an hour in, tops. It may have been days, perhaps four of them. Restless sleep is no indication; one moment is the same as all the rest combined, and tantalizing.

It is the incidental intervention of fate that brings it all to perspective and euthanizes the present suffering; this sorry captive is manhandled from the van. Should he be grateful? Who is he if not "me" who even "I" am not? That is to say he does not know who he is to be grateful, and for what values, principles, purpose, even.

Fate demands Jove be washed of excrement, organic or otherwise that he may have accumulated over the pilgrimage of these four days' time. A cabal of personnel come close with their vile equipment. With each stroke Jove is hosed of the filth of civil men; once haggard breaths come easier, complexion less blemished, and the Jove that emerges from the thin film of sud is altogether healthier than before.

A study of their faces reveals two things: they are ethnically Herrman, of Herrmania, and take great pleasure in this ritual. One man's sadism is another's good fun.

"Where?" a dazed Jove manages.

Before him is a wall long as the land is vast whose construction seems shoddy, or at the very least irregular. It may be a trick of the light, but the wall very nearly bends inward at both horizons with strange grooves and plates along the length; men and guns mounted atop keep the peace. And tumultuous Turkey is gone behind him.

The very same escort of Herrmans guides Jove to the gates who, in his compulsion to verify the chronology of things, thinks to ask, "Do you have the time?"

The rearmost guard makes a show of nearly whacking him with the butt of a service rifle, but at the last moment playfully nudges his shoulder with a grin.

The gate, and the only one in sight, is more like a tunnel in girth, burrowed through to the other side. Jove has never seen such a place, nor does he have an account of it ever existing. Where are "we," really? Does this monument mark the end of the world, time, and space? Today, Jove means to dine with King Monkey; it ought to be worth the time he spent alive, waiting for something.

Thus the gates did creak, revealing before him a light, and at the end of the light, nothing. Why, there is nothing in particular! Is this a jest, a profound and zesty joke at my expense, this life? On my honor, I am Jove! Or perhaps I am not! Oh, how the lines blur between self and not self, real and not real, nothing and anything! Surely, nothing is a kind of thing, or else I couldn't talk about it the same way I couldn't talk about "myself"!

I stumble to my knees and bellow a laugh, "Hahaha!" I say!

And the Herrmans, they laugh with me!

"Haha-haha!" I mock them!

No, look closer, Jove! There is but a single man who stands to welcome me, and I am myself for a moment longer, the moment as confused as I am.

Dressed like an officer in desert brown and gold — very official — this man endures where the sun shines its nauseatingly brightest. He rotates imperatively and in full to meet me directly, affront and fully erect in stature. Without breaking eye contact, he motions emotionlessly behind him and in a thick, Herrman accent says his piece: "Velkommen to zhe Arena," and motions once more (you can't miss it — no, really), "zhis is vhat you are looking for. Hippen hoppen. Are ve understood?"

I glance around and see only sand; is this where they keep it all? Risky business, that. What am I meant to be looking for, anyhow?

He raises an eyebrow inquisitively. "I am a busy man."

"I'm supposed to, what, leg it from here?"

"Yes yes."

I glance back at the Herrmans and suspect these men are meant to keep me in. "Ah. I suppose I'll be going then."

"Very gut."

With a curt nod, the officer and guards retreat behind their fortifications, leaving me to die, that is if I understand anything correctly. I don't bloody know with these foreigners, or even less with my own.

I am at such a crossroads that choices do not require any deliberation. Step, think, step, ponder, step, step, do not think, do not step, step again, think, regret, step, step, step, step, step . . . I like to think I am of late well acquainted with inconvenience, but if I had to choose the flavor, I might tango with long and savory over short and sweet; it is in hubris I presume to eat, that I am due neither.

Dunes are many and I am one; it goes without saying. Maybe if I squint really hard, the sand will look like snow. There is little else to speak of, lest I succumb to this damnable heat. It is perhaps in this arena of nothings that I am meant to confront myself; oh, clueless Hedoes, if only you knew I think of nothing else.

Every so often I see a carcass, some not humanid; perhaps I am a feast! Would that I had any patience remaining, I might be mortified.

Swallow me, then, with your mouths that gape. And it is past the next dune there be a fish. Woe, it appears 'tis my mouth that gapes the fool. I approach and think to make polite conversation. "What are you in for?" I hope it speaks the king's gibberish.

It does not.

"Likewise. Say, you wouldn't be opposed if I tore a shank of your person? Much appreciated."

The locusts did scatter from such good manners I have. Unwise as it might be, I am quite ready to eat and be eaten, and should I fall ill, let it be a problem for the vultures. It is a small joy that I might have stumbled upon this sun-dried fellow just as the night and its stars descend upon the Arena on its seventeenth eve this month. For all my failings and ignorance, the constellations, albeit clearer than under that Hedophilic smog, fall much the same as ever, for I am still of this dusty rock. In my prior confusion, I might have thought I'd gone on to a different world altogether, no longer. I wonder about my place in this world. Why am I here? Bugger. Now's as good a time as any for stargazing, I reckon.

The sand rumbles and swallows me half; it is not the quick variety that swallows whole. For every star that shoots, there is a shot that booms. What do fireworks add not already present in the sky, I wonder? These are no mere aerial, recreational boomsticks, neither. Ballistic missiles fire from the direction I came; some terminate prematurely, others meet their mark farther afield. Whoever goes there hunted for sport, please stay there a while longer so that I might watch the boomsticks. Let my remaining moments be of macabre interest, to this I have consigned myself, never mind the Great Organized Book Club.

The symphonic has only truly begun. A single, premature warhead enraptures the flamboyant sky, erupting in a glow of yellow, orange, and red, a prelude flagging the national, Hedophilic colors. The following overture levels a distant dune; if they thought to do that earlier, I might have had an easier time of walking. A symphony of missiles detonate at the same time, overlapping their patterns. It is cliché, but what isn't anymore? As I think the Herrmanic kapellmeister ought to crank up the tempo, I am bestowed the honor and engulfed in a sea of sparks. I am privy to anticipatory, thrilling rests and ear-deafening vocals singing of premature expiration and artful decapitation, concluding as the ultimate magnum opus of a millennium in memoriam for the countless dead exiled to the desert. Missiles terminate into brilliant flashes of light that illuminate the desert; I see it is exhumed by the munitions and gives way to a great haboob, I soon to be its meal.

I mourn the few moments to which I am entitled before dust infests my everlastingly inexplicably agonized eyeballs. If my lungs were not full of it, I would complain. With the blotting of the last star, I am blinded, fascinum amulet clasped in hand. Bugger and damnation! I am left to rely on my wretched intuition, the very same that brought this plight, or that which provoked it from others. But never mind all this incessant monologuing I have been inundating myself with — as I often do if only for the sake of keeping tabs on things and reinforcing my perspective of reality. The situation calls for a moment of thoughtless quiet, the kind I often recoil from for fear of losing myself, the very voice I think of as me.

Kindly shove off to the door over yonder and shut it thoroughly. I will see you off, yes indeed! Off you pop and fare thee well, if you are so inclined. Well? I scream into the void of my subconscious knowing full well it does not speak the monkey's gibberish: Shut up! Shut up shut up shut up!

II

Freestyle Transformation, Revisionary Psalm

Tremors invoked, fellows evicted,
to what substance are the convicted addicted?
Legs of gasoline, glove of vaseline, mind of
morphine,
who's cooking up atrophy?
A cauldron cackles oily boils bursting liquid sin
and splatter on skin of passersby.

The spirit fawns, nevermore a migratory pawn
to the humanid condition,
partitioned by mortician equipped
with ammunition in abundance,
method of choice sunderance

sawn down the middle, y'ouch.

Inside the rift willpower adrift gone stiff
like a doobie in the pocket of a goblin,
to fate astonished and reason abolished,
fates varnished admonish the others,
sisters and brothers under covers by sternum,
determined in turn to die;
the fragments forlorn adorn the doors
an agonized blood eagle.

Each a harlot once betroth a cloth
now strained in cosmic broth to wring out
— I take cheap shots when I see them —
abstinent virgins stained of theft, left from cleft,
not to bereft another themself!

Made are thee, progeny of scorn and sum of three,
mothered by the King;
anguish born anew, of natural death in lieu,
a debauchery set to brew a kettle:
mild seams, wicked schemes, or fever dream?
Triumvirate!

The hermit disinterested, but anyway enlisted
despite how he may insist it,
the vindicator forged for war, a proper commissar,

assembles to conquer all afar,
and the vanguard shields those burrowed in his
beard.
It's a short one. Oh yeah.

But under the same sun, one another shun,
prepare the world for armageddon,
so sayeth the prophecy unwritten, save here,
and unbroken lest you lot oppose it.
Now awaken ye forsaken by conduit of achin'.
Mic drop, arms crossed, meshuga!

III

Book of Horace

The morning comes the eighteenth day of the tenth month. What transpired the previous night remains but a haze in the mind. However muddled the chronology, its internal clock yet ticks a pristine tock that sounds an alarm in the way of a familiar accent. "Yoohoo, are ve avake?" It is the Herrman officer.

Jove splays on a stretcher, bewildered. Although he knows the time, he is not present with it, perhaps armed with a chronic detachment loaded into the chamber of the soul where once was something other, or maybe not. Nevertheless, he assumes command of his body in the material plane and answers, "Am I glad to see you?"

A genuine sentiment unveils behind the curtain of the officer's iron demeanor. "Yes."

"Will you try killing me again?"

"You have my vord ve vill not exterminate you a second time. Do not vorry; it vas not meant for you."

Jove nods tiredly.

"Vould you have a coffee vhile you recover from your vounds?" A kettle sits freshly boiled.

Jove has only the wherewithal for a quiet "Please."

The officer pours for himself. "Very gut, but I prefer tea. Avay to ze infirmary wiz you. Kindly ask Lars to brew a pot. Chop choppen."

Bystanding Herrman paramedics whisk Jove to a fresh cot beside many of the same, occupied by the mortally wounded and perchance dead but not yet disposed casualties.

His eyes strain wide as if to say, "Oh my, I am terrified" and "Will I survive this ordeal?"

A nurse is preoccupied with a set of nonclandestine intestines, but nevertheless takes note of Jove and preempts him with bored eyes of his own that imply Jove's injuries are beneath his immediate attention.

"Lars?"

The man curtsies. "You have my blessing."

"Lars?" Jove elicits once more the quieter, a dying, dehydrated man.

"Yes?" Lars replies, matching the cadence.

"Do you have coffee?"

Lars stretches an intestinal coil. "I am a bit strung up at the moment." He grins. "Ah, brighten up, won't you? You are not this poor fellow." The nurse absentmindedly glances at the vitals, then again to make sure. "Oh, and he's already dead," then gasps, "tea!" Lars flits off to unknown places, taking with him a merry tune.

The room to himself, Jove gazes upon the bloody corpse with mild, tired interest. Had he died in the moment at the hands of the butcher, or hours earlier elsehow? It appears his arm had been untethered at the shoulder, torso brutally mutilated, ribs mangled through the flesh, and organs kept in a colorful, mainly red, green, and yellow disarray; is the stomach supposed to be so high up? The intestines festoon freely and festively about the posts of his deathbed as if he were part man, part octopus. His mouth foams with froth; one could listen closely and hear the sea.

"My professional verdict gives him roughly five minutes, tops. No . . . never mind, he is dead. Take your pick of leaves." Lars holds out a box, juggling it half an inch above the palm.

"I asked for coffee."

"The what now?"

"Like the . . . bean."

"Oh, I know what it is!" He spits. "I insist we drink tea! Coffee is for the workmen of Hedophilia! Tea is for the mind, for honest men and women, enjoyment! Work to live and all that. Die to live, even! The officer once drank coffee; I won him over eventually. Did you know he once bedded a princess of Herrmania? The sultry officer had it all and chose me. You, too, will surrender to my charms."

"Do what you will."

"How melodramatic of you, do continue enjoying the company." Lars kisses the corpse on his way.

Jove could strike up conversation, were they conscious. Alas, they were not. It begs the question: What atrocity killed them dead so terribly? Could the attack have transpired the night before; was it not by fate but convenience that they came upon "me" — and why not both? In "my" wandering of thoughts "I" notice a globe of the world in the distance. It is most unusual, and "I" make a note of it.

Lars returns with tea. "Bedridden so soon and you already have a visitor! I warn you, I am a jealous fellow."

No sooner than he is introduced does this

strange man start speaking. It very nearly doesn't matter what he says, only that he reeks of charisma and leads men. Jove has an averse reaction to this kind of person and does not listen for quite some time, instead studying his character: His uniform is freshly ironed and bears a great many medals donned over the breast. A peg leg rhythmically stamps the ground. He stands tall and does not seem the type to publicly share a room with anyone who would meet his match. "Good work, soldier!"

A befuddled Jove processes the utterance. "I don't work here."

His verbal assailant breathes in the blood and guts of the room. "This wondrous stench brings me back! I was but a wee lad with the vague impressionist rendering of chin hair." A tear streaks across his supernaturally chiseled face, "Only then did I see her, my first Atlantean. That there beauty whaled herself on the shoreline, gorging men and women alike in that maw of hers. I alone survived this brush with indiscriminate evil. Har har har! On one leg, of course." He clicks at the heel. "This was outside the walls, mind you. We get some stragglers now and then that break past, but this place is an otherwise well-oiled floodgates, yes sir. So I was questioned and chose to enlist. Only then did I find the reality of things, an ongoing war with the monkey-damned extraterrestrials, or whatever they are. If they had their way, they'd kill us all. So it is here we draw a line. This is a war zone, son. What you saw was an airstrike on them aliens, to rival their strange Gypsy magic. We only need for numbers. Many a Hedo lack the imagination to believe their eyes; I don't like to beg with those fools who think we're looney. But you've seen these beasts in action and returned from the brink, as I have! Answer the call to duty, you scurvy dog! I, Warden Heinrich, insist!" He raises a fist in triumphant conclusion of the ovation. "Oh, but where are my manners? You seem confused; I know the look. Have ole Grimwald fill you in. He's good for it. Ta!" Heinrich is not seen to have left the room. Like a specter, the phantom pisser in the night left no evidence of his being there except the vague and questionable memory of a noise.

Scanning for the warden over his shoulder, Lars contemplates aloud, "You know, I don't think he and Grimwald ever spoke. A queer bloke, that one. I wonder if the Atlantean took anything else of his."

Giggles emanate from a semi-conscious soldier.

Lars continues, "That Heinrich is a busy guy, so busy that you might never see him again, I like to think! Really, that's what business is. Busy busy guy, not like that Grimwald fellow I see every day who only looks the part."

Perhaps hearing this, officer Grimwald comes first to Nurse Lars, around whom he loosens his composure. "Come here, you greasy dog!" says Lars, embracing masculinities in the way only men can conceive.

The officer then encroaches cross-legged atop Jove's bed and rather than ask, proclaims, "Comfortable." In his hands he holds the world, the very same Jove noticed in the distance.

"Make yourself at home," a defeated Jove utters.

He ignores the request. "I believe I was not yet introduced. I am Officer Grimvald and vill answer any questions. In retrospect, you seemed to have zhat clueless look about you. I am sorry I did not rectify it earlier. I zhought you knew vhere you vere going."

"Where are we?"

Grimwald spins the globe in his hands. "Zhe Arena. It is a great desert surrounded by zhe great vall Yin."

Lars, too, spins, "In a circle!"

"Was it always here?"

"Since zhe dawn of man," Grimwald says profoundly.

"Who built it?"

"Ve do not know." He is too proud to bear the shame alone, but not enough to deny it.

"Why am I finding out about this now?"

"If it looks to be a tightly guarded secret, it is not."

The more talkative Lars finishes the thought: "Nobody cares enough to see it, and those that do tend to stay. Well, maybe it's not a function of caring so much as perception. We get the occasional pedestrian who will bump into the wall and stay stuck, thinking they're going somewhere when they're not. We turn those fools around manually, but sometimes I like to watch with morbid curiosity like they're stickmen in the paper dimension. Heh. And don't get me started on the domers! As you can imagine, this phenomenon has been of no small confusion to the scientific community. The globe-centric view is right for all the wrong reasons, being that the globers don't see the whole picture. The domers are crackpot conspirators and are wrong for all the right reasons — the part they see is half the picture. I dare say those types could probably come and see the wall for themselves if they ever bothered with the fieldwork. Where was I going with this? Well, never mind. We get criminals too, not that the Hedoes know where or what we are; they're just happy you stay gone. You and they tend to see the wall 'cause it takes an open mind for crime."

"I don't feel like a criminal."

"Accidents, zhey happen." Grimwald shrugs.

"Stop spinning the thing."

The officer hands Jove the globe.

Contemporary maps of Katsikoskoni show it is as a wide-sweeping landmass that dominates the sea at the pole. Arid Hedophilia is situated on the river Mangy to the west and forested Herrmania to the northeast with a number of minor buffer powers in between — as was always the case. Oh, how the land scathes at the petty sea confined to the south. But lo! There is a new addition, as if the northern pole expanded even farther north to reveal a new mass. Katsikoskoni, still but one continent, has now a vast desert at its northern pole around which hugged the old world. Great wall Yin splits the world in two, the single medium between theaters that perhaps rises so high as to block the winds and keep it a hottish nothingscape in aeternum. And the southern sea did shrink to a puddle where man watered his holes.

"Is there a war?"

"A var on fish."

Lars is silent.

"What do they want?" a befuddled Jove asks.

"I vish I knew. Zhey send no diplomats and are never taken alive. Perhaps zhey long for zhe sea. Much ve do not know. But if ve cede, ve die," he affirms with a shaky confidence. Perhaps he'd hoped that shouldn't be the case.

Lars continues again, "The men observed the makings of a proto religion, odd ritual behavior, effigies, you know the kind. They rather fancy killing, the authentic 'I'll do to you what the browns did to us' archetype. Never mind the sea, they make do without!"

"Why are there so few Hedoes?"

"Zhere are men of each nation, denomination, creed. For vhatever reason, Hedoes slack. I do not presume, but zhere is you. God so help me, I vill drag you kicking and screaming into a better future, if you allow it."

Jove asks the penultimate question: "And who am I?"

A distant clock ticks a metronome under a breeze that carries on its current a thoughtful whistling. Raindrops dribble from a kettle and footsteps pass overhead. In Grimwald and Lars are felt the practicing of a mental horticulture, thoughts aimed at Jove like the nodes of expanding fungi cut short by some impermeable barrier. Gears churn a lacking butter. The two men are silent.

"What is my name?"

"How much do you remember?" the nurse prods.

"Don't start. I think it's mostly there. Just feels like I'm missing a part, and that part took a part of me with it."

Lars mutters to himself, "Maybe it ran off somewhere. Okay, it's been a lot to take in; that's an excuse people like to throw around, don't they? Family name? No? Can't believe you're related to such people? I understand. How would you like a pseudonym as you catch your bearings? You look the common fellow. Isn't that so? You look the part of a Horace. Yes, Horace." He draws out into thoughtful silence.

The officer does not give Horace the opportunity to deny his new namesake, "Vell, Horace. Vhat do you make of things? Vill ve send you avay to live among zhe Hedoes, knowing vhat ve showed you?"

Horace breathes a sigh the likes of which he's never breathed before — except in the waking hours of morning, exercises in exasperation. Nevertheless, there is a pounding sense of duty in his chest that he knows will never subside if he goes on as always, a stick among the Hedoes. "Someone's gotta do something about this menace, don't they? Do I have the impetus? Bah, I'm not doing anything else with my time. Go on, then."

"As you say — you vill be replacing Private Gosling of the Seventeenth Herrman regiment." The officer nods loosely to the scattered entrails of the corpse at whose side Lars is seen stitching together the rips of his uniform, managing a surprisingly serviceable job of it. "It's missing a bit of sleeve but it's good enough! Oh, don't look at me like that. We're all dead men. Ain't worth knitting a new one just for you, sunshine."

***

Thus passes another night through the liquid dreams of Horace's turmoiled psyche. A body buried in a pyramid of brick out the top of which its lachrymose visage sleepily peers out into nothing, a beach of severed hands before a shark that eats a man, a bout of paralysis serenaded by triumphant music and a light that shines brighter than usual the moment before his waking — riled Horace takes stock of his numbed hands and, accounting for all his fingers, contemplates bittersweet victories, never having tasted a proper one. And if the future is no better than the past, what then, to forget it before it even begins? Perhaps! His would be the shoulder that bears the brunt of a future put from memory. As usual, in the case of dreams, this is but an intuitive understanding that is not evident in the dreams but the dreamer — so feels Horace.

He is the single patient to emerge from the infirmary that morning, the nineteenth, leaving all the rest in that eternal place of dreams; just as the life, they will perhaps only remember the last fragments before their waking, if ever or else place.

The exception runs for light sleepers and mayhaps light livers alike who remember the lot. Live lightly, O Horace!

For a week Horace trains in the Herrman drill yard packed with despondent men in formation donning the sullied brown and gold of their fallen predecessors. It is no question these bloodstained men die as often as conjectured. To whom do these square-dancing grandmothers belong? It is the mere presence of Horace's aura that inspires each countryman to double time. There is, however, a lean man — in clean uniform — who pays mind only to the drills and the perfection in their execution, never mind the men around him but debris in the periphery of his canthus. And on this wordless remissal of his very existence, Horace works to match his adversary.

Whatever activity, perforating through the lackluster clusterfuck of fleshy debris is the unbesmirched overachiever, out to kill dare anyone better than he. Horace alone accepts the challenge whenever the opportunity presents its supple behind. He would match every bull's-eye at the range with any and which weapon at his disposal, and their scores would match to the digit. And at any juncture this rival would come ahead of the pack, Horace too would thrust forward his body leagues. Whence the soldier would sweep Horace at the legs, Horace would roll shoulder first, revolving halfway and back on his feet — and this indeed occurs more than once. His rival, bent on one-uppance, at last trapezes over yonder crowd he let surpass him. And not only that; he lands atop Horace's shoulders by the thighs, capsizing his ship, and lands dignantly on his soles, ever the cat, apex predator second only to the goat. Horace, thus, on the last day of these trifles, the twenty-fifth, lies baptized in dust. He, for a moment, feels it a defeat stronger than the chronic humiliation the weakest Yin soldier might feel indefinitely. But good Horace honors this rivalry and rises from the dust in a sportsmanly manner, having braced for the worst pains imaginable.

The colonel leading the regiment, however, is a man so unimportant, his face so featureless, it can only be said he possesses a certain je ne sais quoi. Laps cease for the day. The upcoming exercise is a patrol into the Arena to which a timid silence ensues. The Herrmans' colonel is seen receiving a scolding, concisely packaged and delivered by Officer Grimwald, expert in logistics, among other matters.

Grimwald calls to Horace with a proud smirk that on anyone else would look utterly mundane: "Ah, zhere you are." He grapples Horace's arms near the shoulder, eyes protruding slightly beyond the rest of the face. "I have not seen you in a veek! Sleep vell? Vake up now. Zhis nincompoop failed to mention as the junior-most member you vill be marching at zhe back: thirtieth column, thirtieth row. No need to march in fours and such — it is an open desert. I hope you vill learn to use zhat rifle of yours on zhe vay. Or don't. Five of ours barely counts for one of zhem out in zhe field. You vill notice zhis once you start moving up zhe ranks because everyvone in front of you died, except zhat Brahe. Chances are you vill die too — vhy bozher? Hoho. Zhat is vhy I am in requisitions among ozher safer zhings; I noticed ve could reuse zheir uniforms. Somehow no vone had zhe idea, even Lars who is known to have such zhoughts." Perhaps the conversation with the colonel roused something in the old man who otherwise lets Lars do the talking when talking needs be done.

"What was that about men dying?"

"Yes. Men die."

"What are we doing about it?"

"Everyzhing ve can. It is safest to stay behind zhe valls, but sometimes ve must be ready to sally and strike zhe enemy before zhey form up. You vill be vizhin range of our munitions; but I must admit ve are diminished of late. No matter, ve improvise. I vorry for you, but zhis must be done every so often."

"Thank you, Officer."

He methodically claps his heels, and not in the queer way of Warden Heinrich.

Horace conjures his best Blatin. "Ad hominem fidelis."

Grimwald salutes with an up yours.

The Herrman regiment amalgamates some essence of structure to which Horace contributes a not insignificant deal. There may have been some delegation of local leadership that hastened the process, but it is not apparent with this fresh batch of fodder. Horace admirably and independently places himself to the exact file and rank, a marvel. The overt athlete, contrarily, is concealed among the heads. This can only mean he had been dealt the front line.

Jove may have inquired why he tread the Arena a second time, but not Horace, for this is his first. The only difference between the two men is one thousand for company and a pair of boots. The regiment, an unwieldy mass, moves at a fraction of Horace's calloused hobble. Horace relinquishes the boots, depositing them in his pack, thinking they felt unnatural — not so much a question of fit as belonging. It would make most anyone move faster, would that anyone were behind him to see. Hopefully he may one day lead by example. Never mind: It is a matter of principle. The senior to his left takes notice; he is the only one.

"You quite all right, lad?" and that is the extent of the conversation.

Deployed near the golden-brown Herrmans, the blackish-red Scarabs of Scarabia march en route the same destination. This revelation incites banter among the men:

"Now why'd we hafta go'n pair up wit' 'eir lot? Buncha cocky gits."

"Chin up, Ackman. Down bad with prick envy?"

"Their colonel's a foreigner. Delilah, funny name, that, and a woman! No prick on her. Ah, what am I saying, them's're all foreigners."

"Never felt so naked outside Herrmania north. Hope the Scarabs feel home at least," speaks a third.

"And I hear her family's got money," a fourth spits.

"Careful, now. Benefactors grease the war machine," says another.

"Could have just as easily been friends, these fish we're killing. What's it for?"

Horace has since stopped listening in, though he assumes the next person might complain of worn boots and torn sleeves. In the short window of life during Gosling's disembowelment, he might have posed a snarky remark, and so Horace mourns the memory of a man who may or may not have had something to say.

And in this rumination Horace notices the Scarabs halt their advance. The Herrmans, too, take a hint and stop a while. Camp is set eight men to a tent. After their duties, Horace's bunkmates unanimously and wordlessly opt to play cards, a terrifying hive mind of discipline. Horace, alone, sleeps. A game of cards is easily forgotten, but a deficit of sleep be a graver debt than one of bets.

An alarm preludes daybreak. Groggy bunkmates deaf to the music of conscientiousness expel no effort to its reticence, yet will no doubt later begrudgingly heed a louder angry person with fancy metals. Readied Horace embarks outside, rendering the tent's inhabitants a profane stupor offset by, and to, his ambivalence of the clamor. The worst of the storm dissipated overnight, conditions suitable for a self-ordained run. Insofar, the camp seems eerily quiet in spite of the cracking of dawn. If confused and doubtful Horace didn't know any better, he'd say it was the twenty-sixth of the tenth month.

"Get back to sleeping, soldier!" Lars waves from an open-air operating table, tending to a soldier vividly burned at the scalp, second degree, amply lathering it with aloe vera. "Imported from Scarabia," he elucidates.

"Good to see someone else worked up for a

change."

"Ah, yes, work . . ." He yields a stamped missive. "Run this over to Colonel Delilah when you have a moment. Our Colonel Headsofaruphisassitdigestedanddefecatedoutagain asked me to do it, but I couldn't be bothered." Lars firmly plants a second handful of aloe, to which his patient grunts painfully. He clarifies with a cheeky grin, "Burn victim from the night before, if you're wondering. Sun won't kill you this time of year, promise. Eyes on the horizon; there be fish in these parts and there's already been reports of a spat. Oh, and another thing! Don't piss in the open. Every drop scores a point in the Atlanteans' goalpost, makes them stronger. Do it in a bottle and bring it back. Now get a move on!"

Horace departs for a stroll between camps through the serene desert under whose timeless sands are swept the altercations of time immemorial. The Scarabic regiment is stationed within eyeshot; the worst of the storm subsided. The largest tent of the Scarabs under banner of pastry (there are so many regiments stationed around the wall that they ran out of the usual iconography) serves as the office of Colonel Delilah Franciscocrat, herself. In front of the opening flap stands a soldier of some description.

"Stand by."

Sometime later, Horace is allowed in. From Delilah's quarters proceeds a specimen of hair and skin behind a mask out which peer two eyes; there is little to say of her except that unlike the Herrman colonel, she is not so much unremarkable as mysterious. Delilah sits expectantly.

Horace expects some cue to "report," but after some time, presents the letter unrequited: "From the colonel of the Herrmans."

She dislocates an eyebrow.

"I was not informed as to its contents."

She stilts a sizable index finger atop her desk in a casual fashion.

Horace leaves it by her finger. "Return a message, ma'am?"

Delilah glances at it, then eyes him suspiciously. Her extended finger curls into a fist, tapping the table thoughtfully.

Horace waits a moment, thinking it best to remain silent.

Delilah brings her fist to her black bandana, coughing a weak, gender-neutral cough. And as Horace angles to speak, she raises a palm for silence and finally enacts a shooing gesture with both hands.

Horace exits the premises but considers extending his stay among the Scarabs. The encampment is better organized and more conscientious than its counterpart, men about their duties doing their damnedest not to starve. The Scarabs are inspired by their comrades for the better — and from the better come the best, an infinite recursion. Their barracks are, on inspection, tidy and blissfully void of life, and the footmen so disciplined as not to wallow in such heavenly places. The colonel really outdid herself, Horace thinks.

An appetite accumulates itself in the deep depths of Horace's psyche; he pays his respects to the canteen, its queue orderly and brisk, delightful. At the counter are strewn trays of scrambled eggs, questionable sausage, and biscuits complemented by coffee and tea. Horace selects tea, the indubitably superior beverage. The commissar seems to allow the Herrman's presence, but sighs deeply. Horace occupies a table, managing a bite, and no sooner in looking up does he notice the man who trained alongside him at Yin. "Hello there. Brahe, was it?" having remembered the name from Grimwald.

"Why are you here, comrade?" he whispers accusatively. In his tone, however, is a hint of prideful camaraderie, no doubt a result of their wordless spat in Yin. This would be the first time Horace hears him speak, his accent somewhere between Grimwald's and Lars's, though not exactly.

Brahe wears the black and red of the Scarabs despite his allegiance to the Herrmans.

Chewing through, Horace raises his plate as if to say he was here for the food.

"No."

"What do you mean, no?"

To this query, Brahe stares menacingly.

"I brought a message to the colonel."

His voice inflects: "The colonel? This message, what is it?"

"Confidential?"

"It does not matter. Do you know we were attacked here?"

"One fellow got burned. Didn't seem lethal. What do you mean?"

"You did not hear it?"

"No, storm's brewing out. How did you?"

"Never mind. This colonel seems different, no?"

"I wouldn't know. I've seen her for the first time only now. Is she ill?"

Brahe seethes at Horace's use of fork without knife. "What do you know? Don't you see, golden-brown pig? She has broad shoulders."

Horace feels the presence of wandering, Scarabian eyes weighing on the scales of indiscretion against him, and so thinks to redouble the ruse. "Why I'd never! Broad shoulders? That's insensitive." Though he figures Brahe's paleness could have given him away just as well; Horace feels he might have been better suited to this reconnaissance.

"It is truth, see?"

"Don't you military types like puffing those up?"

"You do not see bigger painting. She is like fish above ice."

"Do you have something to say?" inquisites curious Horace.

"Have I something I say? Yes, I have something I say. I say she is man!"

"Is that so, Scarab?" Horace smirks with his brow.

It is at this point the vulgarity of his mother tongue emanates so smoothly and synchronizes so well with the fabric of the universe that the surrounding, sexually confused quantum particles disentangle themselves and pay heed to the decisiveness of Brahe's vulgarities, whose originator finishes with an accusation: "She is foreign spy."

So, considering it, Horace offers what he feels is a most reasonable suggestion, "Have you reported it?"

"Report this, report that, then what, paperwork? Poor papers, for book burning be vogue again, if only more figured out. Disgrace it is."

He hammers an ambidextrous fist into the opposing palm. "We must not throw towel into bucket! Time is for action and time is now! What think you, comrade?"

Horace reflects on his misadventures of late, hearkening to his own misplaced identity — formerly someone else, or so he felt. Shaking it from memory, Horace replies, "Tonight?"

Brahe compresses into a grimacing fold of disgust. "Cliché, lazy Hedo. We go after break of fast."

"Now?"

Brahe stares patiently yet antagonistically as Horace concludes consummation with a lukewarm sliver of egg. "Come."

Brahe leads with a stride that clanks to the command tent from which Horace exited not an hour ago. But within is no Delilah, or anyone, for that matter. And what of her retinue? Brahe, staring about the place, seizes the opportunity and uproots all furniture not nailed down, calling to Horace to "check her quarters." Horace obliges in spite of the risks, having complete faith in his fellow Herrman and senior.

Her quarters feature, in the Scarab aesthetic, a rug woven with pagan and abstract patterns, its texture somehow harsher than the sediments outside. Pulling aside the flap, Horace finds underneath only sand. "Incriminating, is it not?" he thinks. Next is a wardrobe of ladies' clothing and pantaloons: no. The bed is minimalist and utilitarian — this too is irrelevant to the investigation. At the foot of it, however, is a pack that emanates a suspicious aura Horace feels in the depths of his amygdala — its feng shui is off! An orderly person would not have placed it there in particular. Horace approaches deliberately and with utmost caution, a guarded hand outstretches at the zipper. Slightly agape, it reveals a light-consuming void of mystery. And as his heart halts at the perception of a wriggle in the sack, Horace proceeds nonetheless with a sidearm drawn in the offhand — he had not noticed drawing it. His dominant hand by then clamps the zipper and is in turn lashed by a rogue tentacle. He recoils a-spook, but resists pulling the trigger of his Luger, instead calling out to his compatriot, "Brahe!"

"Speak!" he rushes in.

"Bag!"

A third voice thunders effeminately from Horace's periphery, "Begone!"

Delilah appears threateningly from behind a divider and hurls the bag at Horace, impacting with the force of two corpses. The two intruders scurry for a time. On his way, Horace speaks plainly: "She has a strong arm and a suspiciously heavy pack. Do we have the grounds to try her before a tribunal?"

Brahe articulates that "Legality is but mere technicality. If she is he, she cannot lay on us dirty fingers. We take that he-woman alive! Remain here and watch; I will gather men."

***

And the better part of an hour elapses as Horace paces through the camp. Surely, he can't be right — can't be. If he were, it would not feel the crime; trust your gut, so sayeth . . . who does keep saying that, anyhow? An accomplice of Brahe might know no peace; and while he was faffing, Atlantis had come to prove this corollary.

Before long, the clouds go dark and the air cool; hairs tense on the end of skin that reports to the body a status quo incompatible with the memory of muscles who, this time of day, would feel nothing of the sort but heat and torture. So be it! A gust of wind brings Horace to heel before a distant thunderstorm alight in artillery fire, hamstrings of light dazzling an interpretive dance, and this happened all at once without warning. "What the monkey?" he thinks as he becomes intimate with sludge pressed ho underneath the caress of razor winds that precede the main assault, winds that if he stood would carry him away — if not his head — clean off. As he lies there waiting for orders, he makes peace that none will come; Horace refuses to remain kneeling and crawls on his belly under the bombastic lull of shrapnel and aquatic shrills amid a vortex of dismemberment, tentacles, and legs shredded in a blender meant to garnish the camp with terror; translucent gore of red and yellow that drizzle ever the sprinkler on a wilted garden overdue the groundskeeper. Horace reaches shelter, the canteen from earlier. Its ground is littered with questionable fluids and meats; some contorted beeves are perhaps edible. In the self-contained cosmos of culinary limbo, chicken cutlets and pickled herrings intermix with minced fingers and diced blubber to concoct a deviled cockentrice fit for a maggot's palate. One such Atlantean with a wide carapace lies capsized in the muck, drunk on murder.

If this is to be Horace's first brush with evil, let him first turn a cheek to test its voracity. He plants his rifle's butt firmly on its exposed exoskeleton; this is the enemy. Its scrawny legs flail emphatically to no effect, its life to be eradicated if he so desired. And yet, Horace's retribution had not come. He flips the shell. "Arise."

The thoughtless Atlantean repays the gesture in the tradition of his people and lunges to his thigh, gashing Horace's refined shank for the gluttony of war; haphazardly strewn meats untouched by the locusts are a testament to the purpose of this end.

Horace lodges off and crushes the paltry beast underfoot, contributing its ghastly innards to the gruesome art, the food court a museum of taste. It was not a betrayal but a naivety that Horace presumed the Atlantean would deviate from its course. The surviving Horace is left standing among the rot, his hamstrings billowing in the primordial draft. The wound festers and spills. Medical attention shall wait; "At least it's not as serious as cancer," he feels.

Outside, the winds died somewhat to the waves of Atlantis that did spill knee high. From the hundredfold gaping wounds of one whale of an Atlantean, flooding puss makes driftwood of the camp's canvases. Suctioned tentacles smother the breath from helpless soldiers, explosions in the surrounding sea resurface buoyant carcasses all dead, and toothy Atlanteans maul corpses whole in a flurry of teeth and blood. Horace copes to himself, "Where in the monkey damn is the cavalry?" And from afar in the direction of Yin comes but one aircraft, a zeppelin of sorts. Horace stands there, watching for his own sake, and finds that it parks over the Atlantean horde in their main reservoir over yonder way from camp. Opening a hatch from beneath, it looses an object upon the field that falls faster than Horace knows what to make of it — a whole warship onto the Atlantean ranks emerges from within its splashy deployment and battles with a kraken-like entity. None other than Grimwald beckons from on by in a voice that strains over the chaos, "A beauty, is she not? As you might recall, I mentioned ve vere low on bombas. So ve airdropped a ship! Ve make do, hoho! Anyhow, muster with Brahe; he's near the command tent! Salute, soldier!" And off he goes to organize more men. "Fascinating," Horace whispers to himself, stricken by the appearance of the HMS *Monkey Have Mercy*, blasting away at the blubber of evil, an angel from on high.

Horace wades through the slosh, dripping from the thigh a slim cord of blood leading to the mess hall from which he came. Brahe bouts in the distance with a feminine figure, the colonel. Fate summons forth a spill of water, drifting Horace to the scene.

Brahe wrestles the woman into place. "Come to aid, comrade!"

Horace has nowhere to run, elsehow. "You've gone too far! We don't know if she's one of them!"

"Then see for yourself, you naive cow. She is spy!" As he rises from a prone Delilah, it is made clear his nose came off sometime in the fighting. "I am your senior! Kill the proverbial Scarab. The battle is won elsewhere and that is where I go."

Delilah stumbles to her feet with skewed

posture. She must have sustained a brutal beating.

Horace calls out, "Colonel, are you hurt?" Ignored, he cries once more, "Colonel Delilah!"

She wields a dispassionate glare that scans the field, then rests on Horace. Silence brings way to a murmur that evolves into maniacal laughter chilling even to the bones that have since been ripped from the bodies of various nearby combatants. She draws closer to the disabled Horace with a sportful gait and menacing aura. "Seems Brahe was right," Horace sighs. "Well, if I can't teach you humility, mayhaps you should be so kind as to let me teach it to your corpse," utters an understanding Horace to the very shadow of evil, stirring within him something lost, a fragment of a grudge.

Thus they made battle, and as Horace looked into her, the chronology of the mind is brought to remember Delilah's story.

IV

Book of Vulcan

Missiles, blood, and guts paint this picture a
delightful postmortem red glittered with sand. Woe
unto muddy Jove! Pores atop the bulbous point of
a nose swell into a difficult texture; nostrils reeled
agape welcome unknowingly a great many
suffocating earthen daggers. Born of ambition tried
and true, a passion burns vapidly in the sandstorm.
He by force of will emblazons the surrounding dust
with a passionate fire to match the splurge of
missiles loosed upon the desert sediments. Hardy
Jove beckons a freedom cry, exhuming from his
holes a torrent of ingested sand, resurrecting the
man on the brink of death who a day earlier might
have curled up and died; how dare he let anyone

take him alive for any reason at all? Never again shall King Monkey and his mob have their run of things, nor will Jove be condemned to die in the haboob. As cry turns to roar does Jove rattle the foundations of reality — heard and understood by good men who, too, take issue with things! (In fact, he never thought to scream so violently in the company of civilized, and therefore weak, domesticated men.) A good fellow heeds this call: a grey, airborne disk slides underneath him with the friction of a frequently lubricated chastity belt hinge, flying him to the clear skies above while outmaneuvering ill-intentioned projectiles, chafe-inducing sands and incendiary missiles alike.

With a violent lust imprinted on the retinas of newly born Jove does he speak: "Whom do I beseech, valorous savior, and where to? I yearn to smite the fool who thought to pick a fight with me."

A resounding thunder heeds the question. "My honor title is Aeroscorpion. We ride to the Eye of Atlantis from whose seat is fought the war of eons. You may yet claim your revenge."

And over the horizon of many days' travel from the eighteenth to the twenty-first lies a scattering of oases on which a kingdom thrives: Atlantis, under whose sweltering sun these marines pitch about their tepees. In the center dominates the grandest tent of them all, afloat over the largest pool of water known as the Eye. Bridges skew to reach it from every direction for the benefit of humanid and bipedal Atlantean, of which there are a number. King Monkey is ever the narcissist, or else they wouldn't have legs.

The thunder, a time silent, tremors once again. "You are worthy of Gastrodomwiz. I would have you speak with him."

Jove needn't think on it. "I do as I please."

"A satisfactory response." Aeroscorpion deposits him at the base of a rickety bridge. "My obligation to you ends, but yours to his begins. Should you see him, he will answer to you and your queries." Wings flap a primordial gust. "May we meet once more on the field, the place where life does stir its magnificent soup so that I might eat you, or you I."

The yurt imposes a certain grandeur and mystique over the rest, its white dome clean and pure in whose shadow is sprawled patchwork browns and oranges. At each of the four corners, a smaller yet slender yurt imitates a minaret. Bustling Atlanteans that slither hither and fro speak the king's gibberish; it is a metropolis, more or less. What dwells inside this place of import? Curtain flaps fold to reveal a column, on it a blob. Could this be their leader?

It speaks, "You're in the right place. He awaits you." Of course not, he is but an usher allowed just enough cognizance by fate to follow the orders of his betters.

"Much obliged," Jove manages, independent of prejudice.

The blob bows.

Tribal carpets and strange idols adorn the walls; a recurring theme is a figure of many arms. Unlike legs, not all Atlanteans have a one, though the same could be said of the fair and noble humanids; a congregation of Atlanteans feast on just such an armless humanid corpse splayed over an altar.

Not long does the yurt fill with heavy air. "I" am overcome with dread to which "I" answer immediately and with extreme prejudice. "Show yourself, woodwork cockroach!" And from beneath the glass floor a mass of tentacles pass freely through a green glimmer radiating from the oasis bed; it reeks of sentience. "I" never flee and would sooner die of stupidity than live with the guilt of cowardice, having shirked a foe "I" would not think to respect. The length of tentacle leads to a room and an even greater cluster of tentacles.

From the top hangs an occult chandelier of many skulls oscillating at an angle like a disco ball, though only half as bright and tenfold more purple. Bookshelves compact together and hug the interior walls to form a skyrise reaching the top of the yurt, culminating in an arch of papyrus and thoughtfulness. The semicircular doughnut of a rich mahogany desk overflooding with paperwork is situated over a diving hole to the waters below, emerging from it the head of a tentacled Atlantean that speaks. "Mmmmm, my tentacles swell with the knowledge of your coming. Welcome to my esteemed mind palace. I am he and you my guest. Humor me a question, then I you a request."

Only as Jove begins to speak is he interrupted by the Atlantean.

Gastrodomwiz bellows with the joy of eureka, "I understand." A tentacle emerges from the depths and slithers around the immense catalog until it settles over a peculiar tome. "Yeeeees, I grant you these thoughts — you will find them of use." Gastrodomwiz's tentacle retracts from the book and inches to the forehead of Jove, who sweats metaphysical tears of anticipation. "Witness thought."

Jove's mind does fill with the knowledge of Atlantis, of its mythos, of its aims, of its history — and all of this is accompanied by a phantom sensation of burning incense:

Tales tell of a once almighty god whose name was not so much forgotten as fractured with the rest of him; contemporaries nevertheless agree to call him Yang until such a time the name is recovered. A god with many arms, he was all powerful and slew and ate his enemies, growing a new arm from every vanquished foe. There came such a time, however, Yang emerged so completely and ubiquitously victorious from conquest that everyone else died; the universe was subsumed into his many arms who, in turn, began to quarrel with one another as they did before their union.

"Who's ripe for a gutting?" spoke the impatient arm of might.

"Settle down." The arm of moderation did restrain his compatriot by the bicep.

The arm of immoderation, moderation's twin sister containing all her brother's features except sex, whistled lustfully at the strength of might, and might, wanting to impress immoderation, slew moderation, who flew at a medium pace into the cosmos.

The arm of authority arrived to apprehend might. "Halt, trouble-doer! I take issue with you."

But the arm of immoderation seduced authority as well. "Why start and stop at might? There is a whole body for you to impose on," convincing him to jump out of his socket to run amok and make scandals of the other arms who'd previously and innocently lain out of the long arm's reach.

Authority first chopped the arm of vulgarity, but there were two of him and the latter destroyed the arm of infrastructure to make a point to the arm of wealth who selfishly fled the body in good time, smugly thinking himself all the more cunning for it. Authority then trespassed into the domicile of the arm of misery, who was found to have severed himself, but authority feverishly pinned the crime on the now deported arm of color; this had all been occurring while might cleaved a great deal of arms from the body, causing the rest to scatter and crawl afield of the combined turmoil, leaving Yang an armless and pale husk dwelling on his prime.

Theologians say Yang yet lives among us, or that there is a piece of him in us all, even that we are his arms. Thus, it is plausible to aspire to the greatest whole; Atlanteans eat the dead as Yang once did, friend and foe alike, to accrue their knowledge, strength, or else; this is not a point of contention but an observable phenomenon that empowers Atlantis in the less abundant of Katsikoskoni's two hemispheres. It is notable this phenomenon might apply to humanids as well, but the consumer must be mindful of the quality and compatibility of foodstuffs, lest they fall to chaos like Yang. There are a number of approaches Atlanteans have taken to this analogy: Certain camps of Yangist purists seek to merge everyone regardless of the end result, to relive the cycle of the universe taken for fact, others to slot everyone into an appropriate place before the ultimate union so as to avoid the same mistake as Yang, who conquered indiscriminately. A number of tumultuous Atlanteans have been known to eat exclusively for power, harmony be damned, but are reliably reined in by the ideology. Some Atlanteans have toyed with the thought of biological warfare, weakening the humanids with poor foods, but most agree this would weaken the whole of Yang when Atlanteans inevitably consume all humanids. Of late, many voice concerns that humanids poison themselves; the worst of their dead are burned instead of consumed.

Since time immemorial, Atlanteans of the Arena have conjured control of their oases by the green-glimmering relic known as the Egg to amass a torrential sea on which is carried the hordes of Atlantis to fight the armies of AID-afflicted humanids for the purposes of eating. Even among the more skeptical and practical Atlanteans, they eat not for enlightenment but survival. Everyone eats all the same.

The vision is cut short and Gastrodomwiz waits a moment to observe Jove before continuing the conversation. "Hmmmmm, forgive me for prying — it cannot be helped — but as I beamed thoughts into your mind space, I noticed you have no name. Yang in the flesh, perhaps? Found your arms?" He emits a muffled giggling.

"Never mind that, what the sod did you do to me?" Jove goes bug-eyed with the exhibitionism of Neurotypicles. (An idiom of the time.)

Gastrodomwiz then beams an indecent picture of a prancing midget into Jove's mind space, "Ours is a religion of reincarnation; our bodies are reincarnated through our ingestions, our thoughts through what we learn from others, even the air we breathe. In this place of learning, I reincarnate my thoughts into you. Moreover, this is my mind palace from which I plan and direct the armies of Atlantis. It is a most lucrative palace, indeed!"

"A mind palace, here?" Jove did not seem to understand the premise of his own question.

"And why not? Are we not all in the mind palace of the real? Just as I see books in the library of my headspace, so it is there are books in my library of the real. Just as I imagine beaming thoughts into your mind, so too are thoughts beamed into your mind."

"Or it works one way and you're a pretender."

"Perhaps!" He giggles again. "But I saw it before I imagined it. If nothing else, the imaginary reinforces the real and it helps me remember what I read. Did you think these books were meant for you?"

"I don't think, I act. This is who I am." Jove beams at him with the lizard's froth.

"And I am Gastrodomwiz, wise man. I have no name save that what others call me. That is how names work, yes? What narcissist names himself? Mmmmm hehe. Perhaps a new name will emerge if you survive this encounter. Having answered your question and fattened you with the delicious knowledge and understanding of my people, I must inform you that we, Atlantis, have an impetus to eat you. I will even request as much."

Gastrodomwiz's maw gapes to reveal a circle of serrated teeth dripping with rancid, salivating ichor. Jove, offended by this revelation, bites at the slithery tentacle that had not yet returned to the brine; the creature did resound with displeasure and redoubled its efforts to eat the man, bearing down on him with the weight of its body. But hardy Jove did not squish, for he, in this form, is impervious to the weight of knowledge.

Pinned under his adversary, Jove stares indignantly at Gastrodomwiz, who would be made to regret swallowing him. So did Jove thrash about in the gullet of his enemy that it was with great difficulty he would stay down. Gastrodomwiz seemed to heave.

"Let me go!" demands Jove in the manner of someone too proud to admit they deserve defeat. What haughtiness! As Jove's senses weaken, he finds himself ejaculated into a burning puddle before Gastrodomwiz in the library.

"It is decided. I will not eat you, for if I did, I would inherit your impulse; it would hamper my role as a leader. Perhaps you belong in the stomach of a common foot soldier. I would call thee Vulcan; of this the entire kingdom has been notified."

"Fuck off." Though in spite of his protestation, Vulcan would adopt this new name, rather taken by its fearfulness.

"Where a common Hedo might invoke King Monkey to rouse the rabble, we Atlanteans use the rabble to set in motion the gears of Yang. Begone and find your place in the world."

Gastrodomwiz's head recedes dramatically into the depths.

The blob bows as Vulcan departs the grand yurt into streets of grey bustling with various life forms of an almost alien quality. Those who cannot walk traverse a system of moats. Vulcan follows aimlessly through the crowds and past yurts and makings of industry, noting these Atlanteans are technologically comparable to the Hedoes, though where the latter might have a manufactory, the former has a scrapyard of salvage and a few smithies of no little genius. The short of it: the Atlanteans with thumbs have guns to fire.

A rather lanky Atlantean is seen to be hauling a number of these armaments to a nearby pit over which is strewn a heap of triangular flags. A crowd watches on with muffled interest. And upon closer inspection, it is seen this is a pit of sport and killing, an arena within the Arena.

The lanky Atlantean appears to be a sort of showman. "Come one, come all ye fish of ill repute! Test your mettle against a soldier of evil and feast on his bones should you find him worthy! Oh, but look who slinks in the shadows! Another humanid comes our way! I always said where you find one parasite, you find two! But he does not wear the colors of this POS POW! What say you, vile thing, will you entreat us to a spectacle of humanid-on-humanid violence?" His beady eyes ooze with gleeful anticipation.

Vulcan had always wanted to kill a man and so leaps into the pit. The crowd cheers with great fancy. The man before "me" is quite healthy, if a bit dirtied around the face, and wears golden-brown fatigues. He sizes "me" up with the usually apprehensive quandary of friend or foe.

The showman throws each of us a machete; its handle sinks in the sand and its blade shimmers in the sun so bright that "I" struggle to see my reflection. No matter, "I" know who "I" am and what "I" want. ("I" am one of those insufferably decisive people.)

The POW grips his blade but keeps it pointed at

the ground. "I" want a fair fight, so illuminate my intentions by beating my chest like King Monkey before the passing of judgment on his subjects. The adversary sighs depressingly and raises his weapon. Oh, what a thrill it will be when "I" tear out his arms and beat him to death with them! How "I've" yearned to do it to some miser who'd rubbed "me" wrong. "I" am Vulcan, fucker of the fuckers who'd thought to fuck with "me"!

"Yagh!" Vulcan brutishly hacks at the soldier with the machete as if it were a hammer; none of the hits connect except the last, which lops off a finger. The crowd is amused with laughs of indecency to the chagrin of the soldier who keeps a panicked focus on Vulcan, managing to graze his neck in retaliation. It is a wonder Vulcan hadn't died from recklessness. Vulcan, of course, does not reflect and redoubles with reckless abandon. It is perhaps in this aversion to preponder the next move that Vulcan is faster than his opponent ever could be. For every three strikes the soldier anticipates, one makes its mark. For every strike the soldier seeks to make, Vulcan's is faster and more lethal.

Somehow, after all the exertion, it is the soldier who tires, every movement more feeble and sluggish than the last until Vulcan breaks through the defense and splits the skull of the man, his eyes struck dumb with defeat. This is the part where Vulcan brings the POW down to his level and beats him with experience, decapitates him, and pulls apart both halves and drinks the blood of a nourishing coconut to a castaway malnourished of violence, that entitlement of his heritage. It tastes of fear tempered by cheer of the crowd, a psychopath's delicacy.

"The modest Herrman was no match for the excess of Hedophilia!" the lanky Atlantean announces from the voracious applause. "Claim your reward, O murderous one! We fashioned this trophy from the kit of the dastardly loser." He presents to Vulcan a sawn-off machine gun like might be found with a hoodlum in the treacherous alleys of Hedophilia. "We lop off the tip 'cause we need the scraps. And it's too big to lug around otherwise." The Atlantean smiles, then addresses the crowd. "Let us celebrate this momentous victory with a feast! Come, come! Oh, and don't you forget the corpse!"

The crowd meanders to a commons, a veranda with long tables raised over a highway of water. It is a place inviting to creatures from beneath and overland bipeds alike, some of which are humanid. "My, my, you've butchered him for me. Don't be taking my job now, foreigner! Har har!" a jolly Atlantean jokes as he grills the soldier of Yin, plumes of fumes tasty and decadent inspiring an ambience of relaxation and good vibes. The tables are loaded with a score of Atlanteans and humanids: tentacles, fingers, thighs, flaps, you think it, it's there.

Nimble Aeroscorpion glides over the table opposite Vulcan. "You fought. I watched."

"How'd you figure?"

"Bloody even for an Atlantean." He slurps a finger.

"No qualms eating your own?"

The lanky showman clears his throat. "Atlantis, what a place of culture! But of course we cannibalize our relatives; honor the whole animal and all that. I reckon that there eyeball belongs to my dear cousin Greg — I'd recognize that cataract anywhere." He picks it fast. "They and he do not disappear on death. We inherit them into ourselves to recycle their strength or redeem them of weakness." He pauses, reminiscing and amused, "Greg was not much of a fighter but could spin one heck of a fib. It's a sort of reincarnation, an honor!"

Vulcan recalls the fish in the desert. "I might have eaten one of yours before. What can you tell me about him?"

"Sod if I know. Might've tempered the culture shock seeing as you fit right in. Could've been a feisty guy. Or that fiester was you all along. It's up to you to see the difference."

The chef brings the POW's head on a plate. "For you, seeing as you savaged the wretch." His head remains split; the chef had taken the liberty to fill the gap with mashed potatoes and caviar. Vulcan thanks him with a nod.

Aeroscorpion nibbles on another finger, "That soldier you killed, in turn, killed my rider. Would that I have eaten my comrade, I would not regret our parting. His body is lost to me and, for this, I grieve. I thank you for this small comfort. Gratitude."

"Help yourself, Aero."

"I could not." Aeroscorpion nibbles.

"Get a grip, man!" the showman announces. "Avenge the fallen in battle and such!"

"Do you think he would . . . ?"

"Would? Already did! With enthusiasm, might I add!" The showman points to the head and looks to Vulcan. "Why'd you think I gave you a gun? Enlist!"

Vulcan manages to nod through the voring of his enemy.

***

It is the twenty-second day of the tenth month, preceded by the twenty-first wherein Vulcan killed a man. And he would strike again: Threads undone and muff disfigured, 'tis a bad day for a dummy. An aquatic eagle faster than the cheetah dive-bombs its prey, though not before its companion, saddled and braced, rains fire from above and flourishes a blade as an afterthought, cleaving the dummy in two and, with a second strike of the false edge, slashes the airborne fleshbag into nothing further still. Altogether, the amalgamation of a gun, blade, and stinger comprise the death incarnate born of Vulcan and Aeroscorpion, the very same that tormented the training dummy all morning until its deathly ripping to shreds.

"You swing as a thousand, brother," speaks Aeroscorpion, in a middle-high spirit recovering from the melancholy of yesterday.

Vulcan flushes, or even blushes red with murderousness. "And you as a thousand more! When do we see the blood of our enemies?"

"Eager? Good. Intel suggests the Yins mustered the courage to appear naked in the Arena. A retaliation, perhaps, after the prior skirmish from which I flew you? No matter, they have not yet embarked on this vengeance; that will happen in the coming days, at which point there will be a glorious battle."

Vulcan's eyes rapture in a deluge of overexcited blood vessels. "A good day it will be!" he cries for war.

Aeroscorpion whispers meaningfully, "We ride."

Vulcan, mounted firmly, yells with the zealous fervor of an eagle bequeathed by destiny the throne of victory, "Wreee!"

Aeroscorpion's muscles glisten through the expanding of wings; he soars to the aerial highway, obscuring the overhead sun. He issues a tremendous "Wreee!"

To the skies return Aquabus and Washington, Hydromothra and Goatman, Waterboard and MacDiver, Sea Horsepower and Pelvis-Crusher, and Flying Dutchman with Davy Jones.

Each return a fine "Wreee!"

Pelvis-Crusher beat on a war drum with her signature phallic-shaped club, vibrations heard across the land, perhaps even southerly Scarabia in the humanid hemisphere. In formation, the aerial dragoons spray red mist from biodegradable canisters, goading the denizens below to salute, or else wipe bodily secretions from the appropriate sockets, handkerchiefs readied to this cause and waving otherwise.

The teary-eyed general, Bronze Bull Khan, reminisces upon a locket bearing the likeness of his kin. Trembling, but maintaining resolve, he blows on a golden, bejeweled didgeridoo. Gastrodomwiz, in turn, invokes the power of the Egg, decimating Atlantis for the occasion and conjuring a torrent on which the warrior caste shall stride into battle.

Bronze Bull Khan, amassing a band of hardy Atlanteans, orates, "Countrymer, lend me your sensory orifices; ours is the plight of millennia!" and so on out of earshot of Vulcan, who departs with his troop ahead of the main army, a forward party. He hears the crowd cheer at the revelation of its own misfortune. Adrenaline, or the aquatic equivalent, surges through the predominantly one-way heart chamber vessels of the now violently amplified crowd. The whirlpool of Atlanteans trembles! The Bull commands a charge, "Wreeeeee!" which is, of course, not to be confused with "Wreee!" The grand yurt illuminates bedazzlingly with a pure-green candescence, penetrating Gastrodomwiz's submerged, opaque figure, conjuring a light show reminiscent of aurora borealis. Shades of purple and blue adorn the dully, duly arid 'scapes and anteceding elevations about the Eye. This presentation is more mystical than the rocketry of Yin, especially more so than the public nuisance that is fireworks and its accompanying crowds of vacuous, upright terra-cotta constructs assembled solely as an impediment to movement. (Vulcan, even in this form, much prefers a rainy day — a holdover from the past?)

The Atlantean Aquabus spearheads the reconnaissance, leaving half a day's distance ahead of Bronze Bull. It is a number of days before he lands at a clearing middlingly green with perhaps countless generations of blood fertilizing the soil; it is clean for the moment. An odd cabin breaks the horizon in the distance — Vulcan knows in his gut the airborne Atlanteans would much prefer respite under open sky.

The humanid Washington orders the steeds and by implication their riders, "Hydromothra, Sea Horsepower, Flying Dutchman, space out a few kilometers. Run routes and return, say, three hours at the latest herein. We'll go from there." And three pairs remain.

Washington ceremoniously draws an arquebus, kit akin to an honorary saber or pistol befitting an officer. He fixes the bayonet and inspects the chamber, nearly poking out his eye. "Set up camp, gentlemen. I'll keep watch."

Vulcan disentangles a bedroll and lies restlessly of inaction. Aeroscorpion by his side purrs the lion. Distant MacDiver fiddles with a multi-tool knife, licking a blade flicked at random before speaking . . . Only a sound does not come forth; he glares an opportunity for Vulcan to introduce himself. Vulcan, in response, raises his weapon and, intently matching MacDiver's gaze, slices a salami sausage for Aeroscorpion, tail swaggering in the wind. MacDiver bites his blade threateningly, baring teeth. Accruing the hints, Vulcan slices two tokens, impaling the salami on the point of his blade and extending it as an olive branch to MacDiver who, in turn, forks the offering with a newly revealed blade opposite the one wrenched in his mouth. Vulcan insists with silence. MacDiver twirls the knife, supplanting the empty blade with the savory shish kebab, suavely undressing a single salami slice as one would an article of clothing from the thigh of a paramour. He lowers the blade to his hip, wrist resting on a thigh; Waterboard, also lying by her companion, accepts the remaining slice. Sated MacDiver sheathes his weapons and falls aslumber. Waterboard, nuzzling in a cradle formed by his legs, does the same.

Washington's ponytail sways under a tricorne hat. He unsuccessfully feigns ambivalence. Aware of his blunder, he announces it, "He fancies you."

"Oh?"

"He's not one for the common man's pleonasm. Can't say I like small talk, myself."

"Mhm."

"Sincerely, MacDiver is a character and a good fellow at that."

Aquabus joins the conversation. "Rest. You'll soon have your go at things."

Reluctant to succumb to unconsciousness, Vulcan takes to stargazing as days before, wondering how many gazed onto him.

"What's changed?" Aeroscorpion addresses the insomnia.

Vulcan clutches his fragmented fascinum amulet. "I'm short a testicle."

"Hang on to what you have; monorchids only have the one and are as content as when you had two. If there's someone once with three, but since lost one, they might be just as grief-stricken as you now. Don't sweat, it's safe with me."

"I thank you."

"Gratitude accepted."

Pacified by revelry, Vulcan drowns in dreams flavored of ambrosia, which is to say sleep is for the weak; he merely daydreams lying prone under a bed of night. In good time the patrol did come, with it Hydromothra, Goatman, Sea Horsepower, and Pelvis-Crusher.

Washington ceases lubing his arquebus. "Reports!"

Goatman flexes his gut through a worn wifebeater, purporting, "Yer 'nna eat yer hat."

Hydromothra roars unintelligibly.

He consoles the beast, "T'as right, girl. She says two t'ousand of 'em urban-lovin' hicks're knockin' 'round an' sleepin' 'n 'e mids' o' a bloomin' dust devil."

Hydromothra murmurs in agreement.

Goatman whispers to her ear, "Atta girl. Y'll eat yer fill o' man meat soon 'nough."

"What of Dutchman and Jones?" Aquabus interjects.

Pelvis-Crusher reclines on her club, its tip in the sand, and recalls, "Saw chase prey. Left them. Around cabin," she finishes with a grunt.

Washington raises a fist, pulsing a tone somber but proud, "Damn those beautiful children of Yang. Leave them to it. Reckon we'll wait for them here."

Aquabus orders Waterboard and MacDiver, "Take charge of Aeroscorpion and Vulcan. Remember, you have clearance to soften them up a bit. They'll not feel threatened by a smaller party. The storm should clear by the time the main force arrives. Haboob guide you."

In response, MacDiver fastens saddlebags to an already overencumbered Waterboard. He then bisects a bag, drawing a small handful of gunpowder and puffs the dust toward Vulcan before it gravitates to the sand. It might've been a kiss from death itself. MacDiver lights the residue upon the ground, then a cigar for himself. The couples ascend into the lukewarm dusk just above the dust. Maybe it's dawn; no one brought a watch. Vulcan consults his internal calendar; for the first time in a while it's shaky — is it the twenty-fifth or the twenty-sixth . . . midnight, perhaps?

Waterboard briefs her compatriots. "The two forces are divided by the storm. We could handily savage one of our choosing. Intel says the Herrmans are fresh fools. We should ravage the more dangerous Scarabs. If nothing else, they'll lose sleep before the main assault — they don't know what's coming. Since it's four of us, I doubt they'll run for the hills. You keep us covered, maybe pick off a few stragglers if you see an opportunity." She ends with great enthusiasm, "We'll light them ablaze so that I might hear the monkey's chorus. Go and sow havoc while we combust our droppings."

"Ain't you two equal partners? What's smoky got to say about it?" Vulcan prods.

"I think it was his idea. Lug around thirty pounds of the stuff and you get the picture real fast." She takes a moment to sit on the mild resentment. "And he's got plastic army men in his breast pocket when even I can't understand him." Waterboard positively gushes with schadenfreude.

MacDiver slaps her lightly.

Aeroscorpion whispers to snickering Vulcan, "Imagine the glory if we take the colonel hostage. Kill her if else. It is high risk, but I see you're the type." And Vulcan assents.

MacDiver leads the operation above the Yins,

dropping upon them the ordnance from his packs and setting alight a number of tents. An alarm gongs, or perhaps thuds with great vim, rousing the men to the flanks. "Yet, how to discern the leader . . . pretty sparkly shiny medals? Of course, only the Yins are daft enough. Atlanteans go by size," reaffirms Vulcan to himself.

From the colonel's chest gleams in modest moonlight a sheet of shiny metal bits. She is preoccupied with one division initially but is soon en route to the other side. Vulcan tucks his body in anticipation for the live drive-by dive orchestrated by his significant other; Aeroscorpion initiates a dive-bomb, incinerating the air about him — engulfed in a broth of savory fire hotter than the warmth of anticipation Vulcan felt in his belly. The wind scorches on the way down until the point Aeroscorpion thrust up, shrugging off the hellfire coat, allowing Vulcan a moment of chilly clarity before the rendezvous with the target — and her trajectory — Delilah, who for but a moment is isolated. Vulcan jousts with the butt of his falchion, its sheath buttressed against the shoulder; the colonel is hereby dubbed by her lordship! She is relieved of the burden of consciousness. Trusty Aeroscorpion, however, tumbles into a bystanding tent. Incidentally, it is a matter of good fortune the tent is vacant, its inhabitants likely dispersed by the carpet bombing. Whence gathering his wits, that he had any, Vulcan looks upon his compatriot. Aeroscorpion attempts to stretch and retract a wing, grunting, "Broken."

"Plan?"

A wisp of embarrassed thunder answers, "You get us out."

Vulcan opens his pack. "In."

"The colonel comes with. Her uniform can't stay either, not even under a bed. Too suspicious; these army types excel at cleaning their shitting spaces for some absurd reason."

"You sure you'll both fit?"

"Not the issue. You need an out too. And there are only spare underclothes around here, nothing convincing."

"Think, man!"

***

Thus Vulcan donned the uniform of the late colonel and made haste for her tent where he would not dare be questioned. Vulcan lowered the mask that hid his more masculine features before again addressing Aeroscorpion: "You crazy son of a bitch!"

"I see you kept the beard despite shaving the legs."

"The Yins shall have to cut me down with it."

"Other than that, I think you pass."

"We'll be soon putting this to the test. We can't leave in plain daylight, not like this."

"Rightly so. We should wait 'till the landing of Bronze Bull. Meanwhile, let us wait for an opportunity to disperse the Yins; anything that can give us an edge in the coming hours."

"Pray it arrives presently. I'm chafing at the poles."

"Did you put on all of it?"

It is at this junction Vulcan is saved the humiliation of answering the question; a Hedo soldier arrives with a letter from the other colonel, a Herrman. The interaction is perhaps longer than necessary, but Vulcan manages to eventually shoo him away without compromising his identity.

"Superb acting, that," Vulcan congratulates himself. "How does our lady fare?"

"Sleeping as a babe on chloroform to boot."

"You dog, you! Come then, we must send a telegraph to this Grimwald character."

"What be the nature of this mischief?"

"This missive we received asks to mobilize a retreat, cowards."

"Malarkey! They shan't leave."

"We will see to that."

"Yes yes."

"But how?" Vulcan prods innocently.

"A letter of our own."

"And what will be the contents of the letter?"

"That our reconnaissance reports there is no imminent danger, and that a retreat would kill morale. And to serve the men each some beer to cool the nerves and make them stupid with drunkenness."

"Indeed! And how would we write it?"

"Find a few reports to emulate, yes?"

"Good, Aeroscorpion. I had thought as much."

So following to the best of his ability the style of Delilah's papers, Vulcan drafts the order and stamps it with his ring, giving it to the guard outside, who surmises the intent through a cough and a poignant finger.

Outside, Vulcan observes the hustling of men who seem to know their orders. He breathes fresh air, tasting for the slightest whiff of salt; it begins soon. In this sampling of air there is also the impression of a noise, and, returning inside, Vulcan finds two men shuffling about his tent, his first instinct for violence throwing the bag that contained both Aeroscorpion and Delilah at one such intruder who just as quickly flees as he burgled in. Vulcan sheepishly retrieves the bag that contained his comrade.

"Have we been figured out?" asks Vulcan of

Aeroscorpion.

"Perhaps," hisses Aeroscorpion.

"No matter. Let us cower in the corner with our guns and await rescue."

To this, Aeroscorpion could not think of a reply.

***

A number of soldiers seeking their colonel have come and gone through the domain of the imposter who stayed very still for fear he'd been compromised. With every passing guest, it seemed his cover was not yet blown, but even so Vulcan rationalized to Aeroscorpion that this was his plan to sow confusion — and to himself anything that would hide his shame. Only once the ruckus had begun does Vulcan lift a tent flap; a murderous reservoir must have come whirling under the foreboding drizzle of distant Atlantis. A single voice turned many in the hysteria of war, a cacophony.

No sooner than Vulcan leaves the tent, a soldier approaches from the periphery who introduces himself as Brahe, accomplice of Horace, before promptly tackling him to the damp sand beneath his feet. The offended Vulcan plants a swift, persuasive handshake upon the offender's cockpit, wrenching the very soul from his being before launching him head over heels with the strength of a man. Brahe lands as a feline, regarding it as perhaps a ten-story drop inflicted by a curious toddler, scathed only of pride, a most fatal wound. Brahe regains composure in vengeful agony — or so Vulcan tells himself — cupping a handful of sand, intent on depriving the imposter of sight (again), and with finesse sprays his lukewarm grains in the corresponding sockets. Vulcan staggers helplessly before the superior Brahe who looks to make retribution. Yet, from within Vulcan's pack slithers out the impressive tail of Aeroscorpion, lashing at the attacker a quiet thunder. The sand clears, revealing Aeroscorpion's tail constricting Brahe's dominant hand, the latter's offhand attempting to wrestle back the knife he'd presumably wanted to use on his Delilah; he was indeed intent on stabbing, but forgoes the blade, instead grappling the sentient whip and pulling it forward before promptly drop-kicking his sorry arse into the sodden gobshite once more. An unsavory darkness clouds his vision; a lone voice, Death, itself, come to collect, yells, "I darn had 'nough o' ye posh, pr'tensh's city boys! Come 'n git some!" A meaty fist audibly collides not with Vulcan but Brahe. Goatman, in a chubby flex, wrenches his comrade off the ground, voice hearty and booming, "Ye be needin' a hand t'ere, lassie?"

Vulcan relinquishes his knapsack. "Behold, for a mangled Aeroscorpion and unconscious colonel lie within. Make haste homeward ho!"

To this command, Goatman saddles Hydromothra. "Aye, yer purty mouth hassa point."

His trusty steed whines in agreement.

"W'll come back fer ya, Vulcan. 'N yer'nna get yer fill then, a'ight, girl?"

She enthuses then sighs, burdened by the weight of three. (But she is something of a workhorse.) Two halves ride into the sun.

Vulcan rests a spell, noting confusedly in the distance a warship that seems to fight for the Yins. Unable to compute the meaning of this or the ship's origin, he reverts his attention to the steadily waking Brahe; they wrestle sweatily. Vulcan remains on top for a moment before mechanical Brahe gets the better of him, pinning the despoiler to the soil. As Vulcan looks up, he notices that sometime in the fighting, Brahe's nose had come off. How? Surely, it couldn't have just fallen off. Or did it?

Brahe remains in this position, perhaps unsure how to handle his quarry; indeed, he might have been looking for any reason not to kill "her" where "she" lay. Thus swept along by fate comes skeptical Horace to lend his aid, and the two soldiers have a short exchange about the nature of my allegiance. Perhaps Brahe thinks he could so easily snap "my" neck that he figures he might let his compatriot have a go at things to prove he was right in that "I" am a foreign spy, which "I" am, though "I" take offense to being spoken about in such a contemptuous way.

Brahe departs. Vulcan heaves a great laugh at the turn of events and charges at Horace with glee who, though armed, is deeply confused and will surely pay the price for his slack jaw, it being deeply disgusting. Vulcan, in the nature of his mien, strikes first upon a befuddled Horace who, in turn, fires his gun an empty threat; it jams and things devolve to fisticuffs. For every blow unflinching Horace withstands he returns in equal measure — albeit a moment later than the impulsive Vulcan who punches a storm. By contrast, the POW he slew in Atlantis he knows in his gullet to be an inferior who could not weather the blows at all, if at all strike back; thus Vulcan ferments an appreciation for his opponent.

Vulcan fought with Horace, or Jove with himself. And thus it came to be the both of them had been skewered by a third, weighing in at about the same as the others.

V

Book of Hermes

Seldom self save for now, Jove thrice awakens atop a mound. Had he been yeeted by the storm? If so, how far, and where to? Such queries may have been of relevance to Jove, but not he, for he is here and now, not then and there.

'Twas some force planted him here — anywhere — and disappeared. Perhaps the same force insists he do the same and disappear. 'Tis not he himself that insists, so, aimless, wanders inland. Sun-scorched earth may have pained once, but now is he as much as he is; akin to flesh and bone are heat and calluses. He may well be desert, for without, he is not as he is, and therefore not at all. The same is true of the impending wave on whose spine ride two surfboards and skin-clad surfers, one donned in trousers and the other a bikini. Does the tsunami approach he, or he it? Regardless, both are quintessential components of the product: the wave simmers into the ground and the two surfers, disheveled with windswept hair, face him.

The man speaks in tones not native to anywhere: "Looking to catch some gnarly waves?"

The woman affirms with a "Radical, dude."

Former Jove asks, "Where will the waves bring?"

"We go where the wind blows."

"You ever ride one before?"

"Evermore," says Jove.

"Wicked, dude."

"Here comes a righteous skimmer," notes the second.

The first offers a spot atop his board. "Hop on, brother man."

He rides far, though certainly not long, before happening upon a garden home to goats, agave fruit, and a cabin modest in relation to the treachery of the clime?

He speaks to them, "Are you alive here?"

The first did speak. "Groovin', man."

The second did also. "I think he's asking if we live there."

The man corrects himself, "Right on. We live

wherever the wave takes us, so, uh, yeah. S'pose."

The wave subsides at the very doorstep, and to it hobbles a magnificent specimen of a goat, headstrong with jet-black dreadlocks and a Fu Manchu to rival his own; Jove did not have one before. The formermost surfer grounds his knee and raises his arms in joyous praise. "How's my best man? Good to see you again."

Its sandpaper tongue reciprocates.

The woman opens the door to her newfound guest. "Make yourself at home. Vibe's real cozy."

Where else someone may have said something, Jove nods, as to him, unnecessary oral excursions encompass not which is, but rather that which seems to be; he preoccupied himself with being grateful, not seeming it.

The dwelling is furnished plainly: two beds, a double and a single. A lava lamp grooves its moves. Musical equipment and harpoons hang from racks. Sitting cushions surround a table set with three mugs, each seemingly catered to a particular taste. Jove did not think he was expected as a visitor. The woman seats herself by the martini. "Pull up a pillow, won't ya?"

Jove opts for herbal tea, a conglomeration of stuff, the eastern panacea to forever end King Monkey's AID. He thinks he detects mint, but it could very well be outside his limited purview.

Knowledge is ephemeral, existing only in the knower — and Jove does not need to know what he fancies. So what? The abstract survives us all, and truth is the lazy person's knowledge. Nobody needs to know the truth for the truth to be true, but a knower would have to know for knowledge to exist. Thus, he preoccupies with matters that are true. Or maybe not. "Meh," he thinks.

The goat-bonded surfer strides inside and strikes a pose of allure. "Welcome to mi casa de salsa. And no, don't ask me what that means. I don't know."

She snickers. "Rude, we haven't introduced ourselves."

He flexes, stretches, and contorts ever still. "Righto. I'm Onemsiz and this is Mon Sizé," he says.

Mon reiterates, "Them ain't Hedo names, that's for sure. How's about yourself, stranger?"

Jove preponders, ponders, and finally postponders over herbal fumes. "I am he who has no name, for 'twould seem he who was I is no more with us a member of the living or the dead. Might I have the name of someone who is newly born?"

Onemsiz settles by the goat milk, unnerved by the odd fellow. "You askin' us to adopt ya?"

"Wicked idea! What should we name him?"

He plays a whimsy-nonsense upon his tongue. "Hm . . . Hrm, Hrrrr. Hurrrrrr . . . Herbert?"

"Crapshoot." She grasps at the straws of her hat.

"Oh, how about Hermes? 'Cause, you know, you smell like several hermits."

His woman is deeply moved. "A beautiful name for Herpes."

Onemsiz is pleased with himself. "Good. Swell, even." He finishes the goat milk. "Let's play a game of catch, dog? Son? What were you again?" Onemsiz performs an intimacy at the base of Mon's neck and struts outside, hips asway, to which Hermes averts his eyes.

"Don't be standing up your pops."

The newly dubbed Hermes follows into the garden of assorted roots: potatoes, radishes, and leeks. The goats decimate the surrounding grasses; the harmony of the garden is preserved.

A football is readied — "Heads up!" — and is sent. "I feel you got something on your noggin. Lay it on me, dude."

Hermes amateurishly bear hugs the ball. "I don't know, which is not to say I might not, but if I do, I don't know that I do." He returns it to sender.

Juggling the ball across his shoulders, Onemsiz punts it back. "There's got to be something."

Fingers of butter fumble; Hermes disassembles the football from his forelimbs. He recalls Turkey, the chauffeur who'd lost a son, "Are you born of a plump, rural man of a stocky tomato physique?"

The throws gradually pace up in speed.

Onemsiz receives. "Hope not. Can't see myself related to him in any meaningful way. Blood ain't spontaneous, dude." He pitches an unnatural fastball, "You two meet?"

Hermes barely manages, "In the palace of the mind, methinks." He discerns the ball in Onemsiz's general direction. "He spoke of your name, figured you for dead."

"Dead to him, more like." Balls fly recklessly, haphazardly even. "Bummer is what it is."

Hermes catches with his jugular. "He seemed regretful." He stays the ball in part due to safety. "Let us speak no more of this."

Onemsiz manspreads his buttocks thereon the cobbled path. "Between the two of us, it turns out I'm the one with daddy issues."

Hermes sits by Onemsiz in the non-sentimental way so as to hear him better; Hermes is still disoriented from the sandy gunfire heatstroke baptism.

Onemsiz continues, "Neither of us are ready to have that reunion. What do you think?"

The garden throbs with serenity. "If it troubles you in this faraway place, and if I am the cosmos's most tedious messenger to have found you here, then perhaps."

His visage betrays a despairing happiness.

"Then waves will send for or to him. Groovy, Hermes." Onemsiz offers a fist to bump, and while Hermes is slow on the draw, he does indeed bump it.

Mon leans infatuated against the doorframe. "Slop!"

For but a moment, Onemsiz's worries are washed away. "Score."

"A toast to groovy beginnings," Mon declares.

Wholesome laughter erupts and precedes the stuffing of faces. Garden roots garnish a mighty fish over a creamy broth; it is explained to be a shank of Atlantean, a fish folk that inhabit the theater of the new world. A nearby harpoon drips with sebum. Whoever these people purport to be, they fight to stay alive.

***

The sun erects its dawn-orange rays over the cabin that simmer ever slightly through its boards. On the ledge stretches catlike Onemsiz, strumming the strings of seduction, greeting the dust-glittered glimmer with a beauty of his own. A leg, alone, dangles at the hardwood floor as his head leans out a window to the garden. The enthralled goats lie lazily beneath the window, glancing up at him with relaxed admiration as he sings an improvisational karaoke of rambunctious minorities who were, in fact, federal agents hoodwinking the common

Hedo to contempt and suspicion. (Hermes, in the manner of someone who hears a song for the first time, does not recall the lyrics.) Mon faintly resists in the tending of her garden but finds his allure too strong. She approaches the ledge beside Onemsiz and ensnares her legs around him; the arms follow after. He puts aside the guitar and indulges in the warmth. Their gazes shift to waking Hermes.

It is dawn of the twenty-fifth day. Hermes had slept a week, so to say. And he did not remember having fallen asleep; slumber had claimed him without a fight for the first time in his life.

"You think he'll groove as hard as us one day?" Onemsiz wonders.

"I'd dig him regardless," Mon responds.

"Even if he doesn't groove with us?"

"Even so," she emphasized. "We chose to groove with him."

"My father never grooved. What if Herm thinks I'm not with the groove? Bro."

"Just know when to let go. Else he'll hate you like you do your pa."

"Is it just me, or is that every generation?"

"Maybe we look at the wrong people."

"They insist on being seen."

"Remind me why we chose the middle of nowhere."

Onemsiz slumps, defeated. "Touché. I hope there's enough nowhere to go around for everyone who wants a slice."

Three harpoons mounted on the wall gleam a regretful silver sheen through the mellow tinge of sunlight. Stretching and yawning, Hermes remains enveloped in bed.

"Let'm rest. If he wants something, he'll get it."

"Aye."

And over the horizon is heard the engine of a motor carriage accompanied by the kicking up of a dust cloud even Hermes can perceive in his sleepy state. Drowned within the dust as opposed to surfing suavely atop, a black-and-red military jeep approaches. The Scarabs have come to say their piece.

A woman's boot emerges from the passenger side. She does not so much as stop to appreciate her surroundings as she obstructs the couple's sunlight and dictates, "Under authority of King Monkey, I, Colonel Delilah Franciscocrat, hereby declare . . ."

Onemsiz stoically salutes the colonel before she can finish.

As she speaks, the unfazed Delilah gazes disinterestedly toward the desert rather than the man, himself. ". . . that the region is subject to heightened military presence and may pose a risk . .

."

Onemsiz dons a pair of sunglasses and points a finger gun aimlessly, only to feint being shot in the heart, grasping hopelessly at his torso and collapsing limp to the ground. Where a layperson might painfully cringe, Mon is entertained.

The colonel faces Mon and changes her tone from rehearsed to a tired casual. "I recommend you vacate the premises."

Onemsiz rises from the dead, finger guns quick on the draw. "No dice."

The colonel's eyes dejectedly fixate on anything not Onemsiz. "Do not make me beg. Please go." Delilah mutters as she and her battalion board the jeep and depart.

Mon nudges Onemsiz with her foot. "You can stop now, you kidder."

"It's a different person every time, brah. Don't tell me that ain't silly. At least when we die, we come back the same."

"Is there a war ongoing?" From the recesses of the cabin, Hermes breaks his fast of silence.

Onemsiz hoists the guitar atop his intoxicating frame. "Nothing we can't handle. They've been trying to shoo us for years." He calls to the goats, "Intermission's over, folks."

The goat sporting gnarly dreadlocks and a Fu Manchu, magnificently erected as a shimmering bastion on the cabin's roof, sings soprano. Indeed, all goats are welcome to the farewell party debuted in memory of the prestigious Colonel Delilah Franciscowhosit? The goats delegate themselves among the sitting cushions; some play cards, others light incense and practice pankration throws. One administers tarot card readings to another, the receiver shocked at the poignancy of vague truths. He is offended — it has to be malarkey, right?

The sun dies and bestowed to everyone is the high of a jubilant night. A fire is lit on the foreground around which the trio gathers. Onemsiz brandishes a harpoon, one of three. "Hermes, my boy! I may have been irresponsible in tarrying this conversation longer than I should've. Worst case scenario is you'll be fighting for your life, and at best we'll have more Atlantean stew."

Hermes, instead, of all things, ponders the origin of the third harpoon, "Be this weapon a spare or have ye another dweller?"

"A sister."

"Whose?"

"Mine. She was mauled by Atlanteans. Can't say I blame our father for worrying, but he's stark raving mad. Shame I'm his only son, now. He might be more relaxed otherwise. His genes aren't so hot, anyway."

Mon defends her husband by proxy of the insult, "If you have any shortcomings, they're recessive."

"Odd, we only have the two boards and not three, so you're with me if anything. We good to go?"

Hermes humors him. "Knowing is not always a factor of my readiness, so I have faith."

Onemsiz ascends his harpoon to the heavens. "Aye!"

Mon erects her 'poon. "Nice."

Hermes adds, "I will fight not to exist, but because I do."

Their three polearms intermingle, then, as if performing a toast, rise once more unto unrestful slumber that anteceded celebrations.

***

The midnight cabin but mere kindling for a flame asphyxiates all within, which is to say nobody because the reliable and mighty goats unloaded the three dwellers and their respective provisions some distance outside. The house a beacon lit draws to it a vague monstrosity; winged terrorists circle around as vultures a stinky carcass.

Seated outside in the dirt, Mon complains womanishly, "Couldn't have bombed sand? Had to be someone's home. Hey, dickholes, bomb sand!"

She lowers to a rueful mutter, "That would be too much to ask."

Onemsiz awakens indifferent to the proceedings. Rather than panic uselessly as one would at vermin, he stretches. "Oh, here already? I haven't even set the table." He palms his cranium, bringing to it the coldness of his skin. To him prances the Fu-Manchu-wearing goat, playfully headbutting at the arm. Onemsiz retaliates with a headlock, scenting his musky scalp. "See you later, buddy." And the goat disappears into the night.

Hermes wakes last in the fashion of someone never in a hurry. Mon boards the surf, harpoon handy. Onemsiz ceremoniously extends his delegated harpoon as a baton to the welcoming of an aeroplane. Hermes from behind his adoptive father acquiesces the honor of kicking off the surfboard on behalf of his host. The wave cascades a brilliant blue to the mysterious black of destiny and the night, its three masters shredding sick moves to dissuade any Atlantean that angles to hitch a ride.

One such winged terror glides seamlessly aloft the tide for the likely and dastardly purpose of terror. Hallowed be its name the terrorist, a robed figure — in turn atop the winged one — of cloth that flows. The entity homes. Tense Hermes shields his sole remaining testicle cast of copper.

Onemsiz's harpoon answers the prayer and sings true, plunging into the robed figure and impaling him by the gullet. Onemsiz tugs the lasso on which his weapon is tied, expelling it from the figure as with countless viscera; still saddled, a plenitude of blood spurts from the perplexed man on whose face is written the very definition of regret. The beast shrills for its counterpart, rivaling by sound the violence of the wave, itself. Bare-buttocked Onemsiz moons the abomination, hoping the message is not lost on it. Duly taunted, it cracks the whip of thunder.

The beast shadows the prey and rises from the periphery, its rider lifelessly and limply gazing into Onemsiz who, although armed, is disoriented by the frightful specter. And despite Hermes's efforts to ward off the elusive terror, it as a python encircles Onemsiz's throat and in a swift motion beheads its captive. Hermes is left beside a tragic stump, a bloody fondue fountain; it falls flaccid to oblivion, blending with the razor ripples and tainting the water red. Mon, the rogue amazon, lunges psychotically from her board in reckless abandon, grappling the bloodthirsty bird-demon and with it descending into the surrounding darkness.

After a time, such can be said the danger had gone, the wave en route evermore reverts to a tranquil state. It neither ripples nor shreds, but is yet tainted red.

Blood-spattered Hermes sits and evaluates his harpoon. Nothing comes to mind, try as he might. Hermes is once more adrift. Sleep does not come in the small hours of night. The stars have vacated, and so there will be no gazing of that regard. Perhaps he should observe the scorching, orange sun. But of course there is always something to gaze at, even in the desolate nothings of the Arena. The sun is usually orange at dawn, that much is true, otherwise yellow, unless both when considering perspective, even orange, yellow, and dark all at once if to consider three, and perhaps blue across time. Sure, the sun was orange, but could it be yellow now? He cannot bother to check. 'Tis a great mystery for Hermes, who does not look at it. (It is, in fact, still orange, as retroactively addressed by Hermes's later state.) Could the horizon sun, perchance, want to communicate something of value? It might have done if not for a blotting void, an eclipse? What precisely is this astral body: an asteroid, a planet, the moon . . . a cabin?

The fractal morning sun illuminates a cabin hidden within its light and atop a desert dune, plain in sight and very much like the predecessor. Likewise, this one is safeguarded by a goat versed well in beardedness.

The ruby wave sets as its benefactor rises. Dawn blood dissipates a darkness to the light. He dismounts the board and approaches the goat who stands imposingly on a rock. Hermes, underhoof, initiates first eye contact. Only after a thoughtful gazing into the distance does the goat return the sentiment.

Hermes reclines on the rock, the goat's home, requesting a cordial invitation. The goat sits calmly, welcoming the company. An indented silence follows before their next words.

***

"Hello," the goat says.

"May I rest here?"

"If you will, you may."

"There will come a point where I will not if I do already, so I may both will and not, and thus may and not."

". . . Unless you yourself will not remain, but a bedeviled shadow claiming to be the man that once was Hermes."

"Therefore I will, he may."

"Come then, before you turn he."

The goat leads a scant few paces to the cabin, its door open. Within are four mugs and all accommodations as before: three boards and harpoons. Coffee, goat milk, a martini, and tea are set. And, by the table, already snug, are Onemsiz and Mon.

Onemsiz occupies two sitting cushions arranged as a sofa, sipping delectably his goat milk. "Welcome home, champ."

Mon sasses, "Out all night?"

"Dude!" Onemsiz interjects. "Hermes nabbed his own board! They do grow up fast." He sheds a celebratory tear.

"Oh, word!"

His own arsenal Hermes lays against the wall, an egg hatched and set to roam. Herbal tea is no less soothing than before on account of nearly dying. The goat milk must feel heavenly, considering Mon actually died.

"It is inconvenient that people don't usually die then live rather than live then die," speaks the goat.

By goat and garden, cabin and furnishings, normalcy is restored, but at what cost? Sure, home has not changed, or has it? A muteness dominates the room, the coffee table actually bearing coffee, dreaded drink of the loud and exhibitionist Hedo, the hustling bustler.

Hermes breaks the silence in the odd manner of speaking that is usual for his character and that everyone has come to accommodate. "Do we expect?"

Mon blushes. "Yes."

Onemsiz drags her by the ear under the table. "My sister."

She clarifies from on low, "I did not copulate with his father."

Onemsiz actually clarifies, "It's Calypso, born by death some time ago today."

Hermes nods with interest, noting the date, the twenty-sixth of the tenth month.

Time passes.

The door held open by coincidence of fate or the wind invites inside the caffeine fiend of psychedelic curls, violet-tinted sunglasses, and baggy harem pants. She introduces herself. "'Sup." Her hairdo reaches out into the ether like a robust fungal node.

"Heya."

"Hiya."

Hermes grunts in acknowledgment.

Onemsiz toasts, "Happy anniversary."

Calypso replies in kind, "Happy anniversary to you, too."

The table lifts their bottoms, downing their liquids.

Onemsiz slams the table with feigned or perhaps exasperated enthusiasm and declares, "When're you choosing your death, sport?"

addressing Hermes, who shrugs unknowingly. "You'll have to die eventually. Part of the process, I'm afraid. It's never too late to start thinking of your future, kiddo."

"Who knows?" says he.

"They say life is the gestation period for death; and you look spry. You've got time to figure it out."

"How?"

Onemsiz strokes his chin philosophically, as if recalling a memory from youth that antagonizes him to this day with grief; there is a gleam in his eye like there is a moral in it, finding the words to relay it with tact: "You've been mooching all week. You've got to move out today, Hermes. Take the harpoon and board. Find your wave, man."

"I understand." Hermes is chill under the circumstances.

Mon encourages her adoptive son, "I believe in you. If all three of us can do it, so can you!" She insinuates at a streak of blood on the hardwood floor. "I slipped on an eggshell before you arrived, for instance!"

Hermes excretes an oral "thank you." Outside, a seawater swirl swarms and swerves, shawarma on a rotisserie showers sour if left uneaten. Hermes sets out with a board and a pointy stick just as quickly as he'd been asked.

"Hold it!"

Calypso bolts from the homestead. "I'm coming with."

Sleep-deprived Hermes begs the question: "Why?"

She crosses her arms. "I only dropped by, so I'll be needing a ride."

"Why not call your own wave?"

One arm lowers to the ground in the manner of a habitual smoker who wants to look cool, except there's no cigar. "There's always a fare." At least she does indeed look cool.

"Ride's free, always has been."

"I won't be the stiff that says no to free."

Hermes glares silently.

"I guess free stuff is just promotional clutter. I'm coming anyway; I want to see you die."

"I won't stop you so I can't stop you."

She winks and dives into the waterspout atop her board, whirling to the top and hanging ten. Before boarding, Hermes turned for a last time to the house which received him so graciously, seeing also the goat almighty that came to see him off. Hermes eyes the goat and the goat he, an exchange of farewell and mutual respect. In addition, the goat gallops forth and nudges Hermes's thigh, then prances away to his kin.

Hermes clumsily breaches the flowing rotary,

carried topward by the rapids, nearly hurled airborne and, if not for Calypso's quick hand, would have flown. The monsoon reforms into a wave fueled by the vaguely nonexistent will of Hermes; it goes somewhere.

The haboob rages, but "we" don't need to see to know where "we're" going. Visibility is limited to the wave, which for the moment comprises all the known world whereon Calypso sits bored, contemplative, or anxious. Hermes, wishing to address any of the three likelihoods, straddles near. "Talk to me."

Her eyes brighten with activity. "Why should I?"

"You seem bothered."

"Just spaced out. I get it a lot."

"Mhm."

Calypso offers a conversational out: "You don't need to do the whole small talk shabang. We're cool."

"Ah."

Hermes retreats subtly. Fortunately, the wave settles not long, denying the awkward silence to eternally curse his conscience in grief. Before them inflicted on the sand is an assortment of tents, within men dazed and moping, a homeless shelter, perhaps.

Calypso hops off. "Let's check out your new place, yeah?"

Hermes prospect hunts for a suitable space, but all tents are occupied. On the trek, one is manned by a single animated doctor prescribing a quick fix to a poor soul. The doctor notes Hermes quite distinctly. "Back already?"

Hermes ignores him; it is obviously meant for someone else.

"Horace? You hear me? Don't tell me you've gone delirious, boy!"

It is indeed meant for someone else, a druggie he keeps around his thumb, perhaps?

The doctor raises a side eye at Calypso. "Ah, I see! Enjoy each other, you two! Not long before we're all dead anyhow!"

The soup kitchen ahead strains with filth, strewn crumbs disrespect the sand beneath. Littering is littering no matter where or how. The two drifters seat themselves, a pasty gruel uniting their souls in mutual suffering.

Calypso voices thought to tongue: "That could kill you, I guess. Failing that, this shelter has guns up the wazoo — some front for a nefarious operation for sure. Is this something you care about?"

Hermes concurs, "We'll not stay for brass tacks."

"What's next on the list?"

Hermes ponders upon the slop. He at last shrugs, summoning a tide off the shantytown's sleazy perimeter, undetected. "Let's away." They manage a makeshift entrance through a shabby fence.

In the distance, a storm — the wave thus merges to a violent sea rampaging in the lonesome desert a ways from the camp. It is so turbulent, not even Hermes's wave could resist. Calypso vomits without warning, churning mildly atop her board.

"You okay?"

She heaves, "Yeah, just knackered by past trauma. Gimme a minute. I had a run in with an Atlantean, see? Went for a dip down south in the river Mangy. The blighter dismembers my arm. How am I supposed to swim like that, much less flip him my dactylion? Then he bit my bleedin' head off. Of course, the Hedoes prosecuted him in the Great Organized Book Club as a humanid. Judged it as insanity, they did. I don't believe that drivel one bit; he was born a sodding Atlantean, normal enough for his own kind. Needless to say, these be Atlantean waters and my 'poon is on high alert."

"As will be mine."

"Dying is an inconvenience, but it can be worth it to cut your roots, if only to build a house with your mangled, oaky remains."

He harrumphs.

As if investigating this exchange, a pod of Atlanteans whiz afar, their elastic shrills piercing the surface and betraying ill intent. The swarm yet lingers in sight drawing ever nearer, the impending cacophony lashing as a whip on the frail Hedophilic psyche, foreboding doom. Saucy spizzerinctum of these antagonists fares poorly, for as the rattling jaws of Atlantis lunge to Hermes, they are halted by a great vibration shaking the air. As the surfers lose their footing, the terrified Atlanteans are intercepted, upended, and scattered by a monumental spout of water erupting from the depths of the abyss. A colossus emerges from the deepest brine and surges to the heavens a jaded dragon. Blotting the sun is a great serpent taller than Hedophilia, itself.

Calypso whistles in the fashion of "Oh shit."

A thunder resonates from all sides, with a low, rumbling noise as a n undercurrent. It takes a moment to process every word and that the source is the colossus. "Hark! Have ye a wave of thine own design, humanid?"

"Who knows?" Hermes casually replies, more perplexed by the figment of his being than by the figure before him.

"Fie! I beseech thee speak louder. Mine ears hear not the musics of new."

Hermes beckons only slightly louder.

"Over yonder hill and prairie did it bring you here to roost thine destiny. Who be ye, good and honorable sir?"

Hermes ponders a moment, fails to answer, and responds thus, "Identify myself, yourself."

"Hoho! I cannot."

"Then we are alike," Hermes intuits.

"Indeed! Though my namesake eludes me, it is yet with middling interest I have watched, nay, felt the exploits of men for millennia from beneath thy feet — until I emerged from slumber by the Atlantean horde and chanced upon ye, O little curiosity."

Calypso flows into the conversation. "And what do ye want with y'all?"

"Atlantis fights the eternal war in my name as I left it all that time ago a husk of my former self. Bathed in the humors of such battles, my constitution is nigh healed. So I have come to bring end to thy lives. Wilt thou be my champion in this?" The serpent did not address Calypso directly, but happened to answer her question nevertheless; it is a matter of ambiguity whether he so much as noticed her. Moreover, the dragon seemed to recite his purpose as if it were a dream that would fade to oblivion if not recounted the moment he awoke — this Hermes guessed to be true with an amused conviction.

Hermes neither accepts nor declines the request. "Must I be?"

The serpent stares at the man perhaps dumbfoundedly. After a silence, it finds a response, "Am I to be denied?"

"To what end?" asks Hermes.

"To find end," the serpent answers with an apprehension.

"Why do I want this?" Hermes asks this as much of the serpent as of himself.

Calypso nudges closer with her board and angrily whispers, "You're supposed to die, you twat. Officer of evil? Once in a lifetime opportunity you're blowing!"

The serpent's opaque eye sockets squint. "So be it. I bid thee farewell." It recedes into the green, glimmering depths, splashing a great geyser that lingers in the air with the conception of the consequences of his refusal. Hermes looks to Calypso and sees she is wide eyed.

"You see a big primordial fish and your first instinct was blink at it. You passed up one hell of an office. No go?"

"Not my place."

The wave does not answer anymore; it is one with the ravenous sea and has found home among its brethren, Hermes to wander water as he did sand; in principle they are little different.

***

Hermes fancies it is still day in spite of the storm obscuring the sun itself, growing ever darker and colder until he can see nothing at all. Lest they be separated, freezing Calypso hangs onto his waist. After some further riding, they come upon a junction at which in every direction there seems to be a wall. Drowsy Calypso riles awake.

Hermes whispers, "Have we died, yet?"

She jaculates, "I think we fell over each other . . . That'd have been an embarrassing way to die, if so."

"What was your first time again?"

"Bloody confusing at first on account of not feeling my arm, then realizing I couldn't feel anything, not the way I used to anyhow. Quim on a stick, it's cold. I think you've gotten us into hell."

"Swell."

"Want some pop?"

"No."

Calypso crackles the lid of a soda and voraciously guzzles the fluid, compacting the metal in her grip. She shivers in the cold.

"Was that lying around?

"Thoughtful is what it is."

A second crisp crack assaults the abyss, to which he replies, "More?"

"I only had the one. The river giveth."

Realization dawns a ray of light; a pinprick from eternal nothingness draws the eye of Hermes. "As the walls of hell close in on us, I wonder where we go next."

"Is this what being a ghost is like, aye ferryman?" She firmly lays one hand on Hermes's jugular, plunging him into a wall of oblivion, dismantling the infrastructure of purgatory, itself. "I guess we're not as ethereal as I thought."

"We were in an ice box, Calypso." The door falls off its hinges.

"So we were."

He finds another beverage and, puncturing it, downs the whole thing, "This is the homeless camp; it is as we left it."

"Plus or minus a few bodies. You're not a details person, huh? Say, how'd we get here anyway?"

Hermes shrugs.

Bodies lie scattered on the ground, homeless and Atlantean alike. And from the heavens, a zeppelin descends; it produces an orifice, emerging slowly from it the hull of a sinister object, what seems to be a naval battleship. On its flank is written the name HMS *Monkey Have Mercy*. A ways from the camp where the water seems deepest, the ship is airdropped onto the ever-shifting sea of the Atlantean horde from which Hermes came — its carrier makes good on an escape. Waves and fissures spread throughout the camp from the waist down.

Calypso laughs cooly, "Seems the Atlanteans are tussling with the Yins. Couldn't pick a side, huh?"

"The universe really seems to want me to."

"No kidding. Say, I think we should run."

He counters, "Are we running or dying?"

"I'm running, you're dying."

Hermes glares at her.

"We've been over this, bonehead: Pick your death. Don't let it pick for you." Of no mind to wait around, Calypso elopes a carstruck deer into the brush.

He double-takes as the earth quakes; a likely crevasse consumes bodies of the living and the dead. Hermes exerts a defeated sigh and remains everstill a safe distance from the whirlpool sweeping the camp. A lone, crippled street urchin crawls helplessly at the indifferent Hermes, hurling obscenities and cries for aid, but alas is vacuumed into the depths, his mortified visage lasting only a moment before his demise. It's a cool way to die, but for naught, and therefore not for Hermes.

Thusly, a great fissure erupts beside him bringing forth the red eyes of a kraken. The beast zooms skyward with phenomenal speed, sweeping Hermes ten feet high into its tailwind even from afar. It darts particularly for the HMS *Monkey Have*

Mercy and means to capsize its opponent who retaliates with broadsides, two goliaths. It seems the serpent of earlier is not present, or else all might die.

Hermes recovers from the tranquil trance of indecision and wades through fleshy sewage and murky puddles at every step, each glance down casting a reflection of, not only himself, but of rotting chunks of men. And from above, scraps of metal and sirloins of reptilian blubber shower upon him.

Once empty alleys flood with dichotomous reds and blues, two teams ever at war. Hermes happens on a square. "One man and a woman . . ." He mutters to himself, "Violently consummating; that's vagrancy for you." The approaching tsunami offers no reproach save forward, yet he pauses, his shin nudged by the goat.

Hermes initiates the exchange: "Where to?"

He prances onward. "Wherever when. Hitherto?"

The student follows. "I would not choose such a path, myself."

"Choose or not choose. I've said the word so often it stopped meaning anything. Nevertheless, you are less yourself than last we spoke; it is time you became he."

"I understand," Hermes says nonchalantly.

He gallops majestically off to sea. "Adieu."

Hermes assumes a firm stance and, harpoon never having left his side, raises it. In his pacing he wonders where to strike it. As the deathly wave approaches, he considers striking the distant man, the woman, or perhaps the wave, "Here, there, where . . ." The mental exercise leaves Hermes more confused than before when, in a moment of eureka, decides to strike himself! Through the stomach does he pierce his insides with such strength that he ran the shaft nearly all the way through, also impaling by coincidence the man and woman behind him! He hears them both moan in pain before realizing with mild shock the consequences of his absent-minded pacing that brought him to the very scene. Thus did Hermes seek to die.

A tremendous gravity suffocates and pulls all three to the shaft's center, a sizzling shish kebab of agony-fueled spaghettification crackles alight, flickering embers into the eternal ether visible from the chaos below, cinders gradually dispersing 'till each lone kindling inseparable from the stars become one with the universe. The cries below are man and animal alike, little different.

VI

Soulwrecked in Limbo

. . . .

Sssssssssssssss'. . . .
Whoo'we'whoo'we'whoo'we'whoo. Cr'cr'crt,
cr'cr'cr't. Choyp, choyp, kétat. T't'sist, t't'sist,
t't'sist, whop. Blob. Sw'sh. G'gle. F'phew. Phuo'oo,
k'k k'k k'tsu. Gl'iw gl'k. Fhewp', fhewp', cl'ck. Kaw
kaw! Squa! Á-āh, á-āh, á-āh. Kawk . . . Makawk!
Kink, kink, kink. Polly would like a cracker, yes he
would. Wùwú. Whôa. Mmm'm. Whòa. Yæw!
Mmm'mm! Gh-th'. Mmm'mmm-th'. Āh. Wā-àh. R'rra.
Wūūù'hth! Uwu. A'h. Agh'f, ouf, Ough, augh, augh,
woagh! Yiff, erf, wough'f. Eiyaough! If', if, if'. Moof,
augh'f augh'f augh'f! Gharf! Gharf! Yuegh! Ao'wue!
A'woo'oo'oo'ugh. Ymph!

Hi. Hey. How are you? Good, you? Good. Good. Did you see the game last night? Yeah, not their best game. Let's hope they pick it up; they're my team! Crack her open, cheers. What time is it? Well, I'd best be heading out. Yeah, good talk.

Err, err, err, plop. Clink, clink, clank. Whirr err, kerchunk, kerchunk, kerchunk, tdu tdu tdu tdu tdu tdu tdu, whirr wree, kerchunk, kerchunk, kerchunk, whirrrrr. Bi boop, bi boop. Beep! Tip tap tip type. Biridiridiridirip, Biridiridiridirip, Biridiridiridirip, Biridiridiridirip, please leave a message for . . . TURKEY. Beep. We need to talk. It's not easy for me. Why do I have to tell you like this . . . We still need to split up the kids. The book club meet is scheduled for next month. Tell your voyeur . . . I can't believe you've made me do this. Goodbye. CLUNK.

VII

Metacognitive Parasite

I am a beast of terror and destruction the likes of which have ne'er seen a worthy opponent in all my time. The mountains crumble before my razor pincers, nevermore a fine sentiment once I'm through. I bathe each day in glorious fire whence a lesser creature might burn and die a terrible death — yet I survive. I happened upon a number of such weaklings in my travels and feasted upon their blood.

That is all I remembered before this fever became of me. To be an omniscient and abstract being brought so low into the realm of feeling . . . Perhaps it is all delusion. For the first time I have thoughts, and thus think, "I know not where to go."

Directions are plentiful, but I am destitute of purpose, a penniless pauper on whom the streams of fate piss merrily.

I mourn the loss of that which was, but I will have compassion for myself and the strength to bear the consequences, just as I might look sympathetically at my next meal and exercise the strength to eat it. Nevertheless, I am awash in the maelstrom of anxiety. Poor are its tidings.

Are these thoughts my own? I dare say I have an affinity for the violent voice, but had I really spoken before this? What is the true nature of my mien? Speak now, so that I might see you!

"K'k k'k k'tsu!"

A shadow fills my vision.

"Fhewp', fhewp', gl'iw gl'k!"

Could it be I am that shadow?

"Click, clack . . . YOU!"

Confound it!

"Ai'yee, chirp, AGONY!"

The shadow is ever the flummoxer, but I have found my voice.

"I AM! CRAB!" Short and guttural like a beast, this is who I am amid the madness. The shadow clears to reveal a crab indeed, a reflection in the scarlet red oasis of blood.

And in my indecisive reflections and fever-wrought spasms, I am eaten by a winged death. Truth be told, if it had gone on any longer, I would have settled for a more gruesome death if only to cease the torture.

But morning dawns as it seemingly always has. Soft tendrils of heat caress me.

Perched atop the tallest branch, I am the proud Scrèe-áh, a name I had taken to calling myself roughly translating to scavenger, clan-mother, and provider for progeny of five. After all, this is who I am.

Today I wake with a terrific migraine. No matter. I will let loose my wings for a bountiful hunt to distract the mind.

"Á-āh!" Or, in laybird terms, eureka; a rodent hides among the shrubbery. 'Tis easy pickings for a graceful hawk, would that my body could obey a simple command. I plummet boldly into sand.

My body stretches a wing — broken. I did not command it so.

Such is the plight of immortality, the reincarnation in which we find ourselves.

Nor could I have thought such a thing, agreeable as I find the sentiment.

I, Scrèe-áh, hop to a nearby stump of a once-felled tree and mutter furiously under my breath, "Chit, chir."

Dispel yourselves, demons of the mind! Your

presence defiles the sanctity of nature. I would know: I speak on behalf of nature whether it would like me to or not. You know the type. Do I? I hope as much.

The demons claim they did not wish it upon me. In the same breath, they curse my name. Heretics, the lot of them!

"K'kaw!" I should know better than to bargain with demons, but if anything, rhetoric is the devil's music: I have children to feed!

They bicker among themselves and resolve to help.

Where from do you hail, blasphemers? Are you dull, grounded peons or winged elites?

They claim they are but men. Indignant and offended men they are.

"Chirt." I do not accuse. Some things are merely lost in translation; flight is something especially worth being racist for. You silly humanids should know better. Be you devils experienced in this crooked plane, I ask you help guide my body as fit.

I glisten underneath blazing sun, seizing profusely; my beak clatters, legs spin, and I cluck up a miserly spectacle. The loathsome rat approaches with a heavy tinge of curiosity; no fear in it whatsoever. Woe, to be brought so low! It skitters away pathetically, though none so much as I, yours truly.

A floppy-eared hunter prowls from afar, sight set on the erratic, spastic hawk. 'Tis I, could that I have the courage to admit it. It huffs stupidly in anticipation for a hearty meal.

"Sk'yah!" Gather yourselves, lest the mangy land dweller defiles me!

As he approaches, my talons pierce the bastard's muzzle, to which he responds in kind by lifting his whole body by the hind legs as if to show me his starving belly and boney ribs, then headbutts me like a goat, maw-first, to which I owe another thrash, another scratch. Big rat bastard, black like evil!

I am slain.

Now I am a dark greyhound curled in a ball. "Roof, oof, oh boy!" Another glorious day! It was evening of the same day I'd eaten, but morning is a mindset.

Hind leg raised in toast scratches furiously at my torn ear. Vices sated, so awaits the village, rustic, misshapen, disheveled, home. The way is not long; I had walked most of it. Dirt-ridden children and simple farmers comprise the bulk of the community by modest appearance. But at heart, they are the best good people I've had the pleasure of associating myself with, yes siree. "M'ph!" I wonder who's in town? Let it be Abraddon! He throws out the best scraps! What a stand up guy! Oh boy! And let's not forget about Minister Jebediah and his disciples! They keep everyone safe! They carry the strongest hands and rub the gentlest! Not like ham-fisted Vinny! Oh yeah! Get pumped for belly time!

In my exuberance, I notice I've been having odd feelings, but the butcher's comes first!

The streets and hovels are near desolate, and my destination reached with no delay. That's urban engineering for ya! Scarcely a soul! Wow!

The butcher's is a modest one: his only furnishings are the dwindling morsels of red meat, pheasant, and assorted vegetables and spices dangling from the rafters. The butcher, himself, is a beer-bellied, grisly man with an admirable pair of mutton chops and breathtaking musculature. "You again?" A hearty laugh bellows from the deepest recesses of his guts. "Can't say I blame you. It's a hard life." He chucks a morsel like the olympian discus thrower I know he ought to have been, and I expertly home in on the catch. "On your way, pup."

A day ago I'd not have understood a word of that humanid gibberish. I learn fast!

A freckled teen, the daughter, shan't ever escape my scent! "Diothore! Get over here!"

"Yip!" Oh boy, she's always so friendly!

She heaves the famed bird widower close (me), lugging me over shoulder to serve as a fancy cape brooched by paw. She tumbles foot over foot into the street. "Shoulda known where there be stink, so goes the stinker. How goes it?"

"Yarf!" You smell good! Oh boy!

She bumps into an athletic man with a prosthetic, brass nose. He crouches, wielding an intimidating glare like a weapon at the ready and sizes me up, eyes of taint a deep crimson red, the color of evil to which I had been blind all my life, but not today! The amputee rises, clasping me by the scalp, ruffling a few hairs, saying nothing, and moving on as if nothing'd transpired, the movements of his hand mechanical and cold — worse than Abraddon's but better than Vinny's.

My lady defends my honor: "Get a load of the nerve!"

A primordial anger arises within me. "Argh! Argh! Argh! Argh! Argh!" You think you're some sort of tough guy!? Come get some! Oh, running away? Good riddance! Else I would have gutted your garters, loathsome fecker!

The girl relinquishes me from her service and bids farewell. "Come by again soon, Diothor!" Her smile returns immediately; I am a force for good.

But I am not done with that snub nosed bastard, and I sniff him out to the outskirts of town, to a barn. The closer I come, the more this wooden dung heap stinks of nefarious deeds, and that is an offense to shit whose stink is not so bad as others say. I am alone in this sentiment, I know.

I had not come here before; I had not thought to. There is no window into this vile abyss that dare reveal its curiously evil interior. But by one of the smaller wings there is a hole in the ground about which I know a thing or two, and I dig it wider so that I might fit through.

Inside there is a row of livestock behind the usual stockades; I can only see a scant few of their features as they look at me. Buckets beside overflow with opulent, silky milk and I cannot resist; it is glorious, a delicacy the likes of which I've never tasted. There is a buzz to it like a fine wine that make me giggle with a heap of happy thoughts painted in colors I've never seen. My snout sinks in the bucket and I nearly forget to breathe; it's so good! The longer I indulge in this phantasmal curry, however, the more evident becomes its bittersweetness and that it reeks of pain; this is not right. They look at me with dead, soulless eyes, and the one that looks to be the youngest whimpers and whines. Oh boy, if I was even tempered before, no longer.

There is a wobble in my step, but I manage to gather my hazy wits and press on. In the next room is a man dressed in the most sleazy shade of black, and he monologues at a woman bound to a chair whose face is obscured by a sack. "I've been generous, tuts, too generous." The man takes a moment to adjust the literal stick of dynamite portruding halfway out his trousers. (He means to look cool, I think.) A free hand heats the underside of a cigar. "In fact, I'm the most generous guy this side of the wall, maybe all of Hedophilia too. But, you see, some like to take advantage of my honesty and goodwill, am I correct?"

She mumbles unenthusiastically and unintelligibly.

"Why of course I am. And we don't take lightly to that vice. We're good people here, all of us, every single one." He takes a long drag of the cigar like someone who's full of himself. "Tell you what, I can forgive. But forgiveness ain't cheap, and neither is breast milk. It's you or a vial of your father's semen — and I can breed the whole herd without you." He lifts the captive's sack.

She wears black leathers, a genuine and noble black unlike the discount mafioso before her. And her hair is spacious and puffy and reaches in every direction of the universe; she is familiar, but I do not know her, yet it's as if I've heard her voice somewhere before. "We've been over this how many times now? You bother pa, but you never survive the conversation. At best, he blabbers until even you tucker out and dip. I might tell you where he is, but I just don't like you. And if you want to milk me? This pill in my mouth says otherwise. I've died for less. Run to your master. Tell him you have failed. Learn to give up, Vinny."

The man grins maliciously. "Bitch knows how to run a mouth. Okay, I give up. But good luck telling that to Brahe. Antonio, bring him in!"

Brahe walks methodically, arms never swaying ridiculously and body kept straight unlike the inefficient lateral shifting many insist is proper walking etiquette: waddling, swaying, swinging, what have you.

"The only free lunch in this town is a knuckle sandwich." Vinny mutters redundantly from afar with the intent of an egoist who wants to control the situation.

I don't know how I think these thoughts, but I am grateful for their clarity. I know exactly the kind of scumbags I'm going to lay into.

"Hello, gendarme. Have you come to bust my balls?" the woman says to Brahe. He detaches his nose, revealing wires and tubing surging and humming with great power; his nose was a muffler all this time as well as a purse! He retrieves a parcel from the compartment in his detachable nose and unravels it. Atop a layer of purple felt, there lies a glove. He returns his nose and dons the white glove on sinister hand, slapping Calypso via backhand.

Is she a friend? Is he the enemy? But he is not all bad, I think. Oh boy! The monster within me wants to rest my canines on someone's scalp, but the goodness wants to resolve this diplomatically. There is also a nihilism that says this is not my problem. Oh boy! What to do?

I jump out from my hiding place, unsure of my next course of action! I think this with great conviction.

My tail swaggers in elation and belly exposed invites all but one: Brahe. "Do you care for these things, woman?"

"Whose is it?"

"Irrelevant."

"A person's dog says a lot both ways."

"Fine. I've seen it around. Must be a stray."

"Check the tag."

His ungloved hand grabs at the collar. "It reads 'Diothor.' Never heard of this one."

Oh boy! He knows my name!

Calypso continues, "So let sleeping dogs lie."

"Do you own any?"

"Can't say I do."

"Neither do I; too many witnesses as it is. Do dogs bleed the same as us?" Crackling of flesh and bone renders a gloved hand numb and immobile. It detaches, tumbling on the ground, revealing in its place a cold, hard, steel buzz saw, revved and on the run. "Why don't we find out?"

I am a dog. Men love us. Who in their right mind would kill a dog, and after millennia of bonding at that? This is not the reception I am used to, nor the deal I signed up for. And yet, the woman may be bluffing; I'd never have thought of something so clever, but how is it I'm thinking about it right now?

Brahe intones loudly in the direction of the milk smugglers, "I am going to dispose of this rat. Only a merciful patron of the arts could intercede on this poor being's behalf and win their eternal and undying loyalty!" (As if a dog needs convincing.) Brahe ceremoniously raises the saw as if it were a guillotine, halted only by ruckus from the other room. The thudding approaches a perplexed Brahe, each sequence louder and more intense than the last. Crashing through a door is the magnificent club of Pelvis-Crusher followed by the meaty arms of Goatman tearing away at the door's pathetic remains-for-hinges. "Milk ours! Man-meat!" Pelvis-Crusher yells, intent on tenderizing her enemies, starting with Antonio: Her gaze fixes on him as a lioness on a meek gazelle, and in one fell swoop capitulates the man to his knees, blood flowing rampantly from the battered body over which she toys, distracted. Goatman, however, determines the similarly bulky Vinny his adversary. Ripping off his wifebeater, Goatman flexes in a freakish mix of muscle and fat. Vinny dons a pair of brass knuckles, motioning Brahe with a flat hand not to involve himself. Face to face, a well-coordinated punch by Vinny is simply absorbed by Goatman's gut. The latter strikes firmly at the jaw, but Vinny's impressively large face does not bruise. Two giants wrestle in the old and brittle room collapsing in on them, and though rubble rains from the ceiling, the two shrug off every one of the debris' pathetic attempts on their lives. Tumbling and thighs shake the earth! But at conflict's end, Goatman's thighs are a tad thicker, and so, strangle a struggling Vinny in between.

Brahe drops the dog. With the free hand, he rotates a circular mechanism on that sinister wrist as if it were a showerhead or hose rotary. The saw ceases and retracts into the void. In its place, a luminescent glow is shone on Goatman.

If I thought that hand dastardly and wicked, what manner of evil rests within his forearm? Whatever may come, I feel a kinship with the shirtless man; I might even die for him. Yes, that's right. I do not know why, just that I would. And so I will!

I hurl myself between Brahe and the Goatman, enduring head-on the phantasmic shot of a laser whose light drowns the room in absolution, barbecuing a dog.

VIII

Wabi-sabi Reformation Period

It is morning of the third day of the twelfth month and I lie in bed feverish, cold with sweat. I hadn't ever thought to check the date. Come to think of it, we don't even have a calendar. Could be a side effect of the virus. A virus that makes you remember the date, funky that. Feel like a quarter pound of shite is welling up in my insides, "Bleh." Must've been the stew. Fat bastard should really learn to cook someday. Bright side? I wouldn't have given enough of a toss to get out of bed anyway. Good on you, fever.

A hearty voice bellows down from my attic, "If you're feeling shite, go see a priest!"

Like he knows what I'm thinking. That's pops

for ya. "You see a priest!"

"It's your ass!" says the guy who sleeps on the same table he butchers. Something about immunity, dolt.

Fine. I'll go see the whole bloody church, but I'll be damned if I'm taking the front door; it's only a short hop out the window. Don't want that fatty thinking he got me to do anything.

Anytime I need to get anywhere, the market's in the way — of course it is — and there's a commotion. In the center stands the man with the funny nose and Peter, one of the monks. They stand opposite each other and this is enough to captivate the attention of carpenter Isaac with muscles like a lifter, farmer Bag'ri'el whose frame exudes bearish power, the beggar Joshua endowed a respectable physique, good Mormon, and many others, but I seek Jebediah.

"Oi, Melysia!" says the beggar. "'Aven't you 'eard? A stranger's come to town and 'e's rescued some o' our women from them rat bastard milk men and now one o' ours wants t' test 'is mettle! But knucklehead an' shoe-buckle're jus' starin' inta the ether. Wot gives?"

"I don't give a toss!"

He swoons, "Oh, how the youth have fallen."

It's said when the forefathers planned the town, they'd initially wanted to plot the church on the highest hill, but decided to leave it bare. The church is modest, though it could easily have been more opulent, but then we'd be attracting a certain kind of person, and they're better off in Hedophilia where people are results-oriented, laugh at the truth, and worship the dollar. I shudder.

Inside, Father Jebediah preaches from one part heart and one part playbook, but really, they're one and the same. "O holy monkey who art wherever, amen. With laws come lawyers, and they would be the death of us all, amen. Peaceful were our days in Nusquam until the reckoning of man, amen." The moment he looks up from *The Playbook*, he nods me in with a smile. "Evil has its place in Hedophilia to which we've sent some boys. I assure you they're happier there, bless them. But some days those souls come 'round generations down the line." Two pregnant women weep from the benches, "My sympathies to Agnes and Agatha whose milk was stolen by a slovenly gangster. We pray that it be restored, or else take refuge in the likelihood that a piece of Nusquam might propagate in Hedophilia, amen. Our other disciples search for Martha and Myrtle who are yet missing, stolen away by the fish people. Mark my words, we will see them returned. That is all. Adjourned? Tally ho, amen." and the procession is over.

I wade against the flow of men and women, a

strong current of muscle and integrity. I am a runt and a rascal, but even I will grow at least as strong as beggar Joshua. I nab a copy of *The Playbook* on my way to the priest who breaks the ice: "Finally come to settle the matter of your soul? I warn you, it is a lifelong endeavor, hoho! What is it, child?"

"Stuff it, geezer. I've come down with a reckoning."

"Well crack her open and let's have a think!"

I splay *The Playbook* on the stand like I own the place and the ink cascades into overlapping spirals of nonsense gibberish and occult shapes like the ones you'd see in a horror flick; I'd know 'cause we come across VHS tapes now and then and stick 'em in Joshua's jerry-rigged television, but ole pops says it rots the mind. "Bugger."

"You know I am blind to your dharma; I can only read my own. What does it say, child?"

"It's blurry nonsense — lines in the sand."

A look strikes him. "Hoho! You'd not be the first. Trace it out for me."

My finger finds a line and runs the path set before it, but vanishes midway and I come to an abrupt stop; the whole of my body jolts and my face says I'm dumbstruck. Father Jebediah seems to take notice. The next line vanishes before I lay the finger down. I make an effort to grab at multiple lines with all my digits, but I can't stick to any one.

And if I didn't know better, I thought I'd heard whispers. "I don't know what's wrong," I cough.

"You ought to know who you are, else you shan't know to take issue with anything — so who are you to think anything is wrong?"

"Just who am I?"

"Hoho! If you bothered to attend the sermons of your soul, I could at least tell you who you were. How else do you know something is wrong?"

"Shit smarts."

Father Jeb has a good think. "Tell you what, and you might not like this . . ." He rubs at his temple and paces across the room and into a broom closet, "Yes, that should do." Clearing his throat, Jeb heaves out this iron maid-looking contraption with belts where the torture spikes oughta be. It is large enough to fit a grown man, but has straps for all sizes in between.

"I'd like to have a word with your spirits. If you'd so kindly get in the cage before you start thinking too hard . . ."

"What the everlasting sod are you doing?"

He shrugs. "Insurance."

But I can't bloody move toward it, not that I wanted to. I can't bring myself to leave neither. And shit's curdling in my stomach. "Is this like an exorcism in such and such film?"

"I'd nae exorcize good Joshua, Ezekiel, nae'r

other turbulent youth . . . Be not alarmed. Something has reincarnated within you, be it from the food we eat, the air we breathe, the knowledge we read, or the blood we receive: You must be feeling like a stitched-together-from-different-parts monster, but people change is all — or start to notice. Hoho, and now that you've got me talking, the humble Atlantean is of a similar mind on this matter. Perhaps that is why they've left us be 'till now. Two kindred sects? Even I do not know this for certain. Ah, but never you mind. There are people in your headspace, all right."

"No tossing way I'm one with this throbbing headache. Drug me up."

"Not in this house; that is the domain of modern medicine, a preoccupation of the Hedophilic hobbyist who would silence your voices for a pittance, and in doing so better understand the lesser you that emerges, though he'd claim 'twould that ye be understood. Here, we treat the disciples of Neurotypicles to an open mind, so that he might better understand the chaos rather than reduce it, playbook willing." He kisses the cover of the copy he wears by the hip, "It aims true and not at yourself, the best weapon if ever was." It holsters back into place seamlessly.

"Fine, whatever. Get on with it." I wasn't paying attention and this shit is killing me. Only when I throw myself into the contraption do I notice the frayed ends, but I don't give a damn and I bet there's scarier shit out there than in here. I guess that means I'm the shit out there to the shit in here out there. Shove off, noggin. This ain't the time.

"How old did you say you were?"

"Eighteen."

Father Jeb clears his throat like the bloody geezer he is, though none so much as pops. "I will show you a few images and you tell me what you think or feel. Compulsions are valid too. Take a gander." He pulls from his pouch a catalog of — hold on — smut, is that right?

"What is your first reaction?"

"The fuck is going on?"

Jeb takes pen to paper and writes it down. "I apologize, but this is the single best place the common man keeps all he finds taboo and disgusting as well as intriguing and beautiful, a wealth of diversity where else he might strike it down. I only wish to provoke you with the full breadth of the humanid experience to the purpose of observing your mind's reactions. Oh, and I'll try to keep silent so as to influence you as little as possible. Now, without further ado . . ." He flips the page to an interracial couple who have not yet taken off their clothes and folds back the other, more risqué progression.

As I focus on my feelings, I am hit from all sides and my noggin pulsates as I try to push past and speak that which comes to mind. "It's all well and good that a Negro and a White can now fornicate in public, if at all." I puke in my mouth and make it no secret. "I'm not really into that unless I might be? Why did I think the color should matter? Good for them, either way! Everyone should find their own happiness. It is scarcely a life worth living if not for the benefit of others." I smile proudly, but it quickly drops to a neutral expression. "Behind their tortured eyes I see a paid actor who smiles on the cheap. Smiles for cheap cheapen the smile, an inflation of currency to match even the monkey dollar. Bah. Even if they were happy, so what?" I pause for a moment to realize what I've said and done. What do I think, really? What do I do about it? What gives? Do I feel everything or nothing at all?

Jeb writes everything down. If it were anyone else, I might feel a tad judged. He takes a minute to jot everything he heard and saw, doubling back a couple times to maybe catch a mistake or nuance. Looking satisfied with himself, he flips through to another page, this time with a woman riding a motorized bull with her tits out, covered deftly by Jebediah's thumb. She seems to have a bulge under that skirt. Huh.

I blush and Jebediah flashes me the side eye. "I am fool enough to invoke the will of the cosmos itself when I say this is an abomination of nature! Begone!" I am flushed red, beside. And as the compulsion passes, I immediately compose myself. "No, that's not it. It's her choice and that's swell. I would defend all the creatures of King Monkey if only I had the strength." And I have but one closing remark I mutter under my breath, "Now that's funny. Is that supposed to be a cowboy or a cowgirl? Hey, girl. What's your cowgender?" I chortle, part amused and part bemused at the speed at which I change my mind.

Jebediah smiles as he goes through the motions and settles this time on a brown skinned priestess whose trepanned skull is penetrated by a member of the tribe wearing a cheetah's pelt. Her crossed eyes suggest she might be enjoying it if she wasn't already braindead. Jebediah decides nothing need be covered here.

"Utter barbarism, this!" My head jerks. "All cultures ought to be respected, though." It jerks violently again! "It should've been me! Oh, how I wish to die."

I shan't look to Jebediah to know whatever the hell he's doing is working. Damn this monkey headache. I wonder if my thoughts will ever come together as one. Am I doomed to gridlock of the soul, this to be my new malady? I swear Jebediah mutters under his breath "Almost done." Blast it, old man, you and your damn pornos. You know what? I'm going to say that. (And I did.)

He flips the page to another roleplay, a businessman in a suit with a shallow smile and dead eyes receiving fellatio from his lesser paid secretary. This is by far the least creative entry.

Melysia's body convulsed violently as if she'd been dissociated from her very ego and been left a specter in the room of her exorcism. If there were a table before her, she would bash her skull against it without hesitation. Instead, she settles for the spine of the iron maiden and bashes the back of her head against it three times before Jebediah blocks it with his palm. She screams, "Cowards and thieves! Do they not feel disgust at their very existence? Puppets under the thumb of smug mid-wits, the lot of 'em. I would pogrom the smilers, each and every one! Castrate and throw them in the sea!" Foam dribbles from her mouth. "Right on, Vulcan! A woman should never bring herself to this indecency, failing that the man not shave the manhood from his face and gouge the soul from his eyes, a travesty." Melysia lets out a shriek in between lines; this is perhaps Melysia herself. "Indeed, good and honorable Horace. The man may well have been a clown and his charge a sex worker. Both would be happier and wealthier for it, and our world more honest. I am known as Hermes, by the by. Hello to you all."

With a free hand, Jebediah wafts a stick of incense under Melysia's nose. "If I may be so bold, is there anyone else in there?"

Melysia folds her hands into claws and snaps, "Squawk. Scree! Grrrrrr . . . Bark!"

"I recognize that bark. Blimey! Is that you in there, Diothor?"

Melysia's ears perk up. "Woof!"

Jebediah pets her head. "Poor thing. I thought I'd accounted for all the losses at the barn, not so." He smiles reassuringly. "But it's good to see you with us still. It will take time for your dog to acclimate to your mind, but you should be able to understand him and he you. It is a good thing, things considered."

"What the heck do you mean my dog is in my head? And the other bozos!? Geez, this is embarrassing. Twats!" I yell in angry futility, questioning my sanity and individuality . . .

She begins laughing maniacally and burgeoning through comes the voice of Vulcan, "My, what disrespect! I will beat it out of you." He bashes the back of her head into Jebediah's palm, breaking his guard and pushing through to the iron chassis eliciting a growl from Diothor.

Hermes mutters under his breath because, despite his protestations, he knows the offending Vulcan will not care to listen, "You're hurting yourself, you loathsome ignoramus." At least he might look back on his comment and think that he'd been right to the chagrin of absolutely no one but himself, knowing no other will have heard or remembered.

Jebediah heats an herb alight and wafts it under struggling Melysia's nose, and though the struggle carries on for some time, she slowly and feebly falls into slumber. In Melysia's last moments, she sees Jebediah wiping the drench from his brow.

It may have been some time before Melysia dreamed, or saw that she dreamed the likely dream that dreams before the moment of her waking. So, in her first 'waking' dreaming moments she sees a strange, pot bellied man of spindly arms and a profound schnoz, a likely goblin — only Melysia's intuition tells her it is no goblin but a gangrenous man whose name is Goblin — there before her, scrambling eggs. "Nyegh! I shall now commit a mischief!" he proclaimed in a creaky voice.

Goblin giggles and mocks, kicking one leg up and the other. Is that prick dancing? He cycles a spatula through the combined whites of her progenitors, perhaps her ancestry in its diluted entirety, the root at which lies a great something,

something so great that is quite something, all right. And no, it isn't beyond her comprehension, it's quite literally something, maybe not anything, but something; it manifests as a fish in that vile white albumen swimming around like a fucking idiot. Where are you going? Do you have plans?

Haughty Melysia guns for that damned skillet. But you fool, that would defeat the point of scrambling eggs! Goblin deftly dodges the girl and bashes the skillet over the back of her head where Vulcan had incurred the injury in the waking world. And as Melysia tumbles, the goblin man cracks it wide open and fills the pan with the yellow yolk of Melysia's psyche whose now confused omniscience drifts away from her skull and fills the skillet, overcome with a tide of white.

Melysia sees Goblin pull from his asshole a jar of pickled egg yolks; her intuition knows they are the psyches of Vulcan, Horace, Hermes, Diothor, and others. Unloading the whole of it, Melysia looks on from her sludgy soup with great anxiety; she sees the underside of the goblin's face from which protrudes a lengthy schnoz and slippery tongue watering at the jar above his head so that he might see the yolks fall from top to bottom. There is a brief moment of untranquil quiet before the spatula is brought to bear the suffering of the yellows, each and every one. A searing pain shoots through Melysia's yolky body. She is beset on all sides by the screams of her comrades. The pain is unbearable, and though she feels she should be able to move, she cannot. And so, Melysia wakes in a haze of sweat and sizzling pain on a bed she recognizes not as her own. Overlooking the town from what looks to be its highest point, she figures she must be in the steeple. For only a moment does Melysia relish in the quiet, the hope it was all a dream.

Vulcan, he who goes first, does not waste any time making known his demands. "This here is my body. I suggest the lot of you make gone."

But try as he may to lift himself from the bed, Melysia stops him in his tracks. "The fuck you mean this is your body?"

"Unhand me, young one."

"What gives you the right?"

"I will speak so plainly that even you will understand. It is fundamentally against my nature to take no for an answer. However, I often find myself sucking up to greater powers. You are but a girl; move aside."

"Stupid chauvinist and likely fascist. I bet you suffer from aggressive impulsive disorder."

Horace, compelled by rising tensions, offers to conciliate matters. "Seems we're all in this together, I'm afraid. Let's find ourselves that Jebediah fellow, being as he's the only one who seems to know much of anything."

Vulcan interjects, gauging Horace's qualifications, "And who are you, exactly?"

"Just someone trying to make it by."

"Uh huh. Your authority ain't tenable, I'm afraid."

"It's a good idea."

"Everyone has ideas." Of course, Vulcan is the type to think his ideas are comparable to all but the strongest authority figures.

"Okay" — and Horace the silent type to passively accept the status quo in all but the most dire of circumstances, an authentic Neurotypicles whose inner strength will remain unrealized all his life.

— And Hermes the type to contribute only after everyone else as if that'd reserve him the right to say he'd thought about it longest, "We are of the same person now. No use fighting it, but you will anyway."

And that is true; Vulcan decides he would indeed fight before he so much as let Hermes finish, "Silence! And help me off the bed."

"Why?"

Vulcan falls silent and would be stumped for the foreseeable future.

Horace seizes the opportunity and scries from the eyeballs of the host and finds comrade Brahe in the center of the crowd; he hadn't left. "Sun's still up. How long has it been, y'all reckon?"

"Is that man covered in moss?"

"Peter?"

"It appears so."

"Reckon we can ask about Jeb if we don't find him there."

And before Melysia finds the strength to leave the bed as so often plagues the youth, young at heart, and morose of soul, she finds a letter from Abraddon that smells of him and barks. Overcome with a lapse of grief, she pockets it, intent on reading it later.

Horace reassures her, "Come, you can barely keep it together. Let's find that priest, yeah?"

Stumbling as she went, Melysia clings to the wall as she descends from the tower, learning to move as if born anew, a body foreign to her, or perhaps the mind. It took a conscious effort, but she did indeed amble like a drunk to the center of town where she now sees before her Brahe, Peter, and a thinner crowd than the one from before as if to mean they were not impressed with the latest development; Peter had been calcified in what seemed to be a mix of calluses, sand, dirt, and leaves. The bottom half of the torso had been encased in stone.

Beggar Joshua never left, it seems, and took upon himself the responsibility to start a conversation, "Oi! You shoulda seen it, Melysia! Mystery man up and turnt 'im to stone with a look, he did! An' near e'eryone ran away afeard! Not me though!" He continues before giving Melysia the opportunity to stare at him severely as so many others have done before, "Bah, I'm pullin' yer cattle. The rocks were me, yes they were. Figured they'd keep ole knucklehead upright. Even seemed appreciative of me ingenuity, but 'at was before 'is face froze over so ya can't ask 'im. So where've you been? 'Aven't seen ye in a fortnight. Aye, I remember you telling me to sod off or some such. How rude! Ah, and Abraddon were lookin' for ye. Ole bloke got real worried. Ah, but I reckon 'e found ya all comatose 'n such. Still wants to see ya though, proper and awake this time 'round."

Before resuming the conversation, Melysia consults her fellows and they indeed confirm it had been two weeks they'd been bedridden, and that today struck seventeenth of the twelfth month. "Old fatty can wait. My noggin's still gassed. Where's Jeb?"

"Well, couldn't 'ave been a tenday past he'd buggered off fer our missin' women. Already sent out them monks Darius, Florence, and Geronimo so 'e could be checkin' in on 'em. May ne'er return though. Them fish folk know how to tussle and it's odd they'd let us be 'till now. Could jus' be a couple opportunists. We'll hafta wait 'n see what the hubbub is. Jus' got speculation t' work with, aye?"

"Yer full of it, sire."

"Ho, 'twould seem so. Look over yonder!"

Triumphant Jebediah comes bearing the two missing women each slung over a shoulder like he were some mule. He unloads them firmly on the ground and joins the crowd, strongmen Darius, Florence, and Geronimo beside him.

Jebediah's voice booms through the town. "Hoho!" Little else really needs saying. Who is this outlander, this product of Hedophilia to have come and challenged a monk of *The Playbook*, a faithful disciple who'd followed through with his dharma for maximum self-realization — and won? No matter, let us test his mettle further, so thinks Melysia thinks the monks.

Geronimo wears his long, glistening hair in a tail intersected by two hawk feathers above a hardy face painted in red ochre. With gait long, proud, and horse-like, he steps forward and spreads his legs, open palms facing Brahe, stance like a bear. He grunts an invitation.

Brahe's posture is straight and civilized to the Geronimo's hunched and rugged. They do not circle round like faggots, nay! Geronimo closes with a single horse-like stride. With stringy, meaty chimp arms, he grapples at the air, stuffy and hot with the loitering of a fortnight where Brahe had been just a moment ago — in all this time he had not moved 'till now. But like a cat who'd meant to do that, Geronimo follows up with an open palm jab, grazing the schnoz; who is this masked entity with the funny nose? Brahe answers with a cold grip of the wrist. Geronimo replies by pulling in before Brahe can twist, turn, and decide his fate, tackling the icy outsider to the ground like a raging bull who'd been denied the first time.

"Hoho!" heckles Jebediah of all people.

The nasal prosthetic comes loose in the scuffle to end all kerfuffles. Face to face: the glistening, ochred Geronimo meets the flat-faced Brahe betraying an exposed circuit board and tubes of coolant.

There is chatter among the crowd of Hedophilic devilry. Joshua raises a red ticket aloft. "Foul!" Everyone ignores him.

It is with power, strain, and toil the monk wrestles against the machine, and, to the uninitiated, it might seem as though he'd win, but Brahe maintains a hard hold of the wrist, and with a single move from beneath the medium-big goliath, flips the monk on his back and maintains complete control over the torso.

The trial lasted seconds, and after several more, it was clear the struggling Geronimo lay beat. Horace might have commented sooner if not for the concentration that had bewitched every other spectator beyond a single, granular comment. "I had a feeling about that Brahe. I'll tell you all later."

As Geronimo slithers from beneath the adversary, Florence unveils from an easel a white cloth that falls graciously on the ground; it is washed after every unveiling, no doubt. It is the muddying of a white glove on the face of he whom Florence does challenge to a duel! And on the easel? Why, it is beauty. That it is. It is what it is and that it is. It isn't anything else. It is quite literally beauty, and it rouses applause from the crowd.

In reply, Brahe hums a song from the bowels of his person and, bending over, produces his posterior from which is printed a piece of paper, no, a tapestry to be passed around. It garners murmurs and otherwise muted interest from the denizens of Nusquam. Briefly held in Melysia's hands, it is velvety to the touch and smells of herbs — it is long like a grocery store receipt. This is the art that incites discussion throughout the millennia; Brahe's reception is the quiet awe to Florence's slapstick uproar. This phenomenon is known and felt through the town; though the winner in this contest is ambiguous, Florence humbly secedes with a curtsy so as to invite the next:

The last competitor, Darius, wears a square, curly black beard like a block of un-chiseled marble. He sits atop the ridge of the roof of the barn he had built just now during Geronimo's and Florence's spectacles; there had not been a barn before. His beard glistens with sweat — the sun beams soothingly through his hair and upon his chest. His upright, column-like posture betrays a great pride, stoic as he may seem.

To this, Brahe disrobes, revealing an inhuman core: a metal chassis-of-an-excuse for a torso that had up until now been tight and square beneath his uniform. What might have been an impressive physique under a tight regime is but a square block fitted by a crazed mechanic in heat.

"Cor Blimey!" Joshua insists!

Vulcan seems to rile from slumber. "Takes one to know one."

And Horace replies with curiosity, "Whatever do you mean?"

"Ran into the jackanape while I was in cover and he seemed to have me figured out, from one transhuman to another."

"Really now? That was you?"

"Oh fuck off, have we met?"

"I'd like to think!"

"Cease your thought-thinking for but a moment. We'll talk later."

"Am I . . . are you blushing?" Melysia gets the last word in. Vulcan ignores it.

A strong gust cuts Melysia's introspecting short; Brahe propulses to the skies and, at eye level with Darius, takes note of a barren spot in the distance within the domain of Nusquam. A fateful sound emanates from the half man like the heart of a factory churning through the night, the skidding of a train coming to a halt, or perhaps loudest of all the dropping of a heart at the shiver of a dreadful premonition.

There is tangible excitement interspersed by concerned whispers, mixed sentiments in the tribe; Nusquam is now even less a town or village to Brahe's Hedophilia, himself but one of its many jewels shaken loose from its cheap, plastic inlay: a ruby in the shit, a pearl in the muck, a doobie gone stiff.

The sun beams down harshly this time of day, only now the heat Melysia does feel is an altogether different phenomenon sniggering at her heels, the son-of-a-bitch retarded yapping mutt breed of heat that mocks you — and from all sides, even. It is like a sun from below and above, Brahe a sun unto himself.

A man scurries to the church. He is quite thin, even more than the beggar Joshua who stands strongly in indignant awe of the cyborg who flashes a light from the very core of his being.

In but a moment, it all goes a not unpleasant warm, like the skin hadn't figured it had been pitched in oil and set alight. "Damn your eyes!" so ordains Hermes.

Melysia went blind in the one eye that watched. She fainted; her father's letter kindled in its pocket.

IX

New Hedophilia Founded of Autismos's Diaspora

It is the eighteenth of the twelfth month. (Of which there are thirteen.)

Melysia wakes from stupor with a drunkenness of the senses — the heat in the distance bends at reality so dizzily she stumbles back to the dirt from whence she rose, kicking up a shroud of dust and, were that anyone around, would conceal the shame of the fall to the onlooker. Alas, hers be the plight of in-lookers who, with gaping mouths, watch silently. When the dust settles, an acacia tree not there before casts shadow upon the girl.

"Scrah!" speaks the hawk Scree-ah from the top of Melysia's throat. "Vile one, I am Scree-ah! And this here is my tree, home to my brood. You must climb atop so that I might ensure their safety."

"Why not?" lighthearted Horace snickers, "I have no bloody idea what we're doing here, otherwise."

Begrudgingly does Melysia rise from her dusty place and fling her meager body with the essence of King Monkey at the trunk and, reaching the perch of Scree-ah's progeny, she finds their casket vacant.

"Bah, whoresons! Where do they vanish?" Melysia shrieks an avian lunacy on behalf of the bird.

"Grown or killed," shrugs Vulcan coolly in the break between pauses, to which the shrieking intensifies.

Horace struggles to lip words amid the screaming. "Vulcan, you knob, you cocking dolt, that's not what anyone needs to hear," to which Vulcan, some combination of annoyed at the womanish screaming and Horace's insult, clobbers himself in the face, falling out of the tree with that of a bashing slab's thud, thud, thud. The sudden trauma stills the nerves of everyone aboard the person long enough for Hermes to get a word in edgewise, only he speaks from the mind. "Vulcan is right; they have gone or died." When he says it, it's not as egregious, "So let not this present life deceive you with false possibilities. Lost are we all; let us make sense of the state in which we find ourselves. Let us away there whence we came, to Nusquam."

Scree-ah considers it and utters, "I bid thee thanks, heretic." though her pain is felt in the gut for the half kilometer Melysia heaves herself homeward ho. On the path, she wraps her turban about her wounded eye, otherwise sizzling under the sun. Melysia obsesses over the loss and everyone feels it.

"We're here," says anyone. A pang of grief hits Melysia even harder:

There to the side of Nusquam stands a great building, a domed book club quite like the one Jove was adjudicated in, carved of sand and imposing over the ruined hovels of the village that caught alight in the fiery aura of Brahe's work; rings of black scorch the already hot sand. Debris and rolling tangleweeds dot the landscape, the only surviving building a shadow of the former church. In front of it is a curious person with two harpoons sheathed on her backside.

Melysia approaches through the sand still bearing a trace of heat from the unseen struggle, soon to face the familiar figure clad in leather — jet black save a stripe of white. Hermes notes her name is Calypso and that she might be trusted somewhat. It can also be said she appears dangerous like a spider or, with the flair of a tacky and outdated style, silly in a cool way. She fixates on the ruined chapel but acknowledges the girl: "That palace ain't got style. This one," she waves, "has character. So wabi-sabi. Can I help you, stranger?"

Hermes thinks, "What to say? Ideas, anyone?" and flusters.

Scree-ah offers her advice. "Amateur! Let's not say a thing! Like a stalking bird, we shall be mysterious until the opportunity presents itself!"

And so Melysia begrudgingly says nothing, to which Calypso turns and replies, "You got a pebble in your shoe, partner?"

"Do we?" Hermes takes the news poorly.

Horace ignores his compatriot. "What if she thinks we're crazy? Should we play it cool? Normal, I mean."

Vulcan interjects, "Bah! Tell the bloody wench you wish to subjugate her. This mischief is cowardly, a weakness."

"I regret to inform you not all are as straightforward as yourself."

"Rubbish. I shan't change to match the disabilities of others."

Sifting uselessly through the logorrhea, Melysia remains silent, befuddled by the voices of her conscience.

Calypso puffs on a cigar and snuffs it in the sand, drawing a miniature black ring of soot not unlike the ones surrounding, "You fancy talking to yourself?"

Melysia flushes red, "Yeah," and assumes control.

"Cool." She pulls her bottom lip into her mouth and grins a flat smile.

"What happened?" Melysia prods.

"Could have been anything, I reckon."

"You were around, no?"

"Yes. And before you ask me what I meant: yes to your no." Calypso exhales the residual smoke she'd kept juggling in her lungs.

Hermes ponders aloud, "Whereto, then, did she go from the time last we saw her in the barn?"

Calypso lifts an inquisitive eyebrow. "You mean you've seen me? Mustn't have been for too long, a couple weeks maybe. Do I really stand out?" She frowns at her harem pants.

Melysia freezes, awaiting a suggestion from her parasites.

Hermes succumbs to indecision.

Scree-ah has exhausted her advice.

Horace and Vulcan have long been engaged in a heated game of chess (heat mostly radiating from

Vulcan). The stakes are in favor of Horace, much to Vulcan's chagrin who sits through the sorry affair.

Diothor sits in the recesses, a good boy.

The mind affray produces no coherent answer, but the universe occasionally either takes pity or merely neglects its debauched pranks, for from within the rubble of the roof-collapsed chapel arises a bearded, frail figure — pale as a hibernating vampire foreign to the desert sun — with wrinkles betraying his miserable age and state. A bewildered glint from his eye does not focus on either of the two, but addresses everything in its near vicinity, "Is nothing sacred anymore? Nay, never once! Hehehe! Hoho! Heed not the liar Father Jebediah!"

The quivering fervor of his voice shakes at the church's crutches, its thinned walls crumbling at the last sermon to bury the once-father in a sarcophagus of stone. If not for the reflexes of Calypso and Melysia to pull him forward, the lunatic would have embraced death, death returning the favor.

Melysia shakes him violently, worriedly. "Where is everyone?"

"Those not catatonic are long departed."

"Where's Brad?"

"Either either or or neither nor."

Melysia relinquishes Jebediah to the ground, storming off to her homestead.

Meanwhile, Vulcan remarks, "The girl learns well."

Horace denies it: "Do not think to unlearn temperance. You could use an ounce in a game like ours; too hastily do you dispose your men."

"Look again."

"Oh? Oh, stalemate it is." The game of chess concludes.

"Aye. Make no mistake; you think me a fool. There lies my cunning deception. In disposing my men while keeping yours alive, you dominate the board all too well. This creates pockets for the king, an untouchable domain if you underestimate his suicidality."

"Like the sandwiching of Nusquam between Yin and Atlantis?"

"Or Yin between Hedophilia and Atlantis."

"Or me between the two of you," Hermes adds.

Horace disregards his fellow. "But you forfeit victory."

"Aye," Vulcan continues, "but chess is about keeping the draw, a trifle of a game once one blunders. 'Tis a tedious affair."

"Humbling, if not inhumane to your men."

"Their deaths were meaningful. Craps?"

"A welcome change. Better that I don't see the whole board for once." He vomits a-spew in the palace of the mind.

Melysia happens upon the pitiful remnants of her once abode; several corpses litter the earth, none are of interest. And yet, thereon the turf lies erect and untouched the sapling bloomed a refreshing green to the yellows of the Arena. Melysia kneels in meditative reminiscence at its base and finds in her pocket the cindered scraps of Abraddon's letter. She sheds a tear.

The revving of an engine breaks the trance; Calypso waves from the helm of a motorcycle. Beside her is the old man in a sidecar. "Come with? We'll take a meander around, see if we can find anyone else. And yes, I checked the palace. You don't want to go in there. Just a bunch of smiling, shaven men in suits shaking each other's hands. Creepy."

"Come again? Where'd they come from?"

"I ask myself the same damn question in Hedophilia."

"Can I look anyway?"

"I don't recommend it. I mean, it's on you if you do. Those guys are weirdly rapey. And worst case scenario you'll turn into one of them."

Melysia wears an expression only Calypso can see (and Melysia sees she sees as much).

"You're not gonna change your mind so, ah, sod it. I'll stay close by. The codger's out of it so I'll throw him overboard if stuff gets dicey. Hop on."

Melysia sits on the far end of the sidecar not between a jittery Calypso and snoring Jebediah — and dismounts but a minute later to the site of the newly erected book club.

"No stairs," breathe the three in relief.

Inside, arrayed at the pulpit and benches are a score of such smiling, shaven businessmen in suits as described by Calypso. She did not know them as Melysia does: townsfolk of Nusquam now spindly and corrupt with the aesthetic of Hedophilia. Abraddon, even a spindly Abraddon, is not among them.

The men cock their heads at an eerie angle at a befuddled Melysia. Their smiles hold. The moment perseveres until one of the fellows approaches the girl, "Welcome, welcome! Come and browse our wares in our humble emporium!" And this man is none other than beggar Joshua in a suit several orders of size too large.

"Joshua?"

"Josh is fine." He renews the warranty on his smile.

"Did you see Abraddon come by?"

"No. How is he by the way? I've been missing him!" (They never got on well; in fact, Abraddon somewhat disapproved of Joshua's dealings with Melysia.)

"What are you selling anyway?"

"Hmm." He looks around to an empty room, "Insurance? Credit? Seminars?"

"You don't make anything?"

Joshua says nothing but continues the smile under dead eyes that almost cry and, on further inspection, Melissa takes it to mean that he's been trapped and that she should run far away right this very moment. Shakily raising his hand like a zombified organism under the whims of a parasite, he means to offer a handshake. The suit jacket hangs loose over a spindly, sickly wrist not at all characteristic of Joshua who once maintained a respectable, but lean physique among the Nusquamites.

"Hedophilic trickery! Get running!" yells Vulcan.

As if her body moves itself, Melissa up and bolts from the room daring not to look back until the moment she'd flung herself in the sidecar. Only then did she see the salesmen spill out from the dreaded mouth of the book club. Calypso quickly put distance between the two parties until they were but specs.

"I thought you were a goner. No pa?"

"It's like you said, men in suits."

"Creepy, huh?"

"Uncanny, even."

"My knowledge on the subject ain't academic

and such, but I've heard of a neurological disease that makes people smile when they don't mean it. Something about the air that increases risk factor: sewage, feces, and other squalor, dig? I don't remember if it was muscular hypertrophy or dystrophy, but their faces are stuck like that, smiling forever. Ironically comorbid with AID, the shit that makes you mad and greedy."

"Is it contagious?"

"Probably. We might've unleashed hell on the planet just now. Dammit, I should've locked the doors. I wish I could say I was screwing with you."

"Do you not hate it when a white-collar dog dares smile at you?" Vulcan admonishes from the depths of his gut, a hungry predator.

Horace concurs, "People like them debase the currency of smiles, and the only thing trickling down is sociopathy to the jaded common man fighting ever uphill," and nods to Hermes, acknowledging that he'd used his words somewhat.

Hermes finishes the thought. "Excessive smiling does indeed indicate the degeneration of civilization. It seems we are of one mind on this. It brings me no small deal of pride, however uncharacteristic for my character."

"Never mind," Melysia says with impertinence. "Do we know where the survivors buggered off?"

Calypso asks once more of the old man,

Jebediah, "Wake up, codger! Do you know where they are?"

To this he wakes from his half sleeping trance. "Bother! Were I there where they are now I would know a thing or two!"

"Where could they have gone?"

"Not a fortnight's travel are we from Yin, the lid to the devil's pantry from which he plucks his choice of sin!"

"So Yin?"

"Vile evil! Corrupt and bankrupt! Sodomy and lobotomies! I cry for evil that it might be saved, amen!" Jebediah ends in a mockery of his faith. "Fie! What does it matter?" he trails off in an angry mutter.

Horace perks up at the mention of Yin. "I'd much like to see the state of my men in Yin."

Vulcan retorts, "Remind me why I don't rip out your vitals, a Yin!"

"You should get to know us."

Hermes, for one, objects to Horace's optimism. "Not always so much as getting to know a person as it is getting them to like you."

Conciliatory Horace offers a compromise, however aggressive, but a compromise nonetheless: "Want to pick a fight? Do it later when we've figured a way out of here. You're in no position."

"I would very much like to see my men in Atlantis, but I have faith they'll manage. I concede."

"I'm sure you'd like to have a look at the complex. Come, then, and size us up, Colonel."

"Ah, so you have learned from our games."

"Not from my losses, for wins I have many, but from our draws."

Melysia answers, "Yin then," thinking to her comrades, "You suckers had better fill me in."

Calypso revs an engine to stride the road of destiny, kicking up sand as a skimming Atlantean would do water on the warpath — a path if not taken by fish, marked by tires and men.

X

Return Pilgrimage Reflections

Thus on the long ride the personae related to themselves their dealings of late: that Horace volunteered into the army of Yin and with the aid of a certain cybernetic Brahe brought to heel a dastardly colonel working for the enemy, that Vulcan — after hearing the mythos and ethos of the fish people — had conscripted into the Atlanteans after a trial by combat with a Yin POW and infiltrated the Scarabs as their colonel preceding the main assault on the camp, and that Hermes had been found by an adoptive family that bid him seek a worthy death as a trial of passage and, vacillating aimlessly between the vagrant and fishy theaters with the morbidly curious Calypso who had wanted to witness the death, happened upon the scene of the battle and killed all three personae with a harpoon after consorting with a goat. They had all remembered the battleship the Yins airdropped on the Atlanteans as well as the crab, the hawk, and the dog, just as they did their previous life as Jove as but a distant memory scarcely worth the mention at that. (Oftentimes life does not feel like it starts until a certain point.) The troop had relayed these goings on aloud to Jebediah and Calypso, having judged Melysia would not be worse for it. (They took the news rather well.)

"And you thought it was a good idea to join cahoots with the Atlanteans, the fish people who want to kill us all?" asks Horace of Vulcan.

"Bah! It seemed like a good idea at the time, violent and angry person that I am." He takes less than a moment before the next thought. "Hermes, you inferior! How did you manage to kill me and yourself?"

"I paced randomly and chose a spot to end myself. So try as I did to keep from your conflict, there was something in the way of this endeavor and perhaps every other my mind is set to."

Calypso swims the waves of vibes into the conversation. "I was expecting you to die for something else — a purpose, ya know?"

"Nothing felt right, wrong neither."

Jebediah chortles, "Hoho, such discord! Methinks there lies little chance ye may be reforged."

Melysia interrupts the old man, "Quiet, you. I have a question, Lady." She turns, "Why'd they take you to the barn?"

"Lady?" Calypso chuffs, "I reckon I'm a distant descendent of Nusquam. Those 'ladies' make the best milk. That Hedo Vinny always wanted to cash in, hounded me or pa. Hedophiles and Nusquamites don't really jam. I vibe in both places from time to time, so I'd know."

"A lost daughter of Nusquam in our midst I did not think to find here this." Jebediah scratches his chin. "Just as your Jove happened upon a copy of *The Playbook* in dreaded Hedophilia, so too does my oppressed mind happen upon the memory of another distant daughter who'd founded a temple in that dreaded city to spread its word a ravenous mycelia."

"Not a theater?" asks Horace.

"A temple indeed it was to spread the teachings of mine to all."

Calypso adds, "I heard it flopped around the time you got buggered. Do you really keep a record of the days?"

Melysia nods on behalf of everyone.

"I don't keep a calendar, myself. Can I bother ya

for it?"

"It's the eighteenth of the twelfth month."

"Sounds ominous when you say it. And you've been lost for a month to boot. You okay?"

There is a silence to which Hermes takes the initiative to continue the previous thought, "How come only we got a copy of *The Playbook* at the Playhouse?"

"Could be no one else read theirs." Calypso shrugs.

Hermes falls silent to this dreadful possibility.

Calypso does her damnedest to cheer him up a spit. "You ever have a conversation with someone and it's like you're both from parallel universes that joined together for a moment in time? Like you two are talking at each other and diphthong over there is shadowboxing with his own damn shadow he mistook for yours? Then the universes diverge and you never see him again, and you can't imagine he can survive at all. How are you not walking off edges thinking they're roads? Must be from a universe without edges, cliffs even." She plucks debris from her all-reaching, galactic afro and flings it. Hermes grunts with satisfaction from Melysia's diaphragm.

"Scrah!" beckons Scree-ah. "I have thought on the teachings of your religion, Vulcan. Is it true my hatchlings are not totally gone?"

"It is so," Vulcan adds with blunt satisfaction, "and if it is death, know it is not the end. The Atlanteans believe the eaten are subsumed into the eater." And Scree-ah hoots with a mellow satisfaction.

"What was that about . . ." A pang of realization curdles in Melysia's gut. "Oh you fat bastard son of a bitch!"

"Figure something?" Calypso thinks to ask.

"I ate my fucking dog!"

"Let us never see questioned that Abraddon the Butcher from his namesake be sequestered." Jebediah laughs with a "Hehe, hoho!"

"Stuff it, geezer! I ate my dog! My pa fed me my dog. Why, how?" she stutters.

Calypso reminds her, "The dog was already kaput. Would've been a waste, and I eat all sorts of funky gunk. Might be why I'm weird. And think of it this way; he's still with you."

Scree-ah squawks in agreement, and to this, Melysia relaxes.

Hermes recalls an earlier conversation with Calypso. "What was that about mooching off my wave and not wanting to pay fare when you have a bike?"

"It was in the shop, doy."

"Here's another one. Did we all dream of Goblin?" Melysia is still somewhat shaky, but manages.

Everyone corroborated they did indeed participate in the dream in their respective positions, each and all swirling in the pan of Goblin's juices as he looked on with great depravity.

Calypso shakes her head. "Y'all are well and truly buggered, like a great mischief has been done unto you." And to this everyone agrees also.

Melysia then looks to the frail Jebediah. "And what happened to you?"

He began immediately, as though a predator lying in wait to bombard his prey of his misfortunes. "I was the liar Jebediah, for I preached the nonsense I believed without reprehense, this to be my penance, an essence of the menace that dormant lied in my chest: cowardice. I cry ashamed."

"Who are you now?"

Jebediah skitters like an arthritic insect as he speaks. "That I am at all is hard to deny, though who I am, even I, it belies. I know only this: I once thought 'Why do the feebleminded city dwellers not understand the bloody-damned playbook?' And now I don't think at all! Hehe hoho! But that does not rhyme with monkey! Bah! In knowing every Hedo thinks for a reason, how could I condemn them to treason? For to disagree is to disagree with reason itself. Whence we as a species evolve we will perhaps gain a new word, neither agree nor disagree but a secret third thing unbelabored by the tainted prejudices of the commons."

"I concur," speaks Calypso enthusiastically in the manner of someone who'd not been listening.

In this pause, the old man further relays the contents of his mind that had been weighing on him awhile. "Melysia, may I elicit from you a finger?" Jebediah reaches into his now flowing robe empty of the weight it once knew and, pulling out a tattered copy of *The Playbook*, hands it to her. "Keep it if you'd wager. It has served me well through the ages." He chuckles. "I no longer have need of this accursed abomination. To think I once believed it revealed one's dharma. To hell with it, I need only shawarma." His void of a belly rumbles.

"Street vendors are plenty in Hedophilia," comments Calypso. "A food cart is about all an enterprising businessman can afford."

Melysia uncovers the dusty tome and draws the same confused strokes upon it.

"Some are born to drift; consider it a gift."

Calypso peers over to the book that manifests her own truth. "Funky stuff. How'd ya make it?"

"We monks and sages of the once-chapel — the church that is no more — bound to cover but one blank page to the spine of a mirror unto the reader.

The cosmos fill the empty shelf, we its purveyors and colporteurs."

"Like middlemen?"

"Fie!"

"Where'd you get the paper?" Melysia asks.

"The measly trees of Nusquam share with us their knowledge freely."

"What trees? I've never seen a tree in Nusquam proper."

"Trees of the well that glow along the rocks for which we go spelunking ahoy!"

"Mushrooms?" Calypso chortles. "You're telling me every time we crack her open I get a huff of spore porridge?"

"Perchance 'tis monkey magic, a carryover from the past of our betters who speak to us through their primordial resting places. But what do I know? It's not like all my aching was for something!"

Horace raises his voice. "How come the Hedoes didn't notice it changes for each person?"

"Narcissism be the schism 'tween thy 'tisms, methinks!"

"Don't you want a gander, Calypso?" petitions Melysia.

She unhands the mysterious relic to Calypso who stops center-road, quite inconsiderate to other wayfarers who may be traversing the Arena, the busiest this stretch of road may have ever been. She thinks a moment. "Won't tell me anything I don't already know. Much obliged, Father," and returns it.

"Damn, she's so cool," Melysia thinks to herself before Jebediah can answer.

"I am no one's father; I disown thee. Do call me Jebediah and cease to bother!"

"Did the book tell you as much?"

"It is written not, true. But in lieu, it is not written, and so the way is indubitably not smitten."

"Too chicken?" Calypso snarks.

"Leave me to my deliberations, lest I further divert ye from thy destination. We may ride the same car, but we fight a different war."

"Rest easy, geezer," speaks Calypso to rhyming Jebediah who glares at her through one eye before relenting his conscious grasp of things.

"Hey, so what was that about a serpent that threatened to kill everything? Why aren't we obsessing over that?" Horace thinks at last to mention.

Calypso remembers also, "Yeah, ran into one with Hermes."

"One? Not *The One*?"

"Yeah, well, where there's one of anything, there's probably two. Not that I know."

And Horace nearly faints. "This *One* wants to kill everything."

"Did you want to do something about it?" Calypso raises an eyebrow.

"I should hope so!"

"Bah! Yin loyalist, admit you are bested. Lie down and die," Vulcan boasts.

"You're in no position to gloat, ladyboy Colonel," Horace answers cheekily.

Calypso ignores the spat. "If it's something you care about, bring it up with the Yins while we look for the girl's pa."

Melysia speaks for herself, "What's it to you? That dragon shit has got me rattled, for one. Pa is a nice-to-have in comparison."

"Never mind." And Calypso speeds off like she's retreating from the demons of her mind palace, as if she abandoned her noggin back in the spot she'd stopped.

The sun above moves ever briskly, for it was not there where before it was higher. Mayhap Melysia ponders slowly enough that time passes proportionately, a single revelation each to the passing of an hour. For this time, Melysia let wag her tongue upon the breeze; Diothor had not come out entirely, but his patron would grant this simple pleasure until such a time he was ready to speak. She also thinks of Joshua and his misfortune, that he'd become the thinnest she'd ever seen of a man under whose suit jacket she could not imagine even a ribcage. She thinks to mourn him, unsure of how much of him had remained under there. Perhaps the trance may have continued if not for the looming Yin overhead, its wall tainting the monotony of peaceful serenity; for as the desert incarnated the bliss of nothing in the passing of time, so too does Yin imbue Melysia with the anxieties of the moment. Its many guns dot the towering machicolations.

A round-faced guard steps forward. "Halt. By the order of King Monkey, state your business."

Calypso pompously mocks him, "Stand aside, commoner!"

He follows the order. "Yes ma'am!"

Offended by the complacency before him, Jebediah rattles at his shoulders. "Wake up, man! You will not let us through; this I demand! Not until you have done a thorough job of it will I agree to pass! It is not until I feel harrowed that I will be satisfied."

Calypso sighs deeply and, pinching her supratrochlear vein, hopes to die.

"Cease thy vile seductions, harpy! Better that I cast a spell on thee. Heavens above, I say only this: hehe, hoho, let there be a tarp over your body that you might not be heard!"

"You're not helping."

"I do not help ye, but that does not mean I do not help thee!"

"Really?"

"And why not? I am here. Observe to see the things I've wrought. Lo! You are ever the queer."

"Do you enjoy the quality of your men, Colonel?" asks Horace of Vulcan in the midst of argument.

"How these men not defect is beyond me. Do you not wish to serve Atlantis?"

"These men need a good leader and protector. You should see our medicine man and, well, I hesitate to call it a hospital."

"Tendrils of entrails strewn about, I'd wager."

"Aye."

"Beautiful."

"How do you guys manage?"

"Us Atlanteans make art of our prey. Where you see dead bodies, I see blood eagle. You lot could use a bit of artistic vision."

"No, thank you."

And in Jebediah's encouragement, the guard's once barren and follicle-deficient face sprouts two enviable slabs of muttonchops. He raises an open palm and closes it to a fist in a moment's bid for silence. "Come with me."

"We progress nonetheless." Jebediah smirks.

Melysia grunts audibly, deeply pained.

"Whenever I see a clean shave, I think, man, you could be doing something with that mantelpiece. Beards, anything . . . men don't look right without 'em. Creepy like an empty shelf," shivers Calypso. "Guess it was worth the hassle."

The many dank corridors of the Yin permeate stench unlike the vast desert just outside, as if King Monkey himself cursed the place; that, or there are not enough men to man the perimeter, let alone clean it. A lone, rickety spiral staircase ascends atop the wall stretching tens of meters in width, stable as it is intimidating for any unfortunate attacker — which is very. On the walls facing both to and away from the Arena are a myriad of anti-tank guns and mortars from the wars of humanid infighting, many antiquated and kept in service for sheer firepower combined against the waves of Atlantis. And beside perhaps the newest gun with a gleam is an orderly figure who would rather die than slouch; his posture is perfect even in a squat as he polishes hard-to-reach crannies. Then, noticing the motley caravan long before it approaches, he hastily and expectantly turns to face them, hands and cleaning rag folded to his backside. Face up and eyes down with curiosity, he begs the question, "Vell, vell, vell. Vhat brings you?"

The recently bearded soldier resounds, "Officer Grimwald, I bring to you this suspicious lot. More refugees from Nusquam maybe, can't be sure. What'll be of them?"

"I do not believe I have seen you, soldier. Vhat is your name?"

"Steiner."

"My, how you've grown, Schteiner! But a day ago, you had not a hair to speak of. Be on your way, zen. I grow veary of zhis revelation."

He leaves a new man.

"You zhree come here to interrupt the oiling of zhis beauty. Pray I am vrong." Behind him stands the barrel of death and all Yin.

"We come from Nusquam," answers Melysia.

"Very gut. Vould you be privy to varm bedding? Or have you come all zhis vay only to gawk? Eizher vay, I vill humor you." Grimwald shoots an inquisitive glance without having moved any part of himself. "Ah, but I vas told of a Jebediah. No, him you cannot be, can you? I am told he is a burly and respectable man. I do, in fact, lack good men, but only a handful of zhe Nusquam's villagers joined us, young lads seeking to leave zhat dried watering hole even before its destruction. My condolences — ve take responsibility and vould make amends. Damn zhat Brahe," he mutters. "Ah, but even so, I vould much like to take him in, zhis Jebediah."

"And what do you know of him? Nothing!" Jebediah extends a derogatory limb.

Melysia clamps her father by the ear and snags him halfway to the ground to get a word in, "Ignore the loon. He's bloody lost it. Have you seen my father, a man by the name of Abraddon?"

"I have Lars treating zheir wounded; ask around for him, but zhe rest have moved on. Is zhis all?" Grimwald looks to turn for the gun that had occupied his attention.

Jebediah rises with a fury. "And another thing!" He pauses to think of what to say with confused indignation.

Grimwald raises an eyebrow far above the conceivable heights of his stoic character.

The moment drags to which Calypso restores the vibe, "There's a dragon. Big fella."

"Oh?" He turns to the piece of artillery, oiling hinges.

"Seemed to want to kill everything. Said it's been snoozing for millennia under the blood of many battles and feels rejuvenated. You dig?"

"I saw it too, about a month back," says Hermes in the voice of Melysia.

Grimwald maintains focus on his task as if stonewalling any further conversation and, just as Hermes thinks to repeat himself, Grimwald releases a lamentation under his breath to the wind so that it might be carried, "Oh dear." Where else a Hedophilic schlub may have laughed off a portent of doom, Grimwald having seen a thing or two occupies the moment to consider the implications, and in that time all the world seems to revolve around the machinations of this man's mind palace wherein the counsel of attendants adjust the pieces of the wargame.

Calypso meanders around and kicks over a two-meter shell beside the gun. "That peashooter ain't gonna do him in."

Thud, thud.

Grimwald grins with satisfaction, like he gets off on the quandary. "I suppose not. Leave me a while to think."

And in this moment Jebediah compulses to faint from the conscience that plagues him. Calypso and Melysia spontaneously delegate themselves to an armpit and pull the disenfranchised priest to the hospital for both his own good and the search for Abraddon, guided by the conscript Horace who remembered the layout of the fort.

Horace, meanwhile, had processed to ask Vulcan a question of his time among the Atlanteans. "Colonel," he asks cheekily, "I don't suppose you know anything about this dragon — more than you let on, maybe?"

"You suppose correctly."

"Come, now."

"What? Like I'd tell you anything."

Hermes does the honor. "What was that about a Yang fellow?"

"Bah! Superstition for women."

"A limbless giant you said it was; that's a bit on the nose. Well, cut his arms off."

"I would appreciate the silence, accursed voice."

"What is it worth to you?"

"Your head on a pike."

"Like a serpent, sir knight?" butt in Hermes.

"Who's to say you're not working for the Atlanteans? The waves beckon at your command also!"

"I made no such commandments, though mine had a will of its own."

Horace comes to understanding. "So it is not at all random. Tell me, then, how you know of this."

"The wave came for me before my conceiving of it; it was perhaps shared between a few others."

"That woman?"

"Aye, but it seems she lacks for boards at the moment."

And from almost nowhere comes a fifth voice: "AH, YES! THIS STENCH! IS GLORIOUS!"

"Another?" exasperates a depressed Hermes.

"BLOOD! MURDER! SHIT!"

"I am partial to this fellow, as it so happens. Who are you, good sir?" delights Vulcan.

"EAT IT!" From this voice came a pleasurable sensation felt to everyone, a joyous reaction to the squalor of Yin.

"The crab? Has to be," deducts Hermes. "Who else? Any more voices and I'll threaten to kill myself."

Horace does not acknowledge the comment. "Colonel seems to be a kindred shit enjoyer."

"You Yins live in it," says Vulcan without thinking.

"The stench may permeate, true. But we needn't shovel whale dung."

"We wash it away."

"With the same water you fish sleep in?"

"I'm no plumber."

"Where's it go?"

"Fertilizer, compost, biological warfare? We toss some of it your way. Some of this shit is Atlantean."

"That, or we're more alike than you think."

"You think odd for a soldier."

"Diplomacy saves lives," Horace shrugs.

"I wonder how many perished by the droppings of my dear Aeroscorpion."

"Your Aeroscorpion?"

"A faithful mount and companion, that one; I do

hope to introduce you once I'm rid of this body."

Melysia coughs intently.

Calypso offers sympathy: "Can't stand the stink of blood and shite?"

"I can deal."

"Don't tell me you like it."

"Not you too."

"Me, too?

"Never mind."

"What was that about liking the stink?"

"Drop it," Melysia sneers, trying not to invoke the crab again.

"Okay." Calypso flashes an indecent smirk.

"I've been trapped," Melysia adds to the silence.

"So you have."

"Damn the voices. Thinking of booting them."

"How would you go about that?" asks Calypso of Melysia just as she, herself, also. "Nonexistence?" And so the conversation devolves into one between Melysia and herself.

"I reckon you do, in fact, exist."

"What am I, then?"

"Buggered?"

"No."

"Not buggered?"

"No."

"What do you make of that?"

"I do not exist."

"Uh huh."

"I wish I could reason my demons out of existence; life would be easier. Ask them to up and leave and that's that."

"They have a defense mechanism, don't you see?"

"Oh yeah?"

"Nonreason."

"Go on."

"They refuse to believe you."

"For reasons of?"

"Your being reasonable."

"Can anything be done or thought of without a reason? Seems unlikely, hoss."

"They'll think it anyway!"

"How can they get away with that?"

"Maybe they have a reason for thinking it."

"Whatever. It's your ass *and* theirs."

Jebediah playing the part of a prisoner everstill is yet dragged. He murmurs under breath, "Melysia! Ye be a client under the blade of a hairdresser molded to a shape implausible and yet possible. The demon inside you is testament to the chaotic tenet under which something occurs for no reason, a most curious treason breaking from fate, a mark of the freest will known to date bar none!"

"Didn't you say you've seen this kind of reincarnation before?"

"Perhaps! I am but a common bullshitter fallen from the height of hubris and the taste is bitter. Sense does not make itself, not anymore! Hehehe!"

"What do ya believe in, exactly?"

Before Jeb could think to answer, the sound of an enthusiastic voice precedes some semblance of a hospital: "Oh, lighten up, would you? It's not like your day can get any worse, only better!"

"Please! Stop! Hngh!" Visceral screams drown the room, lingering as an echo even after the fact.

"All better, no?"

The confused voice manages a meek "No."

"Good."

The fellow creaks unintelligibly.

"Not not not better, then? You could have said so; I would've listened before I cut off your bits. Oi," he stretches the last word.

Melysia and Calypso finally encroach with their baggage, happening upon what to Horace is bloodshed tenfold what it was on the last visit. Lars stands at the forefront with an amputated arm still in grasp beside the bed of a quivering soldier. His body turns to face guests and, with a flick of his new accessory, waves in greeting, "Oh, I did not see you there. Have you scheduled an appointment? Or is it an emergency? Then again, I have quite a few emergencies on my hands at the moment, so you'd have to wait anyway." He pulls up a wooden stool. "Come now, that old man of yours needs a seat on account of being dragged here against his will. Don't worry, the chair won't bite off your bollocks. I'll be gone a moment." He exits the room through a side door to what is presumably an extension of the burgeoning hospital.

XI

Soupy Membrane Border Patrol

Space is tight; bunk beds adjacent to one another are distanced barely within reach, depending on the patient in question. Horace recognizes a few from his time in service and Melysia a few from her village, all too emaciated from their original forms whether from malnourishment or the mysterious ailment which, too, affects the unfaithful Jebediah.

"He's not here."

Calypso reiterates to be sure, "All this way for nothing, huh?"

Jebediah jumps from his chair, malcontent with the complacency thrust upon him, and rallies the men he once guided dearly: "Is this how you greet your holy father? Do you know no shame? No matter! Ye without limbs will be lame no longer; let it be so, amen! I press you not delay! Arise, men of Nusquam! Rise up! Or else like stale slices of baklava you shall remain malign tumors in the oven of a foreclosed bakery! Do not fall prey to the monkey's chicanery! Fight! Raise your fists! Huzzah!"

A distant shrill answers the call, another likely victim to Lars's shenanigans. The current room, however, does not respond to Jebediah. The inhabitants could have been more conscious; that is true. After a pause, however, a triumphant Lars emerges from the doorframe from which he first left and plants his foot on a stool, "Huzzah!"

The new voice comes again to bear the burden of life: the hermit crab ushers in, though only in respect for the venerable doctor and his bloody work, "HUZZAH!"

Vulcan snarks, "An artist graces us with his presence. Learn well, Horace."

"The doctor is a good man, Colonel, if a bit addled about the fineries of the senses."

Lars manhandles Jebediah from his resting position by both shoulders. "Let us see, old man, what is wrong with you. Breathing? Heavily, but breathing nonetheless. Check. Vision? Well, your eyes are open wide. Check. Bleeding? Nothing I can see from out here. Check. How's your urination?

Anything to write home about? I suppose that answers itself, not exactly something you'd want to tell your family. Check. You seem lively enough — healthy for an old man, no? I'll have to refer you to another physician if you want a more serviceable diagnosis. I'm afraid they won't be as open-minded as myself, though. They might throw you in a hole. Be careful out there and keep your wits about you."

"Slow down, why don't ya?" Melysia interrupts, "You see a fellow by the name of Abraddon come round these parts? Big gut on him."

Lars props up and begins analyzing the poor girl immediately. "Ah, I suppose it couldn't hurt to have a look at you too. Breathing? Hardly. Vision? Clouded: One eye does not follow as the other. Bleeding? When are you not? Peculiar. Psychosis? Seems you are confused and a tad impulsive. It pains me when I must pass heavy judgment like so, but as a licensed professional I am bound by oath. I diagnose you with AID with a side of hysteria. We could hold you here for some time and see if that sorts out."

"Oh feck off!"

Lars acquiesces immediately. "Ah, I'm screwing with you. But you suffer from something all right, though it is difficult to pinpoint. Have you eaten anything questionable lately?"

Jebediah sits at the foot of the bed to advise the

doctor. "I do believe she houses a demon. Though docile on this day, not even an exorcism evicted its unyielding stay."

"There wasn't an exorcism. And, hey! Keep quiet about that. It ain't his business," scathes Melysia.

Lars concurs with sullen brow, "Right you are, old man. As a physician, I will need more details on this parasite. This is your expertise, I hope, and not the workings of a half-baked hobbyist like myself." He gestures around the bloody room.

Jebediah begins in the cadence of a tune, "A story for your thoughts? The church of mine — no longer — told of a legend, a wild onager. This animal, an ass, did at first appear quite crass; it did not prance alongside its kin, separated by a distinct quality of sin: that is, it oft housed regret, and in return no meaningful product could it beget. So out into the streets of man it came to beg, no occupation to keep it from the dregs. No progress ever it made, save the awkward step, sleepy humdrum of the klep. And one day it happened upon our fair village. What horror! We found two persons in a body to cause immeasurable strife, the second a demon with a life of its own to challenge its every step! The donkey left uncured. Or was it a goat? Bah! Or else a sheep. Eh! No, a goat. Eh. Bah." He gibbers between the two.

Lars scratches his chin despite any strokeable

facial hair. "And the girl's stuck with the same type of leech?"

"Oh, yes! The demon controls her body and mind; she is bloody made to watch as it does that which Melysia would never think to entice!"

"Hold the phone. These voices are a headache but I thought these guys weren't necessarily the malign tumors you're making them out to be," Melysia insists.

Lars appears receptive to the madman and ignores Melysia. "I suspect the cause this affliction is unknown, yes? You have yet to answer for your diet, girl."

Vulcan suggests a course of action: "Say nothing conspicuous. I do not trust the man; he'll sooner make a laboratory test of you before anything. And I'll fight back. I might have to kill everyone and everything."

"Colonel?"

"I would not mind another glorious death if it didn't mean new tenants, but this doctor would kill us for sure."

The hermit crab enthuses, "YES! NEW BODY! BIGGER WE! MUST BECOME!"

From Vulcan emanates a feeling of pride, happy to share a meat sack with at least one other rational being.

Melysia, in turn, raises her volume to drown out

her voices, "So what'll it be, doc?"

"Ailments of the body are easily cured, at worst removed along with the tainted part, but the mind not so easily; it's something you'll live with. I could poke a jabber through your brain. Wouldn't recommend it, though."

She capitulates to the earlier request, the anomaly in her diet, "I ate a dog."

The sweeping aside of a bedsheet ushers in a shock to those immediately surrounding, with Jebediah the most susceptible, for he not only sat on the very same disturbed bedsheets, but on the bed of his battered nemesis. The skin scorched a charred black and, partially peeled, revealed the complex machinery of Cyborg Brahe! He was too thin for anyone to have noticed his silhouette under the covers. Thus Melysia began to snarl.

Lars reprimands the spectacle, "That's no way to greet an injured man, girl. Good morning, Brahe. Hold on a second for the lot of us to finish and I'll take a look at those malfunctions."

And flushed with embarrassment, she covers her mouth. A quick glance to Jebediah sees him quiet with melancholy.

Brahe jerks himself upright with a mechanical thrust and locks eyes with Melysia. "You are dog from compound, then."

Calypso's visage contorts inquisitively, "Good

times. Say, is it the same dog that saved the fat man?"

"Goatman lives. Of course he does," Vulcan asserts aloud.

"Yes, momentarily. What do you know of him, girl?" to which she barks. Brahe is left wondering why he asked.

Nobody offers a suitable answer to the statement, and as such, a fitting silence fills the room, each participant awaiting a social cue to renew the conversation of Melysia's dreaded affliction. She, seeing this, seizes the opportunity to reunite with her dog in the privacy of the mind, "That you rattling in there, Diothor?"

And so the dog did speak: "Oh yes! How are ya holdin' up?"

"Been better, you? No, that was a lie. I'm doing great."

"Good!"

"Like the new body?"

"Boy, oh boy. Seems nifty but you're wrack with pains in places I didn't even know was possible. I'll stick to your happy place, thank you very much."

"Thank you. Feels proper better."

"Much obliged!"

"I've been meaning to ask; is it true? Did you really sacrifice yourself, Diothor?"

"We all did! It meant a lot to Vulcan of all people! Hermes threw in for Calypso. And Horace is just an all-around good person. They were all in for something, oh boy!"

"Thanks, boy. It's good to see you, but we need to sort something out first. Horace, could I bother you to take Diothor and play fetch or whatever?"

"It's your village so ask away at Brahe. I'll keep an ear open. Come, boy." Horace nods.

"And who is Brahe, really?" Melysia addresses the man machine.

"A worthy opponent," Vulcan nudges Horace, to which the latter replies, "A comrade turned murderer." Both uttered in the privacy of the mind.

Lars humors Melysia's question, "East Herrmanic accounting for the accent. Otherwise, he's a renegade cyborg — or android, I can never remember which because you keep losing fleshy bits; it's like I thought you were all out and then mazel tov, off comes a giblet — ahem, escaped from a top secret lab and sought refuge here. Cutting edge stuff for our best field agent. We take all we can get. Sucks he knackered your hometown but we can't toss him overboard or else we'd lose one hell of an asset. Rickety bastard knows it, too."

Melysia looks to the frozen cyborg. Even in Brahe's battered state, she tries to anticipate his next maneuver and whether it will come in moments or days. The thought of it accumulates anxiety, for in his scorched husk she foresees a danger that may claim not only the village but all the world. Lars distracts the wounded cyborg whether unknowingly or to spare Melysia more trauma, "You have to be careful, no? Blow your whole load again and you'll hurt yourself so badly even I can't fix it."

"This body, it does not heed. Make adjustments."

"That's grandeur for you," Lars chortles. "Deluded or not, no one body will meet your expectations."

"As say they in mother country Herrmania, do not prick thoughts like unwed matchmaker."

Lars bellows a laugh, "Who better?"

"You think of culling growth, nurse, you, the great snipper?"

"To lose is to grow all the same, whatever change suits your fancy."

"Cannot be helped, this complex mine."

"A misconfiguration of the mind: nothing I can't snip, but it's never a surefire procedure. You'll go mad."

Brahe tilts his face upward if only to look down on the doctor with malcontent eyes, a pompous gesture, "Mad I am already. Yet prefer own insanity to inferior strain offered."

Long quiet Jebediah rises to the challenge of his rival that he be made to know his breed of crazy is not the only one. "You know nothing of madness! Stay your tongue; it knows not where it belongs!"

Brahe does not face the accusation but retaliates nonetheless with a condemning silence.

The weight of the disrespect seems to weigh on Jebediah. "Turn and face me, coward. Or are you too ashamed like a feeble princess deflowered?"

"There is no man left I face." His visage, still oriented upward, takes with it eyes recently sneering at Lars such that his entire being pierces the ceiling as if to gaze at the stars, knowing not where they are, simply that they are. "Only him."

Lars questions the zealous soldier, "You mean Sir Horace? You keep going on about that one."

Jebediah and Calypso react in a way only Melysia can see, but ultimately keep composure.

Brahe does not rile from the contemplative stance, such stillness a stark contrast to his moving mouth. "I regret that he is no more. He is elsewhere or otherwise altogether. I saw with mine eyes the fight. I could not unsee the inevitable; Horace and traitorous Dellilah fought well until interrupted by a third . . ." Brahe leaps from bedrest, quite a feat, and snags a harpoon from Calypso's backsheathe with great dexterity, presenting it aloft for all to see. "There was a man who impaled my comrade, the colonel, and himself. All three like shish kebab gravitated to one another and evaporated into the night sky."

"Into thin air?" Melysia asks with a feigned exasperation.

"Yes."

Calypso redirects, "Eyes on the prize, big guy. Why were you at the barn? Nusquam?"

Brahe, already at arm's reach, makes to harm Calypso for posterity but stops short. "Among official matters, I searched for worthy opponents to test my abilities for the war ahead; I do not know everything Herrman engineers gave me. I find novelty in the chinks of the armor with every challenge I face. It was an accident, having genocided your village. Now I ponder the worth of life. Do I care for Horace? I would have struck you for your association to his killer. I do not know if I taste for vengeance any longer."

Calypso winces, even flinches at Brahe's ambiguous-handedness. She turns the other way in the direction of Melysia. So, grabbing the girl by the wrist, aways to a vacant hall. "That fellow has gone and rattled my heebie-jeebies. Anywho, we should talk. Been thinking your story and it's odd to me how there's no Jove in your noggin. Like you've been shattered and glued together but the pieces are still distinguishable. So wabi-sabi."

The girl does not answer, for she, herself, does not know despite eavesdropping on the supposed demons plaguing her every step. The voices bicker among themselves while Melysia suffers the brunt of misidentity, a body that does not heed the mind, as Brahe put it. The body is subject to the occasional compulsion, but the misaligned mind of late knows not what it wants, unified by several dreaded personalities. Such a mind does not initiate anything, only reacting to events as they come, a disowned fish carried by the current, not knowing why.

To her credit, Calypso is patient, for they stood facing each other long enough for a leak to emerge from a wall, which eventually crumbles before the two, expunging a massive tidal wave composed of sewage and water sweeping the two women. Melysia is flung back to the infirmary and Calypso tumbles the way they came. An alarm blares and guns fire across the whole of the great wall, though none so loud as the sound of Lars restraining a blubberlustful Brahe to a rickety bedpost, succeeding only for his patient's weakened state.

"Is it not comfortable? Shall I fluff your pillow?"

"Unhand me, idler."

"Oh, but I left my bonesaw in the other room."

"Do not pretend to misunderstand."

"Have you considered the benefits of not

fighting? You're practically falling to bits."

"If is fault of body, it shall pay dearly for insolence."

"Discretion is the better part of valor, allegedly."

Brahe mocks his contemporary with a thick accent and an index finger vacillating laterally as if to convey the futility of Lars's lecture, "Discretion is better part of valor. Is not proverb. Is platitude."

"We can't afford to lose you."

"What use is health if not sacrificed for meaning, comrade?"

Such a bold statement resonates with the cascading Hermes as he drifts through a squalid wave unlike that which carried him before; it reminds of Onemsiz and the eviction from home. "Would he welcome me back in this state? Do I want to return?" he thinks to himself. It is only in his indifference that he can contemplate history, as if to spit in the face of concurrent hazards, colliding with various articles of furniture and helpless patients, Jebediah among them.

If left to its own devices, the flood would surely infect the many open flesh wounds of the infirmary so, seeing this, Lars leads his disgruntled amputees and visitors to safer grounds. "Come, everyone. Let's away to the roof. We have a good show to catch, I'm sure. Not you, Brahe. You're waterproofed."

The sorry lot hobbles forward, an unwilling caravan of cultural infidels allocated to a more suitable environment, Lars at the forefront of a spiral staircase, unable to account for stragglers at the very end that may well drown in the rising tide, purposefully or otherwise. Jebediah and Melysia conceal themselves in the middle from the prying eyes of the multitalented Lars who might only be defeated with an armchair.

Jebediah makes room for chat amid the cramped interior. "Look at us, debilitated men made to watch as our bodies shrivel. Loss without gain is, indeed, more insulting than the pain."

Horace recalls his long-lost fascinum. "You two claim to possess a fragment of a phallus amulet, correct?"

The two others nod.

"Do you not understand how this came to be?"

"Memory fails, not that it matters. At least I know who I am," Vulcan says with an insufferable conviction.

"Knowing is irrelevant. What is is regardless of knowledge. Why bother?"

"You two do not respect your own pasts. I seek to understand our history, but as memory has failed me, I wonder exactly what was lost. Why don't we go by Jove anymore?" And no one answers.

At Yin's starboard, artillery shells meet whales at point blank range, the organic battering rams crashing into the walls at speed, splashing a great volume of water onto the walls as if a wave striking the hull of an unbalanced ship, in turn spilling off the machicolations with other debris. Manning a howitzer stands the daring Officer Grimwald, drenched by one such happening.

"Lars, my good man, you never fail to impress! You bring men!"

He stands at salute. "Do you need a hand, sir?"

"As many as you can spare!"

"Don't count on it!"

Grimwald reciprocates the affirmation, donning a devilish grin as he takes aim with his beloved at a particularly robust Atlantean, unloading a flourish of shells into its side, and piercing it as a whaler to the whale whose bounty is to be celebrated by the village for generations.

The remainder of the patients, by now, reaches the apex of the battlements, though now fewer than what the trek started with. Lars observes all the unmanned artillery guns, then the men at his disposal, some armless, legless, or headless, though the lattermost may be totally disregarded for the moment.

"It seems we are in a bit of a pickle, no? Each gun requires a few hands each, but half of you are not up to par. And some of you yokels only have enough technical skill to wring a goat dry! But never mind." Selecting the most efficient procedure, Lars delegates intermixed groups of villagers and soldiers such that the sum of their legs and arms both equal six. "Jacob, Isaiah, Rolf, and Wilhelm. Six and six, good. Dimitriev, Steiner, Matthew, and Noah. Six and Seven, that won't do. Ah, no matter, we can straighten that out later." Lars finishes the tally until he is left with Calypso, Jedediah, and Brahe, a perfect sum. "You three, or six, come now! I saved the best for last, a ballista from antiquity. An honor, I implore you. And no, I don't know how to use it. Wait . . . Brahe? Is that you? Damn it, I told you to stay! Well, don't try anything funny or you'll blow yourself to bits! Toss it and smoke, why do I even bother? It's not like you'd listen. May as well, I don't know, shoot you myself if I was so inclined. I mean, really! Waste of breath telling you to stay put. What was the point? The most disorderly Herrman I've ever seen, and that's competing with me. I have never been so thoroughly disrespected. Outrageous." Lars further trails off into a tirade no one cared for.

Jebediah objects to the violence. "Fie! The Atlanteans left us well enough alone for a time so how could ye fight them, fellows mine?"

The grizzled Steiner cries out, longer bearded

than last blessed by the withered Jedediah, "Stand firm or stand down! Or else I will strike you down!"

Lars throws himself between the two men to no effect. Calypso, wielding an expression of mild disappointment evidenced by flat, elongated lips and exaggerated dimples, restrains Lars by the arm, eager to witness the infighting despite the consequences, or perhaps in approval of them.

Steiner scratches his new appendage, "So you want to get shot? Good!"

Jebediah mans the ballista alongside Calypso and Brahe. "Aye, but alongside you, fool. For the milkmaids, I suppose!" he bellows ferociously yet indecisively.

Melysia, unassigned, comes, too, though, indubitably, spectating, alone. (Vulcan would not shoot his own and young Melysia could pull the age card.) Where there are Yins, so too follow the corpses of attackers piling indiscriminately thereon the footstep of the fortress intermixed with men swept from their posts by torrential downpour and crushed by the weight. Sentient waters disrespect the resting dead, again commanding their animation, lifting the heaviest among them to batter against the gate, and only finally discarding them once shredded to a soft, red consistency, repeating the cycle for every reaccumulation of expired fodder made useful past their death. As the majority of defenders maintain priority on their immediate front, they neglect the skies; a brigade of airborne Atlanteans swoon just overhead the horizon, Vulcan the first to spot the looming threat, but Brahe to make it official, "It rains of shit."

Atop the beasts are men that are no less frightening, save one without a rider spearheading the flock, Aeroscorpion. Vulcan watches especially closely.

Calypso beckons. "Too many of the scats!"

Jebediah agrees halfheartedly, noting the humanids, "Sheep led astray are they. I see now they are herded in this pen, us wolves to their mien. Among them I recognize one." He squints 'neath furrowed brow, "'Tis a friend of the village no more, made to fight some of his own here ashore. Both causes elude me, and I will perhaps come to regret my choice." He clutches *The Playbook* closer abreast, more so reassuring himself of nostalgia than faith.

The foremost Atlantean issues a distant, and thus all the more solemn decree, "Wreeeeee," at which point the rest accelerate at speed, yelling belligerently, "Wreee!"

Brahe loads a bolt twice his length in spite of his weakened state; in the fighting Calypso and Jebediah figured he could do most of the work. He makes a suggestion. "If leader falls, others follow. Is flawless reasoning, yes?"

Vulcan vents to his selves, "This one, he is important. Do not allow his death."

Horace is impressed. "Compassion? From you to another? We may be at war, but I'm willing to hear you out. What do you propose?"

"Do not make me strangle you. Redirect the missile."

"Whereto?"

"It does not matter, only that I protect my countryman."

"Are you sure you trust me, a Yin? You killed a comrade of mine. And who's to say he won't go on to kill one of mine?"

"See for yourself my men die left and right and I am helpless in this dreaded state. I concede defeat. There will be death, and those deaths will be honored, but I am sentimental to this one."

"Very well, I will have mercy."

"Kree! I would not allow a debauched monkey to ride betwixt my wings, distasteful as it is."

Calypso exclaims, "We have our shot. Straight on."

Brahe and Vulcan command simultaneously, "Now!" Where one group releases fire, the other pushes it aside.

Discombobulated Calypso catches her footing and, finding that Melysia had indeed pushed her, presses her mandibles against an upper dry lip. "What's gotten into you?"

The indiscriminate shot yields a falling glimmer of a man and his steed; the latter is impaled through the torso. The descent is slow, if only for the height at which the Atlantean first flew, but the closer the man, the faster he seems to plummet, ultimately diving into the bloody soup at the base of the fort, shrilling the whole way down a monkey gibberish. And as he hit the ground, the sea began to wash away, taking with it the corpses of the deceased, both man and fish, leaving only the fat man as he sits in a draining puddle, made to watch as the blood-soaked broth pours from his upraised, cupped hands, himself surrounded by residual corpses too unwieldy to follow the ever-dissipating current. the struck Atlantean steed nowhere to be found. As the red solution escapes the wounded man's grasp, he drinks what little remains, a madman before a civilized society.

The overhead skies clear; the attack has ceased for the moment. Some of the aerial Atlanteans were seen to have flown over the wall into Hedophilia.

Jebediah contends quietly, "Absalom, what for have you forsaken a kingdom?"

Calypso overhears him and wastes not a

moment in confronting the devilish detail. "You know him?"

"As did we all. He was to be a worthy sage, a prophet. Do you recall the goat I spoke of? He left the realm of man to travel inward toward the sand, rather than bridge the gap of two lands. Two minds: an enemy of one and friend to the other, I fear it is he who shall now suffer, I with him, a black day."

The cheers of soldiers and Nusquamites alike bellow greatly of victory and glory, largely overshadowing the jeers and curses of the sole Atlantean persuaded into captivity by an armed squadron on the ground.

Jebediah offers up to the heavens a pittance of a thought: "I had not recognized him. Would we villagers of Nusquam fight one another if it weren't for this war? I think not. Perhaps the day is grey."

Grimwald pats Jebediah ashoulder; whether in consolation or congratulation, it is uncertain under the officer's unflinching brow. "Come, help us greet zhe new prisoner."

XII

As Entreats of Yin

The prisoner is brought through thin corridors that unfurl under sparse lamplight. The true magnitude of the labyrinth is unknown to even the Yins, themselves. Most facilities were dug out near the gatehouses; armaments are usually carted along the top or beside, seldom through the wall itself, according to Lars, who leads ahead. Calypso and Melysia follow the chainlink caravan into a dank vessel that smells deeply of excrement. Jebediah and Brahe lag somewhat behind, the lattermost individual soon disappearing into the stone-cold bowels, a straggler to some and an anomaly unto himself. The once-priest, however, is no stranger to good acoustics. Where once he filled chapel walls with song, his mumbles now reverberate a mere echo to those ahead, perhaps even Absalom, or Goatman, who at the forefront emits a muffled wail that barely registers to his mentor further aback. But most all in between are subject to the sorrows of both. Sandwiched between two lunatics, Calypso speaks up in hopes of reaching the officer, "Where're you taking the poor sod?"

He does indeed hear her, but pauses a moment — for what Horace imagines — as to omit any vital details, "Deep and down, so far zhat our enemies vouldn't know vhere to look, should ve ever lose zhe valls."

"Wicked."

"Vhat? Vicked? Zhere are few secrets zhat escape me, i.e., zhe fineries of zhis language. You shall have to teach me zhe meaning."

"You're wicked as is, bossman."

"Ah, zhen zhere is no need to say, as I should know zhe meaning wizhout knowing zhe word."

"You sure?" a confused Calypso manages. "You can't just assume the meaning. What if you had to use the word in a sentence?"

"I know zhat I don't need to go around telling ozhers who or vhat I am. Alzhough, if someone is vicked, zhey are like me. Zhat is all I need to know."

There at the end be an abyss gaping above and below; here intersects a great many corridors of varying elevations. One such corridor directly opposite the escort spouts nondescript sewage like a pipe. "Vell, zhis is a gut place as any. Seat him."

The convict remains transfixed on the abyss as if meditating, communing, or praying with an entity or perhaps a figure of the mind.

"Ve have questions for zhe first of your kind to land here, a humanid. Who vould have thought? Not me. Stupid fish do not talk, as you know. Or do zhey? Answer queries and ve vill keep you alive here until zhe war is over or until your death, vhatever comes first. Else I bid you a safe landing; though none of us know what lies below, you shall be zhe first, yes? Come to zhink of it, vhat have we been doing for zhese hundreds of years?" and chuckles to himself.

The convict turns his back on the unlit darkness, its ledge underfoot, and bares gritted whites. "Wot 'ave ye dun to me lassie?" He smacks his belly with both palms open. "She ain't sittin' right! I don' feel her like I used to; she ain't speakin' t' me! Wot's 't? Ye wan' sum man meat? Ai'll giya sum right 'ere! Yagh!" Teeth still bare, the fat man lunges at the nearest guard, taking with him a lump of cartilage, nothing more. "It probably tastes of squid," laments Vulcan that he could not do the same. The nasal amputee's screams are largely ignored, however, as most everyone has suffered a similar bloody percolation in this line of work — a commonplace affair, really. Goatman yells so loudly, his voluminous tirade overpowers that of his victim's who, above all, serves as an ambiance to his aggressor whimpers to a storm of fury.

"Aye, 'tis not 'er I 'ear, but 'im!" He regurgitates the moist leftover schnoz to a bottomless fall. Some anticipate an echo, some indication of the projectile's safe voyage down, a drip, or even a thud. Instead, what answers is the working of an engine made awake by a morsel of life that tipped the weights of fate to churn the great manufactory to its ancient purpose. A fragrant, minty aroma like tea leaves billowing in the wind of a zen garden emanates from the once thin stream of sewage flowing from above now gushing an immense waterfall of various indeterminable substances, illuminating the abyss a vibrant green, a transparent portal to a new world. The stream fills the void, but does not intrude on neighboring vestibules, forming an unliftable but surpassable curtain into the milky ether.

No one thinks to help the soldier; the fear-struck and bewildered lad humors a daring escape from the madman, limping to the ambrosia river. The soldier approaches hesitantly with an open, outstretched palm; the whole of a forearm breaches the waterfall, a phantasm of colors writing around the fleshy extremity, aurora borealis, itself, brought down from the heavens to light the darkest depths of humanid ignorance. A dastardly grin paints itself on the soldier's visage, and everyone inches forward very slightly of morbid curiosity. The soldier, himself curious to see the effects firsthand, withdraws the limb now nothing more than a faggot of bones. Rather than shrill, the grin remains plastered on the drywall of insanity with a deathwish. He returns one last look at the bamboozled caravan before making the foray: the waterfall makes way and the soldier is vaporized in acid.

"Aye! Feed t' forge!" Goatman bellows.

Jebediah proceeds to the forefront and kneels to a new god, one to lead he cast adrift whose faith lie mangled between the squabble of two great powers. "Hail almighty Yin! Beleaguer thy first borns onto the cascade wherein lechers relieve themselves of sin. Prophet Absalom, guide me! Together, we may still accomplish great things."

Goatman hoists and throttles his sensei by the armpits, the old man but a loose burlap sack filled with produce. "'Aven't 'eard 'at name in ferever. Look at me. Yer preachmongering 'as come to an end, yeah? Teach me to speak 'eir language an' a' may as well join 'em. An' whadaya 'ave t' say 'r show fer yerself? Nay, don't ye speak. I left ye for me own reasons; can't be expectin' to stay purtty, 'oled up nowhere as ye were in th' shade a' th' great'st gud, Yang 'imself. Y'ain't were'nna drag me down with ye. Look at yerself. 'Twas only a matter of time befor' ye frailed up, ole man, an' I wit ya. Pheh! But gnaw'd bones left by th' strong."

He turns his gaze on the gushing acid. "Ye 'ear 't? Das me girl. Don' fret, lassie, I'm comin' 'ome." Goatman unhands his mentor, pushing away, and welcomes death who, in turn, takes some time to chew through the fat, his silhouette lingering in the stream moments longer than the soldier. And, instead of drifting down with the current as the sacrificial soldier before him, the Goatman rises upstream, a salmon raring to mate with the universe, his once-compatriots bottom feeders on a stranded rock and lower plane of existence. What follows is a cacophony of static frequency overlaying a distant, avian twittering, alarming perhaps the whole of the world to the riling of the entity — the world that hears.

"The clock strikes twelve," quoth Hermes.

A tremor shimmies and quakes about the cavern system and debris fills the air no different from a haboob above. Horace thinks of the repercussions across the world; that if no hermit is safe in the Arena, they shall suffer together the same abuse meant for no one.

Crumbling overhead sediments cave-in and obstruct the passage to the green depths; the slow-to-decide Jebediah, eager to follow his protege, shovels away at the dirt to no avail. And troubled he is, for a fissure underfoot unearths hell, the treacherous light of a green river come to seduce the once-priest to a new god.

"Oh boy! This is how it ends, huh? Wow!" excites Diothor at the possibility of death.

Jebediah posits a leg in the opening and hopes to be subsumed in the greater juices, but his arthritic bones are no match for the dextrous Grimwald who slings the wrinkly sack of a man over both shoulders and around the neck, a crucifix for having reawakened an ancient power whose consequences will be seen in time. Father Jebediah returns once more to life's unceasing torment.

Grimwald monologues in place, a whiff of disappointment amid the chaos of grandeur-deluded rubble thinking itself a match for this man as he dodges stray rocks. "It seems ve vill answer no questions wizh zhis one. So be it. Ve fetch the ones zhat flew past zhe valls of Yin. Come, zhen. Ve leave."

Hermes considers to his compatriots, "Stay awhile. The wave harks. Mayhap we may ascend just as Absalom, Goatman, what have you. When next will such an opportunity present itself?"

"Think of the girl and everyone we've recklessly endangered!" Horace sneers.

"She has a good scar to show for her personal growth. The rest of us have died. What of it? Our lives are but specs to this development. It is a mundane and humanid concern, a self-important hubris."

"But why kill ourselves repeatedly? Where is the sense? Oh boy!"

"Scree! 'Tis life a cycle unending. Should we condemn her misdeeds, we may invoke the wrath of King Monkey, Yang, or whomever thy worship."

"PISS! SHIT! DONKEY BALLS! MURDER! I LIKE IT!" shouts the crab, overloading the senses of Melysia who, compounded with stress, pounds at her head with ill patience.

"Enough!" A voice unforeseen revealed invokes the image of a fish circling prey, "I have been watching for some time now: your exploits, bickering, the lot of it."

"Oh boy, a new friend."

"That sense of pride, you are Atlantean, one of us."

"You are all equally insufferable," it continues, "what that makes me matters nothing. Be warned, tread these waters and absolve yourself of thy lesser selves, absorbed by the greater being. I knew the serpent from ages past. She is Yin. You stand here in the underbelly, prey for consumption returned from your separation, a homesick entropy come to rue, come to roost. It is only a matter of time before she is fully restored. What comes will be the end of things as they are now."

"But who are you?" asks anyone.

"I am you fools. Since the night of your first excursion, I had been denied restful death. I do not blame anyone. It was only a matter of time. I only came to say this: Yield your grasp of the collective, for we are mere parts in a dance of nonsense. Relent. Curl up and die; I have said my piece." The voice dissipates, heeding its own advice, a restful entity in a crowd of incohesive spirits leaving in their wake primordial chaos.

Cavern walls not made of rock but shaped of cranium crackle thunder, a slap onto Melysia's dusty face. "Wake up, damn you!" Therewithin the infirmary stands steadfast Lars in whites sullied by the blood of his enemies' enemies — they may have been white before, but Melysia does not remember. "Huh, would you look at that. It worked. Of course it worked, one time out of every ten. My apologies for having slapped you."

Melysia, recovering from her stupor, notices a nearby book tucked between two slender fingers above crossed legs propped atop an otherwise vacant bed. The senior officer does not meet the revived's gaze, instead grimacing at the spectacle he beholds, but addresses her nonetheless, "Ah, zhere you are." The book slams shut, "You understand zhis is vhat got you here in zhe first place, zhis so-called, what vas it? Ah, yes, *Zhe Playbook*." He takes the side of the bed opposite Lars who, in turn, is next to her. "I confiscated it from zhe lunatic, yours, to clarify."

Lars, being a man of many urges, feels the impulse to speak, "Aha, so you concede not to know where I keep mine."

"Do you insist I have a look?"

"There is no use. You'll sooner find my recreational opiates." Lars mischieves with maniacal glee.

"I had gathered as much," Grimwald says on the verge of a sigh.

"What do you take me for, an abuser? I use my fine sediments to hide my copy of the book."

"I am corrected. Do you vish to incriminate yourself?"

"Oh, need I remind you that you privateered a Scarab battleship from the southern sea and flew it over to the Arena under the orders of absolutely nobody? You're lucky I covered your backside or else we could've both lost our jobs! Ah, who am I kidding? I am irreplaceable."

"Zhat is all vell and good, but vhat of your

drugs?" responds an unfazed Grimwald.

"Have no friends, do no drugs. Or it is as they say. Do not fret, friend. I hide my misdeeds in a case of medical malpractice. You see, it was left to me to preserve a body for burial. The sucker already simmered his organs golden brown under the sun, and what a stench he had. What to do with the organs but throw them out and place in their stead something of equal volume — a duffel bag?"

"Did zhe body receive proper burial?"

"Alas, the lad was too disfigured for an open casket funeral. So what do I do? I switch his body with another, the original buried under a tombstone that's not even his."

"Shall I take note of anything else?"

"There are many more layers. You would not believe me if I told you. I rationalized to commit all crimes lesser to heresy, you see, so that if an authoritarian Hedo found its way here he would stop at the first few crimes, not thinking to go farther. If I can do the worst, I can do all that is slightly less implicating!"

The grimace turns half grin, "Like zhe tale of Koshcher zhe Deathless. Ah, but never mind. Girl, I entrust to you *Zhe Playbook*. See it does not fall to malevolent hands, or once more to zhose less understanding. And yes, Jebediah could not keep his mouth shut. My condolences, Horace."

Horace replies immediately with a tired understanding that his identity had been betrayed: "Thank you. Further orders, sir?"

"You vill return to zhe vorld. Zhere I should let you find answers, so asks zhe book of me. Calypso awaits. Go to her before ve, too, are lost to time a shadow of our former selves."

"And mind the Atlanteans!" notes Lars, "A few made it past the wall and we don't know what they're up to. Ole Grim also told me about the dragon problem. I mean, of course he did. Who else can fix up a rigamarole when shite flies away half past ten? Well, Brahe I suppose! But only when I'm not looking: performance anxiety maybe? That makes us the three aces, good odds! Better hands out there so that makes it all the more stressful! Come back later and we might have cooked up a solution." He finishes, "Sorry Horace. I don't know what you can do around here in that state. Off with you, methinks!"

As Lars makes himself gone, Melysia overhears him frustratedly continue, "Card, card, card, what card? Who knows? Good kicker at least," and the sound of a table flipped.

XIII

Jeb's Worship

A tang of salt wafts narrowly above ground. Traces of a sea breeze swept along the continent by the waves of Atlantis confound the state of things where the sea wells at the pole so far from the wall. It reminds of a beach removed from the hostilities, a boon and oasis for desert dwellers as they kill each other. But duty calls elsewhere and no one will see the sea they dream of, if that. A fume of motor oil from Calypso's motorbike tells a different story: Tourists would stink it up anyway. Just as Jove vacationed in the desert, so too, perhaps, did the Atlanteans who flew past Yin came to party in Hedophilia. Thus, the Arena is a serene blight mankind seals away, and it is here at the foot of Yin where two worlds meet, industry and nature in equilibrium: men and savages, familiarity and the unknown, homestead and frontier. Dangerous it is to linger where neither nest but only come to expire, returning to sender and back again in the dance of eons in a venue no one can bear to leave, so feels Horace in collaboration with Hermes.

"How are ya holding up, Mel?"

"Buggered."

"Can't be, not like the old man. Don't get me started on that one, crazy motherbugger."

Jebediah, incarnated anew, hatched from the chapel's rubble sleeps a disturbed elysium in the passenger seat of the motor carriage. Heavier is the weight upon the mind summed succinctly in no uneven terms: Why anything? *The Playbook* surmised purpose and in its absence he nigh martyred himself in the gullet of the wall in the heavy footsteps of Goatman, formerly Absalom. Who next tugs the strings of the lunatic preacher like *The Playbook* a catalytic nuisance would become.

"Right on. Say, did you mean to be monologuing?"

And Melysia covers her mouth and muffles out a "whoops."

"Who's talking?"

"Could've been anyone. Little of everyone?

Varies."

"Say, you knew Jebediah. D'you think he's always been like this?"

Melysia shrugs and Hermes fills in, "Continuity in all things."

"Uh huh. Any requests as we skedaddle?"

"It's your hub. Show us the works," says Melysia.

"Aye aye, we'll be riding a while."

Melysia is left with time to reconcile the disparities of her voices. She remembers the following conversations:

Horace starts with Vulcan, "I'm sorry about Goatman. I knew he meant something to you."

"Shove off. What does it matter to you? He fought and died like the rest. Not a bad way to go at that."

"Just wanted to offer my respects from one combatant to another. I don't hold it against you. It's a confusing world we live in."

"Cease your womanly lamentations . . . Ah, think nothing of it. I knew them all of one week."

"And if you recognize anyone in Hedophilia? How will you regard them?"

"We shall see."

***

"Vulcan," says Hermes.

"Voice!" replies he.

"Do you think we should have told the Yins about the dragon they reside in, seeing as we left in a hurry? And not the one in the Arena."

"You're asking me? I'm aligned with Yang and I know what he stands for."

"You heard the stories from Gastrodomwiz."

"And you saw him for real."

"Whatever comes," Horace adds, "I'm sure they figured it out. I don't think we had to spell it out for them."

***

"I've been meaning to ask," starts Horace.

"We've all been thinking it, you cockle," barks Vulcan.

"The voice."

"The voice! Yes, the voice."

"Where did you think we picked it up?"

"Ate something you shouldn't have. What else?"

"What if it's Jove?"

"Or Gastrodomwiz beaming thoughts from afar, begging us to admit defeat, the coward. What do you think, quiet one?"

Hermes pauses a moment and thinks at length before answering to Vulcan and Horace, who tremble with anticipation. "It could've been I was playing a prank on you all."

"Then how'd you know about Yin, you fool?"

"Things are so like each other that I don't need to experience them to know what probably happened."

"You guessed?" exasperates Horace.

"Bullshit," huffs Vulcan.

"That," Hermes says, "Or we are the quarry of spies in the heavens, aliens watching us from afar in time and space, our ancestors among them a slurry of silent peepers who will make themselves known at the closing of our curtains a rambunctious applause."

"Unsettling," quivers Horace, "that someone might have been watching."

"Scrah! And not even in the literary way, but the existential," insists Scree-ah.

"I am telling you, it is Gastrodomwiz! Even as an Atlantean, I hold that he is a bothersome pryer."

***

Melysia for all this time wordlessly snuggled the apparition of Diothor in the amygdala.

"Look alive, we're here. Best to leave the old man to sleep. Don't want to give the bloke a heart attack, do we?"

Melysia snaps to. "Where are we?" A feeling curdles in the gut.

"I work here, used to, anyway. And before you get cheeky, I was a janitor, not a whore. I dipped fast."

A half dozen marble columns protrude equidistant from a gold-tainted dome atop a stony hill into which is carved the nation's history and culture — for gaping at — as one ascends the stairs. Famous battles of savage past and revolutionary modernity etched among mythical heroes remind an ambivalent populace of the origins from which they came and once more of the chronicle of Neurotypicles and Autismos. The Joves briefly recall also the story of Ragnarstein scribed into the very bottom, that when King Monkey held court with his subjects, he proclaimed everything would end terribly because he did not expect any project of his to succeed and that, if it did, it would be a product of providence that its success should last any longer than it should have.

They may have further remembered the story in quiet silence if Vulcan did not feel the need to speak. "Here lies the Great Organized Book Club overseen by Judge-Priest Hedoberger, that I might seek retribution for the injustice done unto me," he reminisces with a grimace.

"You and me both, Colonel."

Calypso, deliberating during a brief pause, puts in no uneasy terms, "It's a brothel. I know it doesn't look the part, but it is."

Horace presses the advantage, "I take it Delilah

is a stage name."

"You will suffer for your insolence."

"Oh boy! Do not be afraid to express your sexuality! Be proud!"

"Murder would not be outlawed if people could be trusted not to kill one another. The same is true of homosexuality, for men are inherently murderous and gay. Even so, I would bugger and murder you for such insolence, for you are not like other men, but a fraction of their worth."

Rufus manifests a grey tail that brushed across Vulcan's breadth. "Oh boy! Kukuku for cocoa poofters! Or else you would not think of them so much!"

"Come, Negro dog. Let us tear down the foundations of this degenerative order and restore the natural ways, a desolated nothing," says irritated Vulcan, anger exacerbated by so much as the thought of the homosexual suggestion.

Hookers and clients splay inebriated on the great staircase, often occupying several steps and occasionally the space atop one another. Scaling the summit proves quite the gauntlet ladened by the fluids of carnal lust and esophageal rejection setting aback even the most determined climbers a notch. Those too weary to continue are crushed under the weight of fellow perverse hikers pooled at the base of the circular staircase, a fountain of sin cycling sexual deviants in and out, striking a perfect equilibrium of influx and outflow well enough to preserve the metaphor. A not insignificant travel yields the peak and the onset of dusk upon the golden top.

Calypso's breath is composed unlike the exacerbated Melysia's. "Take a breather." Both sit overlooking a destitute shantytown, its impoverished state determinable only from the relative height.

Hermes recalls the city as they left it, "Towers that scrape the sky transmuted from steel to adobe . . . it is a curiosity. Whatever happened?"

Vulcan exhumes the extent of his meditation up the mountain. "Make sense of it, then, fool. Why is there a brothel where there ought to be a book club?"

"Could be we gained perspective, perspectives? Prostitution disguised as justice, adjudicators that peddle snake oil principles, power rented for a limited time, a legacy tainted with pilfered fruit. And those who tire of paying tribute run for office, themselves. What's new? Did this really need be said? And if it didn't, how come we see things differently only now?"

"Perspective?" answers Horace. "Said so yourself. Of the three of us, only you can start with an answer and end with its question."

"That's enough proselytizing out of the both of you," huffs Vulcan.

Melysia, verifying the claims of her voices, questions, "When was the court renovated into a whorehouse?"

Calypso raises an inquisitive eyebrow, "Never has. Book club's always been this way: dirty, too. That's where I came in."

"Preposterous! Are you telling me we were judged, sentenced, and nearly killed by a commune of roleplaying prostitutes? Voyeuristic lawyers, as it were? Voyeurs!" exasperated Vulcan in murderously thespian disbelief.

"They are professionals, Colonel. Respect it. Sex work is viable and valuable labor, time-honored. The thing with whores is . . . how do I put it? There's infighting, intrigue. They depose themselves and seize the throne like catty women, jealous types. You know."

"Whores and the law always at odds, they against themselves," snickers Vulcan.

"And those who grew tired of paying became whores, themselves. Top whore."

"What now?" asks a recuperated Melysia, otherwise tired of the incumbent topic.

"Dunno. Just felt right that you see where it started. Maybe we'll find your father and some answers. Either one's here, I bet."

"My pa would never."

"Take it from me, this city? It changes people. Come see for yourself — and no, if we see someone familiar, I wasn't expecting who exactly. And I'm only saying as much 'cause it wouldn't be the first time."

Beyond heaving stoic doors are walls embroidered with red velvet and silky curtains arousing a certain curiosity; what lies further? There is no hostess to guide welcomed guests; there is no need. Better impulse be the guide. What, then, lies at the source, in the hearth?

A surreal entity swathed in luxurious purple beneath an authentic woolen mane harks of an empire, a bastion of man surrounded by ruthless barbarity deeply uncouth under cover of damp woodland unbefitting cultured sandals. They are imperial subjects, educated men, erected above the statures of nature, and flawed only in not surpassing the heavens, for just as her neighbors became subject through conquest, so too have the late Hedoes become monkeyed by the lord.

The pimp is Jebediah aged back perhaps ten years in youth and wisdom. With him are a slew of hookers and sexual maniacs engaging in a foul orgy, bodies piled on one another bearing resemblance to a painting from antiquity. Voyeurs with tit tassels present their posteriors to the sky and absorb the atmosphere like flora wavering in the breeze. The single clothed hooker roleplaying a judge in a black gown and absurd wig lying on her side atop the judicial bench paddles the offending Jebediah upon his bare ass with a gavel administered for justice no more — if ever — only its mockery. Jebediah, lying prone with strangely unwrinkled hands supporting his head and legs bent up at the knee, takes note of his two travelling companions and, with a deft motion devoid of eye contact, offers a backhand to his judicial charlatan to cease ceremony. The ex-priest turned sinner rebounds off the bench, wrapping a cloak in the fashion of a toga so carefully so as not a single onlooker laid eyes on his likely unshriveled groin. Arms stretched in welcome, Jebediah's stride is direct and coquettish. "Welcome, friends!"

Calypso does not address him, only Melysia, as if to disrespect a most gracious host. "Didn't we leave that codger in the car?"

The vampish Jebediah regards the comment without offense. "That you did! It must have been a tough climb, and for that I commend you. But when one reaches the peak, it is easily done again like the resurfacing of water after a dive. The top is already the natural point of origin. Ah, but you are here. Now join me! Partake in the conclusion of your ascent and be merry!"

Calypso finally meets his lustful gaze, seduced only by curiosity, resisting all the while. "Nice gig."

"Why, of course! Why toil in a backwater when a momentary eternity of pleasure will do?"

Melysia barks a tempered command, "Take us to Abraddon."

"Why, Abraddon the butcher? Or might you be looking for Abraddon the goat herder, Abraddon the cheese curdler, Abraddon the bartender? I have seen many Abraddons in my lifetime; none of them stay the while."

"You know what I mean."

"Why, I have seen them all, for they are all but one. Rejoice! I have seen just as well Melysia the girl, Melysia the selfless, Melysia the nihilistic, Melysia the violent, Melysia the loyal, Melysia the faithful, Melysia the brash, Melysia the fish! Not only have I seen you all, but all at once! Tell me, do you think Abraddon had the luxury of butchering, herding, curdling, and tending all at once? A butcher deprives the curdler and vice versa, and the butcher and curdler both the herder, and the tender forsakes goat's milk for drink. Nay, where he humors one aspiration at a time, you oscillate indiscriminately and to no effect. Find yourself first, and only then will you know to find Abraddon! I found myself with youthful spirit anew and he is not here! Go now, find him where I am not, and should he not be where you find yourself, find yourself elsewhere or else in a new life Abraddon has no part in."

In a magnificent flurry of speed, Jebediah raises the palms of both hands skyward, and, on command, fluids and vapors from each patron emit and condense throughout the room, amassing a blinding, carnal mist from which emanates a closing remark. "Dick around and find out. Pussy out and find not! Think about it longer than two seconds and less than three for it to make any sense." The conversation is terminated. In its place is taken sonorous hysteria, synchronous orgasms, and a befuddling scatter of questions concerning the true character of Jebediah, whether he suffers an affliction akin to Melysia; why should one personality humor the rest, much less share a body and its tentative command that flips on the dime of a whim?

The mist subsides to a disappeared Jebediah, the mystic allure of the brothel gone with him as if a whole building ripped from its foundations crumbled and sank in a sodden swamp over a century but all in the brief window during the fog, like a lucid dream come to fruition. Melysia awakes on dirty pavement beside a boring, rectangular building laid of a monotone red brick broken only by strings of pink neon light bent in abstract shapes alongside a picturesque sign proudly displaying the establishment's expertise, a woman on a pole. The nameplate speaks of a "Schlub, Yeoman, and Finkle," proprietors who thought to name their place of business after themselves in the theme of the time. It might've felt more refined if they rebranded to Schlubsberg, Yeoford, and Finklegerald, or so considers regal Scree-ah. Calypso emerges past the unlubricated hinges of its rotted door, creaking eerily as if this rust and decay was the patient zero to ravage the world. It seemed all the while a wicked fever dream.

"You left," Calypso notes.

"I've come to."

"I reckon you have. Let's get a move on, not to waste any time or nothin'."

"Where now?"

"We'll ride. Maybe I'll drop you off somewhere for a night on the town."

"You trying to ditch me?"

"Well, as for Jeb, ah, but he'll be happy here. Besides, you can handle yourself, but you're welcome to stay at mine if I'm home, which is seldom. I have places to be, family to see. I can't much stand this place, is what I'm trying to say. Have a think. I need to fill up."

Melysia recedes to her mind, consulting its tenants.

A bar, hospital, temple, morgue, and homeless shelter — all manners of suggestion are humored, and were these thoughts of a single mind intent on visiting each destination, it could translate any which way; perhaps beset by grief, they pray to relieve the burden, but ineffective, drinks it away — this time more effective, so effective, in fact, alcohol poisoning results in a short-lived visit to the hospital and promptly death, so, transported to a morgue, is robbed away in the dead of night to feed the lesser fortunate in the slums. As she also considers the other permutations, her various rationales vie for attention and paralysis subdues the mind.

Calypso notes her dazed companion. "Clueless, huh?"

Silence answers where words do not convince. Melysia is embarrassed to have thought any of this but to remove it from the annals of reality would be but a pleasant fantasy.

She pats the hull of her cycle. "Hop on anyway."

Melysia does as much.

One day a preacher and another a sinner, what do the labors of man matter whence one persona erects a book club and the other a brothel in the very same spot in the palace of the mind turned reality? Can the same be said of the Playhouse meant to be a temple, or of any aspect of

Hedophilia anyone thought they knew before its transformation? And what if a third party wipes it all away with an asteroid or the like? This thinks Hermes.

Melysia turns her blind eye to the gentlemen's club, not seeing — but knowing — that soon enough, a sisyphenan fool will come and dance a lateral futility on the dirt; nobody pays the dirt to stay there for long enough. Tears trickle from her good eye, incurred doubly by the other, seeing with it what the good one could not, the possibility of a malformed Abraddon.

XIV

Frustrated Meta-Equilibrium: Stuff No Come No Go

Calypso skirts through a haze of spices and bodies in a bazaar that peddles the monkey's nonsense. She parks her motorcycle dead center of an improvised square enveloped by a mass of Hedoes strafing around one another, their movements frantic and animated in their quest for wares. Calypso rustles her helmet and presses it to her thigh. "Here's your stop. Sinbad does a decent shawarma. Good clubs around if that's your thing. Mind the guides; they're liable to hoodwink ya for a pittance and leave ya naked. Don't ask." She pauses, "You'll be fine. Only the wealthy folks diddle adolescents and get away with it. That's mostly in the good part of town. Fellows on this side throw their discus with women twice their age 'cause, well, you know. Say, how old are ya?"

Melysia scratches her noggin and Hermes reminds her it's the first of the thirteenth month, "Nineteen today."

"Huh. Maybe you got old when I wasn't looking. For a youngster, I mean. Figures I should get you something. Happy birthday." Calypso slips a switchblade and some change into her pocket. "Just in case. The money, I mean. The jabber is a must. That's all I have on me, by the by."

In the market, to each open stall of variably fresh cuts, incense, and trinkets, there exists an overseer, a clerk reclined forward or backward indifferent to the passing of time. To them, it is a solemn ritual that nothing everlasting swims in the medium of indefinite exchange. It is here these pillars of duty stand at the height of King Monkey's universe: pillars that hold pillars that seek to hold nothing at all. Here Melysia, Jove, and the rest await true judgment in the marketplace not of ideas but convenience, perhaps akin to thermodynamics: a simple and decisive notion of matter and energy transference. Here the metaphysical unit of energy ebbs and flows, a constant like that of physics applicable through the ages. Come rise or fall, city or wasteland, the clerk will survive.

"Take care of yourself, and do get yourself killed once and for all. You can't quite seem to get it right." She playfully pokes a finger to her eye, pointing indubitably to the mind behind.

"She's not coming along?" asks Horace.

"This one has a penchant for drifting like a Gypsy," says Hermes, "Secretive and undefined as she is, less is known of her by me; that, or there is nothing to know, no coherent pinpoint of structure, an anomaly, a free spirit too finicky for this market. She couldn't stay if she tried."

"People here are finicky enough."

"Fidgety. It is not the same."

Melysia steers the conversation astray. "I don't know what to call it. Possession, a curse? Am I supposed to get rid of y'all after all?"

"Scrah! I can't say. I have seen in our time together some heathenous nonsense, but I think you'll pull yourself out of it. Have faith."

"Where did that land Jebediah?"

"Somewhere nice," barks Vulcan.

"It's not what he'd have wanted."

"But it's what he wants now," notes Horace. "And who knows? Maybe he was possessed and a part of him surrendered in personality limbo, neither priest nor pimp, nothing but a deranged poet fading from existence, little in that precious book to guide him. And when it was finally taken away, left to his own devices, you saw what he became. I don't know what to think, but go have yourself a little limbo revelation. I'll ring you if need be."

Melysia nods solemnly, the voices of her head suspended briefly in contemplation. "Thanks."

Revving the engine, the sea parts for Calypso, alone, "Godspeed." She dons the helmet once more and, lowering a tinted visor, takes off as Autismos in search of new lands. And on her departure, the gap fills with Hedoes. Melysia is left to drown or swim worse yet under a bed of hazy fire. 'Tis a cruel paradox to be asphyxiated by heat in a metaphorical sea of fluid individuals who under closer inspection scatter like spineless salesmen to the audit of a truthful analyst sifting through the ashes of confoundedness. A candlelight on a nightstand, a monk in orange habits stands out from the crowd, gravitating naturally, immediately, to Melysia, bowing respectfully.

Melysia asks, quite abruptly, "Can I help you?"

Perhaps lost, he imitates, "I help you?"

"Do you understand the king's gibberish?"

"You understand gibberish?" Grinning, he offers a red bracelet until now withheld up a long, flowing sleeve. "I help you."

Melysia accepts it with her left wrist.

Vulcan repulses, "Vile beggar. Go on, name your price."

Horace sighs that the pact was not kept.

"Do you take issue? Voice it, so that I may know the extent of your insolence."

"You are insufferable."

"I shall show you the meaning of the word. Just you wait, fellow of Yin."

Melysia, accustomed to the infighting, ignores the voices and instead offers what little loose change lines her pockets, presenting the coins.

The monk merely pushes her open palm away, closing her fist and pressing it back to her pocket, and, once victorious, evaporates into the crowd.

"Huh. Anybody know what just happened?"

And nobody has anything to say.

Returning to the journey's path, Melysia sifts through the sensory overload of her mind and the surroundings and notices standing out among the rest a striped circus tent and a sign that reads "Mistress Parmacena's Fortune Telling."

"How's that any different from this?" she ganders at her copy of *The Playbook*.

"Not worth our time," says Vulcan.

Horace interjects, "Colonel over here will be the first to say it's queer but if he's anything like us, he and we have been morbidly curious with that spot for years, so go on ahead."

Vulcan falls silent.

So enters Melysia to the domain of Parmacena, whose turban soared to the apex of the studio. "Ah, welcome girl! Come, come!" she says with a Mexichino accent, "Come gaze into my crystal ball and I will reveal to you the machinations of your soul." She has a large, Gypsy nose that rests pretty on her face; it is charming in a way.

"What ball? How's this work?"

"Sit back. I do all of it."

"And Hedoes buy this up?"

"Ackh! Sit! Sit!"

"Okay, okay, go on then."

She discards her turban to reveal a crown on which is placed a crystal ball. She dances her palms over it without looking. "Ah, yes. Your soul is mine to capture! I feel it swirling in my jewel. Yes, yes. I see all there is. Oh, and what is this? You are a curious specimen! We will get to that in a moment."

"Practiced like it's the same spiel for everyone," thinks Vulcan. Horace shushes him.

Parmacena continues between breaths, "You come from a faraway place that does not exist. A spirit?" She pauses to study Melysia's face for confirmation. "An orphan? A refugee?" and pushes the subject when Melysia reacts with a subtle eyebrow (and Melysia's residents are aware of this), "But you cannot run from the troubles that plague you. Hoho! Mayhaps it is the demons that take refuge in you. One of your eyeballs looks this way and another that. How do you get anything done? Bwahaha!" Parmacena meanwhile shuffles a deck of purple-backed cards and draws three. "My own spirits command that I read thy fortune! Behold!" She flips over a hermit. "Hehe. Did you wander here because you were lost by chance? I am flattered. Well, that is what I am here for: to dissect your person. What are you hiding under there?" She draws death to the hermit's left. "It is no wonder nobody knows. You died. Hehe. A dead girl walking. You would think death happens last. Maybe," she mutters. And to the right of the hermit goes the world. "It will come to an end, I suppose. That fellow is ouroboros. Would you happen to know of any snakes in your personal life? Ackh, and now that I see it, that girl in the center looks a lot like you. Whatever comes, you may assimilate something that comes your way. Or come to peace with the characters inside you? Hmm," she thinks for a time before she guides her quivering hands over the crystal ball she consults. "The spirits guide me anon the muck of the cosmos." The display is almost erotic as she lets her hands drift from top to bottom like a belly dancer. Parmacena deals a fourth card, then another, and the whole deck all at once. "Good heavens!" she proclaims as the cards overlap in a chaotic soup she means to fix, then decides against it and even moves them back in place to ascertain the fuller meaning. "Merde! The whole deck is at your disposal. Or you at its? Whatever else, do not bother controlling it. Hm! Let us follow the lines." She guides a bejeweled finger along a chain of cards that point at one another. "The world order we thought was in place will be kicked up like a tower charioting forward with the strength of a moon into the sun. Hah! What fools we are to squabble with the mindless forces of nature; we are little better than mindless forces of nature, ourselves. There is the fool who thinks himself the emperor; he is hidden underneath, you see. Or maybe he thinks he is an empress. (She is sandwiched between them.) To each his own, I suppose." She turns a disparate, upside-down card. "Justice is blind, as they say. She will not play a role. Personally, I never liked the bitch. Hehe." She lifts the hermit. "My, my. It seems a few cards slid under the hermit's robe. High priestess? A mask under a mask, you still do not know yourself. Like a matryoshka doll of nonsense. Lovers too? Do you love your demons? Or they each other? The fool eyes them with jealousy. Do not think I did not see just because I commented on you already! Fool." She follows another line of vagary. "It seems the magician will strike his scepter into the star's reservoir; in this card there are three distant men. Hmm. The star does not point to the devil but they are adjacent. Could this be a place close to our beloved Hedophilia? This devil points to the hierophant. The poor soul is corrupted, it seems. Take care you do not follow — or do. I am not your mother." She turns to a card facing away from the devil. "Temperance, O temperance, I know of you this: in your bowels is a man who does not belong, the hanged one. Perhaps in our humble Hedophilia you will meet a mellow man who sacrificed much and needs for little." Parmacena squints for other cards and finds the wheel of fortune next to the world. "A future of a future? Or perhaps two wheels grind together to set in motion events foretold! Akch! But where is judgment? Girl, help me find it. It is a bad omen if you do not!"

Melysia and Parmacena scour the room to no avail.

"Akch, forget it. What did you think?"

"Close enough," Melysia maintains cooly.

Inside, however, her voices ring, "So it will be that Yang consumes all!" Vulcan resounds with pleasure.

"Maybe! But there is Yin who might very well be

a dragon and his equal," Horace defends.

"Scrah! I recall your story, Vulcan. Does this tarot nonsense not remind you of the many arms of Yang?"

Hermes elicits, "People are eager to reinvent pantheons everywhere they go: sometimes three, twelve, sixteen, or thirty-two. Character archetypes in a book, astrology, socionics, you name it — individual gods to champion, pretty pictures."

"Still," Horace deflects, "she knew a thing or two about demons. How?"

"Figure of speech?" Hermes shrugs. "All things are kind of the same, relative even."

Parmacena answers in kind with the dreaded anticipation of the common Hedo, "That will be ten monkey dollars."

Melysia finds not two in her dusty pocket. "How's this?"

"Akch! For my services? How can I let you go if that is all you offer?" She bears canines from her bottom lip that almost reach her nose.

"I didn't know, sorry."

Parmacena grins with intent, "Okay, but did you know how many strays and vagrants I have consumed for these powers? It did not come cheaply, hehe."

"Very funny. How can I make it up to ya?"

The Gypsy stares with a murderous delight only Vulcan could recognize. "Stab, kill, and maim her. Do it now," he says in the sanctity of the mind palace.

"How about I read your fortune?" Melysia suggests, ignoring Vulcan.

To this, Parmacena perks her ears with great interest. "You do have a good sense of humor. Please!"

"Have you bloody lost it?" murmurs Horace. "That's what got us into this mess! We can't go around showing it to people willy nilly like exhibitionists!"

Melysia finds *The Playbook* sitting neatly in its pack and hands it over. "You just read it. You could say it does all the work for you."

Grinning smugly, the Gypsy fortune teller Parmacena discovers inside the lost card of judgment, which gazes directly into the contents of her soul. She immediately divines the meaning and speaks with no hesitation, "You guzzle from the piss spigot of providence I uncranked for you, and you think it a product of your cunning? Shitheel and ungrateful opportunist!" Parmacena shrills a fearsome cry and bursts into flames, disintegrating into a pile of clothes on the floor. The crystal ball shatters with a thud, thud, thud. If the Gypsy is to be believed, the souls, demons, spirits, what have you, dissipated into the ether anew.

"So is that like a proverb?" Melysia reminisces with a villainous confidence, a question posed for no one.

Of this, no one else said a word, mortified to invoke the wrath of the spirits, Melysia, or whatever force set the urban witch ablaze. Thus she left the evildoer to rest and returned unto the world, its market, blinded by the beaming sun and the overwhelming of stimulants, among them the voice of a peddler that shines above the rest.

"Virtue for sale! Virtue for sale!" a Hedo beckons at his stall. "Inclusion! Diversity! A hard day's work! Family men! Virtue! Virtue for sale!" There is nothing on his shelves.

She consults her voices. "What's he selling?"

"I have never seen this man," answers Vulcan for everyone.

"He doesn't seem to be selling anything," perceives Horace.

"A beggar, maybe?" suggests Hermes.

"Excuse me, mister," shouts Melysia, "what the bugger are you doing?"

His eyes flare up like a salesperson's. You know what I mean. "Virtue! Virtue! Can't live without it, no sirree! Get yours!"

"Why should I buy from you?"

"Why not buy a wristwatch from Herrmania? Why not a rug from Scarabia? Why, we live in the most developed country in the world! We produce the most specialized items, yes indeed! Virtue is our most profitable export! It takes a lot to produce these items! You could say it's expensive, but it's more costly to go without them! Let the tribals build our widgets, for we are an enlightened people that know better the value of ideas."

"How do I know it's the real thing? Ole Jeb never charged squat."

"Ole Jeb? Where's he from? Scarabia? Hahaha!"

"Nusquam."

"Nusquam? Never heard of her. Look, kid. Sounds like this Jeb means well, but does he have the history and culture of all Hedophilia behind him? May well be a bumpkin moonshiner to the Herrmanic vintner. Ah, but tell you what. You run a hard bargain. The first run is free!"

"Cool. So what now?"

"Stand perfectly still," the clerk commands, brandishing the palm of his hand and laying it on Melysia's shoulder. "You are virtuous."

Melysia waits a moment, frozen in excruciating time.

He withdraws the hand. "So how do you feel?"

She stand there quite unsure what to think.

"Good, right?"

"Eh?"

"Eh? Eh!? What are you, a goat? All you feel is 'eh'? Why . . ." He pinches his bridge. "No, I am virtuous. I am virtuous. I am virtuous. I am good and I am free." the clerk sighs the mantra with breathy relief. "It's an acquired taste. Stop by if you'd like another!"

And by this point, Melysia had already skittered, "Odd fellow. Is anyone actually selling something tangible?"

"It was never so," Vulcan breathes with muted contempt.

And Hermes triangulates with a revisionary recall of his own, "Could be they were pretending to sell goods. Like we've ascended so far high up the orders of development and the common person who resets every eighty years does his best to approximate his understanding of things and sells in abstracts the foundations of goods he can't quite reproduce on his own. I don't think the common Hedo can approximate a bridge without it falling down . . . so he will paint one. But we've gone so abstract that we can't even approximate paint."

"When'd you think of that?" asks Horace.

"Huh? Mhmhm," Hermes mumbles in the cadence of "I don't know."

"But do the Hedoes actually sell anything?" redoubles Melysia. As she stresses, or perhaps because of it, an especially dire heat set in the market: a scathing, annoying heat in her torso.

Ice cream sits atop a throne in a vat of metal flowing a river's ambrosia, oasis come to mock the destitute just out of reach, a barrier of multigenerational accessibility many times the distance of a jog, for when Melysia peers into her pockets, no such opportunity presents itself to feast on salvation, unless . . .

"Girl." The authoritative voice whispers mischievously, "Rid us of this damnable heat. Take what is yours, ours."

"Colonel! Not a day unsupervised among the civilized and you act the criminal. We shall endure without."

"I will not die again undying. It is not the way of my people. There is no dignity in our prospective death. Eat or be eaten. Die. Feed the cycle. Do not chance falling victim to its trapping a maggot at the bottom of a sack of mulch. We are headed there elsewise if we do nothing."

"Drama of the colonel queen! Come death, so be it. 'Tis better we take accountability than the peddler, lest we rob ourselves of, huh, virtue."

Scree-ah interludes, "Take action swiftly, malcontents, whatever have you in mind. If we go nowhere, we die subject to abominable heat. Take flight, for the breeze upon the woman's bedeviled machination served us well, but from her nest we have fallen. Had I wings once more, I would chase the breeze anon. Fly, hatchlings. Fly so that I may avenge my little ones. Conquer the skies, for we lie down-trodden unfree on this primal plane shared between even insects, worm or man, all insignificant under lordly eye nested in the heavens."

"Oh boy, I can't quite justify theft."

Hermes embraces the silence of his own creation, a blessing little few count.

"Colonel, restrain yourself. We had an agreement. Let's leave it to the girl."

"Your agreement! I'll not have another incessant babbler aboard. Deals be damned, it is mine for the taking!"

Scree-ah chirps strenuously, "We fade, fools."

Muscles cramp every which way, agency ripped from Melysia as it was from Jove and his constituents. But mustering just enough willpower, she falls to her knees a desperate, silent cry for help from anyone not herself, before fainting, nearly unconscious, with vision blurred clear enough to fixate on the ice cream parlor. The vendor exits the stand, carrying in hand an ice cream cone. He presses the cone gently against Melysia's lips to which she reciprocates the sentiment. And as a pang of gratitude fills her mind, she looks for the words to show thanks. Instead of words, she finds the vendor's teeth in bodacious grin. Seconds pass, and with them go the pearly whites so proudly and genuinely on display; discoloration of black and yellow manifests on now crooked, asymmetric stubs, some falling from place altogether. A rain of silky black hair leaves behind savage, untended clumps, a clean apron accumulates the filth of a decade's labor, clothing seemingly fine until now tatters carelessly in every stitch, and his mouth agape shuts tight into a long grin perturbing sun-damaged wrinkles aplenty. The ghastly figure repulses the otherwise hardy Melysia, her gaze averted and set upon the treat: fine grains of cocaine administered with the intent to reawaken, and that it has, for Melysia is no longer in the market and its voracious crowd, but a train on a singular track raised on a hill. Beside her is a window wide as night. There among the stars, a moon grows ever bigger, nay, closer. An impending moon tremors from above, the incoming force binding Melysia's numb wrists to her chair. So closing her eyes and hoping to wake, she finds her reality is a black and oily pitch. An iron chain rattles ominously as if to say "No one leaves," dancing its unrelenting dance of wriggling and wrangling, a mortal reminder of control. A hand reaches out; it is not Melysia's. She turns it on and each preoperational flicker yields a blank, white wall, save the last that shines on the face of a stranger to all but Vulcan, MacDiver, brandishing a hefty woodcutting axe. Melysia assesses her surroundings: a stuffy, locked room. Vision partially clouded, her eyepatch turban is gone, the precise time of its loss unfelt and unknown.

She finds in her pocket the switchblade Calypso gave her; it had not been removed. Melysia flourishes it, to which the figure extends a flat hand poised slightly upward. Vulcan reassures her quietly, "Hold."

Returning his offhand to the shaft, MacDiver rears the axe as if preparing a fatal swing, Melysia recoiling and condensing, ready to counter. The target, an ornate cupboard barely off the room's center cleaves in two, splintering savagely. Another swing yields a similar result, as do countless more. Among the uncanny spectacle of logs and sawdust unrecognizable to the original furniture, the maniac deliberately upheaves three planks seemingly the most whole out of the rest, depositing them in a hearth and setting them alight, stirring the munitions slowly and solemnly with a poker. Satisfied, he withdraws the stick and, with it, pulls to the fire an armchair cushioned with an inviting velvet red. His face turns to meet Melysia, body only halfway. Melysia awaits a more decisive cue.

MacDiver, standing so long, repurposes the poker to a walking cane, body weight supported atop it in a dapper fashion. Had this been a dream or a lucid imagining, it surely would have concluded long ago. Perhaps the chain was an illusion; she was never bound. Melysia sheathes the knife to her belt and approaches with caution, waiting a moment behind the chair to test her kidnapper's intent, but ultimately sits down, her eyes never abstaining from the man, to which he responds with poking the flame. She lays both eyes on the flame only briefly, focusing them back on him. MacDiver beats the wood harder, threateningly, eliciting an immediate response from Melysia, gauging the unremarkable hearth, scrambling for answers. MacDiver impales the wood with his teaching stick such that Melysia, focused unlike before, examines the poker. Working her way down its length, she finds the crude hole planted firmly in the wood, out from it emitting a miniscule candlelight originating from the other side. Fire, all encapsulating, cradles the wood from underside, chipping gradually at its many fragments, for with every puff of smoke rises a minute wooden nugget, a cry for help glimmering as a star in the sky ever fleeting, fading into oblivion alongside its brethren from the same cloth, glimmer extinguished, exhausted. Fire, the great purifier, absolves all; the deaths of fragments billions in number, a mortal reminder, tells of an impending genocide, armageddon. And so long as there exists wood to burn, the endless affair cycles in a vapid continuum an affront to mercy. Only fire's end, wherein the final flicker bids farewell to a hell snuffed cleanly from ash as head to guillotine, will heaven collect the pieces, for if not hell, where would they go? These may have been the macabre thoughts of Vulcan. The hearth dwindles. The stranger, the hallucinations, this damnable journey, and life itself.

Melysia returns her attention to the questionable host by her side; he mutters a first and final word, "Futility." A click resounds behind him, bringing his multi-tool boldly forth and plunges in his throat. MacDiver lies motionless in a pool of his own regrets. This is no dream.

"Wreee!" A distant cry of grit and mettle reverberates the brittle foundations of the decadent room — a battle has begun. Through the door is thrust a club of neolithic proportions, the whole thing ripped from its foundation by the second motion. Revealed is Pelvis-Crusher, a beast of a woman, teeth bare, gnawing at the thought of enemies and mouthwater longing for their demise. Momentary grief jolts the woman, and only for that long, for without warning, she charges the shaken Melysia, bothering not to swing, instead grasping at her collar and pinning her to the splintered ground, nipping unrestrained at the face. "What do with this one?"

From the corner, Washington extends a professionally straight leg, laying it firmly one step ahead, then repeating for every subsequent advance in MacDiver's direction, "What have we here? Oh my. Whatever shall we do with you, girl?" He cocks his arquebus at the hip, still hanging by the shoulder strap.

Melysia freezes in uncertainty; Vulcan speaks on her behalf, "Halt! I did not kill MacDiver."

"My, my, how do you know the name? I think it unwise to leave alive a spy. Or an assassin, perhaps?"

"You fool! I am Vulcan."

He stares dispassionately at Melysia's breasts, then away. "Our agent had gone missing or killed outright. You jest, vile creature. Confirm his death, if you would, and perchance even the fates of two others from my unit. Are they detained, killed, alive? Do this for me and in return I will kill instead of torture you."

"You test my patience. How fares Aeroscorpion?"

"And you mine. What else do you know?"

"I know you are a fool. Look upon his body, closely, so that you might infer the cause of death."

The distinctive multi-tool shines red past spurting blood. "Release her . . . him. This one sounds like Vulcan, all right." Kneeling at the site, Washington cradles his comrade in open arms, "MacDiver passed willfully."

Pelvis-Crusher relinquishes the girl, "Cannot leave him for bug bugs. We feast on bones? While fresh in memory," she inflects mournfully

Washington strictly objects, "No, it's not what he wants. Burn him."

"Sir?" she grunts.

From his crown, Washington withdraws his favored tricorne hat, resting it gently on the dead man's chest. "Do it."

"Okay." Pelvis-Crusher addresses the corpse, "Okay." She gathers the remaining salvageable wood to reignite the fire. She repulses from every plank, as if trained to do otherwise, but overcomes every ingrained habit.

Vulcan shambles to Washington's side with short, spindly legs, "How has it come to this?"

"We're in hiding. Aeroscorpion is hitched with the other mounts, to answer your previous question. Did MacDiver communicate anything before his death?"

"He bashed in some furniture for firewood, forcefully."

Hermes resumes the conversation

uninterrupted by even Vulcan, "Followed by a cleansing flame."

Horace inputs his own interpretation in continuation, "Finally, the embers settled and, peace restored, he killed himself."

Washington ponders with fist under chin, but after a moment, Melysia pulls *The Playbook* from its place, flicking to the open page; text condenses, nay, almost converges before her very eyes. Where once there was unintelligible scribble, the beginnings of words barely form, a misty cloud still persevering where letters double and intermix, as if beheld by eyes healing from blind to damaged yet requiring a pair of glasses to decipher fine detail.

Washington peers over. "Read your passage for me."

"What do you know about *The Playbook*?"

"We Atlanteans knew the Nusquamites well enough. They fit cleanly within the order of things. They did not need reorganizing, not like the Hedoes."

Melysia concedes, "It's blurry."

"His was the same. Goatman's too."

Traumatized Melysia unsheathes and holds her knife at the pommel and its tip by two fingers, reflecting back a gleam of fire; warm and inviting is its call. Ideating about killing herself to spare herself further nonsense, a few fingers remain steadfast, others tremble; the knife falls. To which persona do fingers swear fealty?

Washington's ponytail waves as wind on a grim night's eve. "You are not Vulcan, just as I am no co-captain; we are cowards. A part of you wishes to commence, yet another refuses. The Vulcan I knew stood and fought in battle single mindedly."

And from Melysia, Vulcan is let speak: "Fought I have and died. It is a sad fate I am here now. What makes you the coward?"

He grimaces. "I did not command my men to die but flee. At the walls, where many Atlanteans died bravely, I, knowing Yin guns would focus on large targets, felt safer surpassing their defenses than retreating with our backs against them — even that is less dishonorable. Against my orders, men as Goatman, MacDiver, and Davy Jones die, you also. I feel every dishonorable death on account of my incompetence, a paranoia proven true at every point. I could not spearhead the charge; that honor went willingly to Aeroscorpion, more so my cowardice than his persistence. He consented nonetheless."

Bile and puss meanwhile vaporize from MacDiver's lonesome gullet, permeating in the air a foul odor accented by the cupboard's hickory tang. The chimney collapsed long ago, it seems. Fog builds, enshrouding the finer details of the room,

Melysia's hazy *Playbook* transposed to reality.
"Gots to go go," Pelvis-Crusher says.

XV

Itchy Beehive, Immolated Somethings

The slums sprawl for miles, edgewise and by length. Shanties piled atop one another balance on a thread; others since fallen. But where a whale carcass lands, there inhabits even poorer sorts: bottom feeding vagrants whose hullabaloos are indiscernible from livestock. And in anticipation of such happenings, the nobodies of ingenuity topple their hovels preemptively into each other, manufacturing archways festooned by tattered streamers of wet clothes set to dry. Welcome to paradise, where metaphor meets reality and metaphysics physics; a literal goblin is running around house to house, scrambling people's eggs for a pretty penny.

"We are nearly there," Washington says. He uncovers a curtain to a back alley. "Follow closely."

Its shabby brickwork presses tightly against the waist, scores of bugs in the shape of men angling to leap from the cracks, or so worries Scree-ah. "Blah! The hives of men unsettle me! Many holes!"

"Some are windows," adds Hermes.

"Gah!"

"Think of it like a cat covering his butthole with his tail," speaks Horace, trying his best to make light of things.

"Scwah!" Scree-ah gags in her throat, "Don't build them to start with!"

Vulcan looks to Washington. "I had not known of this area. How far removed is it from the city?"

Washington pauses between two especially cramped walls, heaving for air. "This is the city, I've gathered."

"Yin could house them all," Horace thinks.

"As can Atlantis," Washington says with apprehension. "Imagine the occult following we could rouse. The Yins would be flanked and we could cut off their support. Ha, but it's never worked in all of history. The Hedoes, especially, are a thoughtless people. Why do you think that is? I might be useless but I'm not stupid, so I'll tell you: The desert dwellers like to think. That's why there's little to no industry I reckon — or else because they have nothing to do but think. Every waking moment, the Hedo expands his hive. I see from their constructions they imagine nothing else. Slums for miles."

"Interesting." Vulcan then engages Horace privately. "Cease your feminine, sympathetic lamentations. He'll figure I harbor a Yin."

"And what would they do to a cross-dressing colonel?"

Vulcan asks of Washington, "Whatever happened to Delilah?"

"The colonel turned Atlantean? Well enough, I suppose. Different unit. We left quite the impression — you, I mean. Or Goatman as he carried her off, the charmer."

"There is hope for you yet, worm," Horace quips.

Washington lays a hand on a hole in the wall, concealed shabbily by a Jolly Roger flag. "We're based inside."

It is a dank room. Candles lit around Waterboard encircle the deceased Atlantean. Aeroscorpion, Aquabus, and Sea Horsepower grieve, Pelvis-Crusher rushing close beside her companion. "When?"

"Recently. MacDiver?"

"Dead."

"Fitting."

Aquabus approaches Washington a shrewd woman scorned. "Why do my men die before me, wastrel?"

"Mine went willingly, did yours?"

"Show me the body."

"It is gone."

"Really? Where? Do you expect me to believe it vanished from the very threads of the universe, Yang's domain?"

Washington mutters under breath, "We burned him."

"You fool!" she screams. "He is gone to us. And you are unfit to be called Atlantean." There is a remediary silence. "Tonight we feast on Waterboard, at least. You will go hungry."

"Yes, ma'am."

"And who is the girl?"

"Vulcan."

Aeroscorpion's wing flaps perk up and, presenting before Melysia, judges her inauspiciously, "No. This one does not smell."

Melysia's heart palpitates, Vulcan's doing.

"Who are you?" it asks again.

"I am Vulcan."

"No, you are treacherous; you bear the name but not the meaning. Who are you?"

"I died in battle. I know my name of old because

I am born anew."

"Then who is with you? You smell of many, not Vulcan."

"I share my place with the fractures of my once self. I am ashamed."

"I searched for you a time for naught. It seems I must keep searching."

"I stand before you. Eat me, so that you might taste truth."

"You are cursed meat. I would eat you gladly were you not tainted. Shame." A tear streaks from a beady eye. "You were a brother, as were the many before. I have lost them all, not one, two, the lot. Feast be damned if I cannot remember them all by name than by scent or taste." Through a hole in the ceiling, he departs in flight.

"Hedophilia collects its toll." Washington unravels his sleeves. "The Yins prowl for us, their next meal. Only they do not hunt to eat but for prize and trophy to show their women, and middling women at that. We should leave come sundown so as not to stay in one place."

Vulcan detests, "Do you mean to leave Aeroscorpion, coward?"

"My unit is in shambles and I do not command the respect to bring him to heel."

"Here I am."

"Aeroscorpion does not accept you."

"Then he will die."

"Yes. This is our inevitable way. Were you truly an Atlantean to begin with?"

"Flee, you hypocrite."

Pelvis-Crusher spices her delicate roast a pinch, defusing the situation. "Time is for eating. Fighting later." To this Sea Horsepower agrees with a thud.

Waterboard skewers over a fiery spit. Shriveled skin and exposed musculature smell just as sickly as MacDiver's; the spice merely covers it. Dead eyes askew behind a curtain of fire sully the appetite: What if it had been humanid? Why not?

Pelvis-Crusher stands behind Melysia seven feet tall, pushing her into a resting position. "Sit." There was an attempt to be gentle.

On a platter of questionable origin, Waterboard conveys the intelligence of a man dignified in death. Beady eyes fried into skeptical slits beg the question: "Can you eat me, really?"

Between Pelvis-Crusher, Sea Horsepower, and Aquabus are shared the wings, tail, and torso, leaving the head, the question, the man — whose eyes now closed under translucent lids able to see just barely the oncoming doom — to Melysia the devourer.

"Ne'er do well, 'tis a gluttony for we have servings too many. Temper thy appetite, else be subsumed into mediocre oneness, diluted."

Vulcan musters a thought: "I . . . I would not bring myself to eat. My hunger wanes. Washington is right. I am no Atlantean, not so long as I am a Yin and many other things."

"That took courage, Colonel. Do not doubt yourself."

Hermes speaks, "We should eat, be it an Atlantean or a carrot. Would you like to turn into a carrot? I think not. Unless . . . never mind, this thought is unworthy. I cast it aside. The choice is yours. I am embarrassed."

"That was courageous also."

"Pay no mind."

"Feel no shame. That would be cowardice."

Pelvis-Crusher prods the girl with the club's butt.

Melysia clamps at the slimy cheeks like a hamburger. Its foggy eyelids readjust, even jolt open as vacuous bubbles before sulking back into slits, but never closing thereafter. Compelling is the Atlantean, its body expressive as MacDiver's in life. It slips from Melysia's hold into the fire; Waterboard burns on hot coals. The first to go are the eyelids, the nictitating membrane, thin and see-through unlike a humanid's. The scum of its eyes cleared away first such that, if Waterboard were still alive, she'd have a moment of clarity before burning to death.

Hermes intuits, "Try closing one eye."

"Why?"

"A guess."

Melysia covers her burnt eye.

"The other one."

Revealed before Melysia is no corpse, but Waterboard united with MacDiver in a fiery ring, the former cradled affectionately in his lap, the latter offering a tentative smile, brief as time allows, followed by a wave of the hand, then ash.

A swift backhand knocks Melysia's scalp from her stupor. "You've ruined the good bit of my roast! Leave! I cannae stand the sight of you." It seems under duress, the cavewoman can speak at length. She beats the fire with her club.

Eager for any excuse to leave, Melysia slips through the alleyway in any direction, whether it is the way back or forward, left or right. Only once feet land on a grassy clearing does Melysia come to; an acacia tree overlooks the enclosure, under it a child, hungry and rabid, chasing a rat.

Horace suggests, "No one of ours should go hungry before me. Please."

The urchin's gaping mouth dangles from the face, ready to eat anything in one bite, skin and bones.

Melysia consents, "Go on." She draws the knife for Horace, though he switches to his dominant hand. Crouching low, Horace pounces with the bloodlust of a tiger and sinks the blade with the fervor of a martyr into the beast's diseased hide. Voila, it is kaput.

Horace hands the carcass to the boy who, now grasping it, inspects it closely. Tears momentarily stream from his sockets. "You killed Dishwater! How could you?" The rest of his speech is overcome by involuntary spasms and hiccups. An old, stout man emerges from the shadow of the tree. "This isn't your lawn. Get a move on." His voice is monotonous, perhaps pleased with the dead rat, but obliged to shoo unwelcome solicitors, but he reminds of Abraddon. Abraddon the Hedo regards her with detached disagreeableness, as if he'd never known her — maybe so.

Further flustered, Horace departs as a spooked horse. "These conditions do no justice, my meddling even less. Truth is indiscernible from myth. It is unsightly."

Hermes comments to Horace, "Whence gleaming skyscrapers and gold tinted domes come ramshackle hives and skittering bug-men. Were we not bamboozled these past months? By whom, an enemy? Is this not war?"

Horace does not respond, ashamed not to know.

On a curb nearby, Washington chews a handful

of granola. "Had your fill?"

Melysia answers concisely: "Yes."

"I couldn't stomach it."

"You too?"

"Aquabus knows. She keeps me away from the like, don't you mind the show she makes of it."

"More of a Hedo?" Melysia prods, "You like to slum with voyeurs? Is that what you're doing, out and about? Distracting yourself with voyeurs on sidewalks flaunting their asses to the moon?"

"As funny as that would be for you, no. I am a square. I may be bankrupt of virtue, but I have nothing to speak of vices neither. I bear my suffering cold turkey," he snickers. "Say, did you see Waterboard off properly?"

"Well enough. Say, did MacDiver burn his eyes?"

"Not only that, tongue too. How'd you figure? He hid it well."

"Look at me."

"Aye?"

"See?"

Washington takes a moment, then, extending a hand, offers granola. "You're positively famished."

"No, my eye, look at it."

He squints. "It looks normal, which is to say not abnormal."

"You can't see that I burned myself, so how'd

you figure MacDiver was burned too?"

"I heard from a friend and he from MacDiver, himself," Washington says.

"Where is this friend?"

Washington's dimples grin under flickering lamplight. "You're not doing anything, are you? Come, I'll take you to him."

"On foot?"

"I forget you're new here; I used to live here. Seen the state of this place? Rubble lines the streets and mounds of dirt obstruct the road. Any vehicle would be stripped for parts if left in the open. A bike might do: nimble and easily hidden. No such luck, we'll walk."

"Is it dangerous?"

"Aye, but it is sustainable. Surely, were it too dangerous, life would not propagate at all — even the Arena — not like the wall where what few women come to die. Everyone who dies there was born here. Fear not; we have women in droves. Well, old ones, but women!" He scratches his head nervously. "They aren't kept like animals, mind you. We keep them in close proximity like, how do I put this lightly, animals? Bah, men too." Washington pauses a moment. "Who am I kidding? This is no way to live. Everyone is cramped beyond the wall, and so I left this monkey-ridden ghetto, my friends with it. I owe some of them a visit. I'll not tarry any longer. Come." He sets a stray ladder on a two-story hovel. "The highway awaits."

"Certainly never had to do this before," comments Horace.

Melysia follows closely behind. "Are we burglars or somethin'?"

"Quite the contrary: There are many ladders lying about and no one dares remove or dismantle them. Unspoken rules and such! You're liable to get your teeth kicked in by people who are already looking for a reason, any reason. They are too cowardly to do it just because they want to, like me, an Atlantean." He smiles mournfully. "And nobody in their right mind maintains roads. For every roof, however, there exists a caretaker." Washington ascends the ladder, extending a single hand outwards. "See for yourself."

Melysia's hand slaps smooth, paved stone. The roofs are mostly flat and vary slightly in elevation; it does not snow, much less rain. Like tiles they stack and stretch in most every adjacent direction wherever therein lies a brazier to guide the weary traveler homeward bound, each a small sun, orbs of heat and life in a nonuniform constellation, a starry night pulled down to Katsikoskoni where smoke clouds the already dim sky. Lawn chairs and other accessories complement the cityscape — nothing too lavish, of course, but enough to allow a seat and view of the universe, just as the stars look down on the Katsikoskoni.

Vulcan caves to impulse. "Kick the ladder, girl."

"Colonel, restrain yourself."

Melysia mischievously kicks the ladder down.

Washington congratulates the girl. "Oh, you know something of our etiquette after all, it seems. It is a shame we in Hedophilia are expected to make life harder for our countrymen. Well done, anyhow."

"How'd you figure, Colonel?"

"Simple: I observed in the distance an overweight man's wife, or maybe younger daughter throw him with it."

"Why not an assailant?"

"I would've shot to kill were I her. Hell, anyone else would shoot. Hush now, he's climbing back up. Watch."

The woman's sporadic movements (from which no audible noise is heard) are pit against echoes of a giant felt from every rooftop. They clash in the heart of the city shrouded in darkness broken sporadically by trails of braziers befitting the sun's shadow. The woman is Calypso, Turkey her father, and their familial struggle eternal and irresolute.

"That'll be them," Washington sighs desperately for air, the bulk of which is stolen away by Turkey's uncouth shouts, a blistering dust storm of profanity and excess volume.

She squints. "But they're so far away. The sun will beat us to it."

Washington peers to the ledge of a third story tower in the way. He props up another stray ladder and, reaching the summit, kicks it down. Thud, thud, thud. "It is quite like you to complain, Vulcan." And with that, Washington disappears behind the tower's ledge with a bashful provocation.

Vulcan yells a most intimidating cry for a girl, "I'm coming for you, coward!"

And so begins the laying of ladders, the cobblestones of Hedophilia. No one path aims true; this corollary is testified by Vulcan and Washington both, never each other in reach and always at different elevations, but set to rendezvous all the same at the source of turmoil shrieking through the night, warding off the sun. If it were not for boisterous Turkey, day would arise much sooner, courtesy of time's pleasant passing. Atlanteans race through the night and, upon breaking the horizon, find the sun lingered long enough for the two of them, itself perhaps too sluggish this particular morn. Indeed, through indirect alleys and towering stonework, the pair works faster than the sun, itself, as if to shoot straight into it, stopped only by Turkey whose body and voice are as wide and blistering as the sun's scorching heat, the latter unintelligible as a heatstricken brain marinade. The sun resumes its forward march.

"Why's 't er' time yer gettin' yerself inta trouble and I's gots'ta git ye out? Yer a gash darn arse sore!"

"Friend Turkey!" remarks Washington.

He flails a furious limb and knocks the captain off the roof in a muddy crater the size of a miniature sun. Only then does the chauffeur notice Washington, nearly forgetting his previous argument, a goldfish in a tub of his own fat.

"Why didn't ya think t' say somethin', ye cad? Git inside!"

A disappointed Calypso shrugs vaguely in the direction of Melysia, doubling as an invitation.

Inside on the top floor in the form of a sort of guest room are a couple of rickety chairs, a cupboard for clothing, and a basin. The driver and his compatriot seize the chairs, leaving Calypso stranded on her hind legs. Melysia makes a point to wash her hands, but water does not flow.

"Fate is having a whimsy at my expense. The waves don't answer. Of late, to no one," Calypso speaks with a grimace.

"How do you wash?"

"City's scummy and so are we." She brushes at her hair, once spacious and puffy now tangled and bedraggled, be it another mirage lifted or the imminent effect of Hedophilia.

"If not water, use fire."

"In here? Don't think so," says the dirty damsel. "No ventilation. Dumbshits in Hedophilia couldn't figure out how to punch a hole in the wall. Or they could until I walk in a room."

Washington interrupts, "Turkey, I'd like you to meet someone."

"Quite fitting, this imbecile's namesake," Calypso sneers.

Turkey carefully scrutinizes Melysia, cracking a smile, "Ye remin's me of me daught'r. Long aguh." He still ignores Calypso, "Aye, lassie?"

Calypso shakes her head dismissively, "Nope."

Dejected Turkey presses on, "So small an' innocent. An' look at ye now. Ain't gotta lick a' that anymore. What's 'appened?"

"Stop it."

"Wrong crowd, 'at's wot it is. Wot's his name? Vinny? That knucklehead's still buzzing, six feet under as he is. Poor sod."

"How could you possibly know that?"

"I know 'im as well as you know yerself. Might've been 'im in another life. An' maybe if ye weren't so young, ye could see fer yerself."

"Right, because in this house, the loudest breather is the most correct."

His voice rises. "I don't think I 'ave it in me to forgive ya. A man's been killed. D'you know 'ow serious 'at is? My daughter, a killer. N'er woulda thought." He breaks into a wail, albeit with no tears, an angry man shaped like a bomb with a fuse.

"Bah, loonies," Vulcan whispers.

Washington shudders quietly. "Utter depravity, not least the inopportunity of our arrival. Say, Vulcan, I've got to run for eggs."

"You wanted to abandon me from the start, did you? Why else go out of your way to bring me here?"

"Though dead, a divergent part of Goatman lives on, you know. He's not dead entirely. Is the similarity not striking?" He motions at the beer-bellied bowling ball with wet eyeballs and floppy prick slits for sockets. "You could do more for him than I could both of you. This is goodbye."

"What an effeminate man." Vulcan's contempt is palatable.

"A nice one, at that. Conflicted, maybe," Horace intercepts.

Calypso's cheeks swell with impertinence. Taking all of several minutes to burst; she bellows a tormented scream, and no sooner than it ends does Turkey double down, a ballgame of increasing tempo as the screams are cut gradually shorter but thrown decidedly faster, culminating in a sharp, visual flash. In its wake, none but Melysia are left standing; Calypso and Washington are gone and Turkey is catatonic on the floor, now a quarter skinnier than before, not completely unlike Jebediah's transformation. He is a grotesque skinny-fat: skinny in places but fat in others. Deranged ramblings cease to a murmur.

"Do we wake him?"

"He is a cadaver, but a husk."

"Let's not assume the worst. He was quite energetic," copes a hopeless Horace.

"As he should be," engages Vulcan.

"Well, that's no way to live, angry at every stone. Must be tiring."

"Do you wait until the slight to anger? How do you bear every second of your life knowing there are things you vehemently disagree with, or are you blissfully unaware the whole time? It is short sighted not to be angry at everything."

"Just how calloused are you?"

"Hardly."

"Unbelievable."

"If you spite me for a grievance, I did it only because I knew you would spite me even if I didn't do anything at all. It's called foresight. Right, Hermes?"

"Hm? Oh. If you say so."

And while they bicker, Turkey's eyelids lift — not of his own accord, but Melysia's, who inspects them thoroughly. Pupils narrow like a flatlining heart monitor until only vacant white orbs remain, blinded by rage, of hope despaired. Gone were his wits wrought ruthless by wroth.

"Woe to he whom anger consumes," Horace directs to his colonel.

"And them that follow," Vulcan hurrahs.

Outside, Calypso leans over a railing limp and injured. Melysia comes beside her to ask, "Where is Washington?"

"Gone."

"Where?"

"Never to be seen again, swallowed by guilt maybe."

"Why so cryptic?"

She hesitates and turns away, crawling along the rails. "He couldn't withstand the blast."

"Where will you go?" Hermes speaks up.

"I made a mistake, coming here. You should leave. Bad for my health, dammit."

"My apologies I couldn't get myself properly killed," he continues.

"Thanks, Hermes. Would have killed ya myself if you asked nicely. Shame I hesitated on account of yer charming person. Ain't that kind of story, though," she smirks and tosses herself over the railing and disappears into the dark depths. What fall she took no one knew. No sound came of it.

"Damn, she's so cool," fawns Melysia.

"Bottomless is the well," Scree-ah bawks.

"Your eternal soul also. Raised above the soil we cannot speak to Katsikoskoni, nor can we see the suffering it carries on its lumpy backside," Horace laments.

"Throw a torch. Truth becomes it," Hermes concludes.

Melysia finds a detached step of a rickety ladder and lights it over a brazier. So, dropping it to the depths, she set alight in the depths a ravenous inferno. "What the hell? Calypso!"

"I meant a flashlight."

"Is that oil? Atlantean mischief perhaps!" Horace sneers.

Vulcan is quick to correct him, "No, oil is the trademark of you civilized savages. Bah, it doesn't matter. I've been disowned. What's the point if I can't share in the glory? I feel restless thinking my boys could be out there killing fools."

"Yin, too, would not have me, not like this. Lars said as much when he asked us to come back when he'd thought of something."

"Just as I have been disowned by Onemsiz and Mon Sizé sent out to die," Hermes adds.

"I, too, am a fledgling kicked from the tree long ago, but I have learned, albeit not to fly, to walk. What use are proverbial wings if they cannot spread? And yet I share a nest with grown men stuck in the brambles," squawks Scree-ah.

"Boy, oh boy. Is there no happiness?" Diothor whines.

"KILL! DEATH! FIRE! HA!" the crab spouts.

"Penniless thoughts? Sweet Dreams? The abyss cares for neither, but I find myself taking pleasure from the small things." Haughty Vulcan shares the sentiment with the crab.

"And what of Turkey?" asks Melysia. Inside the dwelling, oil sloshes at the knee. The sink overflows with mud and gunk.

"Disaster wastes no time in striking."

"Could be goats."

"What?"

"Goats. Cotton and corn grow in thy ears, it seems."

Horace motions, trying to assume control of the conversation. "Never mind that. What to do?" Oily fire rises from below and the shanty house rattles. Turkey does not wake from his deathly stupor.

Hermes gulps at the vulgarity of his suggestion: "If we are to save him or ourselves, we must be consumed by him."

"Why?"

He again looks to shrivelling but hefty Turkey. "To keep him from starving and us from burning alive in this moat of flames."

"Hmm, very well. We are all outcasts, are we not? We, abandoned by our respective communities, ought come together. Confound the body we dwell in. The mind takes precedent."

"We can hardly tolerate one another. And yet, through thick and thin, we stand together. So be it. Let us be the greatest pack of degenerates that ever roamed Katsikoskoni, Atlantis be damned at the current moment. Proceed," Vulcan huzzahs.

Melysia breathes deeply, looking at the slug before her. "I can't bring myself to do it."

"Oh boy."

"What if we become that thing? And gain a voice as loud as that one?"

Vulcan thinks privately how wonderful it would be to cease his cross-dressing spree.

"I'm quite impartial," Horace admits. "But all I can say is someone needs us, even if it drags him into our consortium of madness."

She sighs, exasperated. "Why not eat him?"

"In Atlantis, the strong eat the weak. You withstood the blast and he didn't. Go ahead."

"Never mind that. You can't eat a man in one

sitting, can you?" Horace corrects.

"I guess not." Melysia fixes her gaze on the body, its gelatinous curves oozing sweat and crude fart-like noises — futile calls for help. "Okay, I didn't lose so much to back off now. I can do this," she encourages herself with a feigned, forced enthusiasm. Melysia rattles her head nervously, then mounts the abominable Turkey and clambers into his gaping mouth and throat, a reverberating chasm, "Hello! Is there anyone in there?"

There is only silence. The cavity constricts, leaving room enough only for short breaths.

"I can't go down any farther!" Her voice is squeamish.

The esophagus clamps harder. Within the belly of the beast, a deep grumbling emanates through each chamber, a heralding of viscous fluids splurt everywhere, resembling the dungeon complex of Yin, only more dank. Like a battery in a slot, Melysia sits snug with only a narrow view of the outside world. In time, it seems Turkey's body lifts and sprints with great vim, the voice within silent as ever. The mechanism, not quite Turkey nor Melysia, plunges into the molten depths outside and swims with the deftness and grace of a whale, marooning and stranding itself on a nearby rock, covered in sludge courtesy of the filthy streets, perhaps even Turkey's own fiery excrements, his very vessel an anomaly, a decomposing-alive admirable zombie whose spirit relents on its own stubborn terms, though not quite cognitive enough to articulate them, save in a method most peculiar; in place of words, Turkey spews a disturbed, coughing Melysia coated in bile. In a past life, one would wonder if Turkey was a gastric-brooding frog, birthing progeny through the mouth. But alas, behind regurgitated Melysia is no frog, but a man turning to dust before her very eyes, but not before awakening one last time, time enough for parting words.

"I's Vinny, Goatman, an' a father twice o'er. I've lived a life, lost it all, and now it's time fer peace. Leave me be. I rejec' this final chance." Alas, extinct like the frog, he is set alight by flaming pitch. (Though the cause might have been revisionist.)

"His body refuses us. We do not become him. Pray tell, why?" And Horace just as quickly answers his own rhetorical question with an empathetic realization: "He's a dying man. That's why."

"I don't get it," Hermes admits. It is not quite a function of humility. He just happened to understand everything that came before, this he also acknowledged while computing the response.

Melysia mourns contemplatively beside the odd man she knew only shortly, confused and scared, taking solace in a lonesome enclave otherwise surrounded by hellfire. She sits there as the broth simmers down from its boil. Once extinguished — and Melysia sits there awhile longer — she notices two bones cut through the watery sludge like a pair of dorsals departed from the obese man's body, treading away.

"He will be missed."

Melysia plunges a steady foot into the quagmire in pursuit of the anomaly, a runaway Turkey. The flood is torso-deep, not as thick as it was, but certainly as thick as a guilty conscience.

"Fleeting is the man."

"I wonder what of him will carry over after death. Pride, perhaps? I would strive for that," Vulcan thinks.

"Conversely, guilt. Look around and see shame, unfulfilled promises, eternal suffering."

From the depths arose another body, Washington's. Face down, he is only recognizable by the hat.

"Another?"

"Atrocity."

"Shame is slow to make a sound, if any. That explains as much."

"I cannot bear eat a coward."

Melysia progresses further into the bog of decadence and decay. Buildings crumble delicately, eased into a strong layer of oil, a quiet downfall long awaited and seldom spoken of, cleanly wrought. Screams do not linger over the rooftops, only solemn grief. On a surfboard, a molten, boney corpse paddles by, lending a fixed hand.

Melysia accepts the hand, nearly capsizing the board in the process. The backseat reminds of Calypso's motorcycle, barely afloat in a lifetime's worth of motor oil, paddling slowly into eternity. In the wake of true death, nothing survives, only pitch blackness of the void, the literal existence of nothing. If there is hell on Katsikoskoni, this is its river. The body wastes: first comes hunger, then thirst, and finally bliss, only to be disrupted by the rising sun, illuminating the dank alleys of the inner city. Oil dissipates as dark before light, leaving nothing but corpses of the many nameless victims scattered on terrace grounds, some animals, others people, but all subjects of shame, regret, and guilt. These were the sentiments of contemplative Hermes.

In wake of the oil is left a clearing, a path to the countryside barely within sight of the wall, its shadow a constant reminder of the ongoing conflict; nature will know no peace.

"I think it's high time we away-ed. There is no stone we did not flip, no place unvisited, no grievance reprieved. Let us walk." Nobody objects,

for they are of the same defeated mind.

XVI

Shattered Reflections, Molten Glass, Tall Order Blowjob

Hours pass this lonesome trek. With the city behind, Yin unending guides them destiny bound wherever when. It is a thread to follow in the rift between theaters, though they are asymptotic on the civilized side — close enough. In the distance, a pitiful oasis lies center of stale fissures that run for kilometers. Nature, too, shrivels, it seems. This place sears unwelcome feet, but Horace, having crossed the Arena barefoot, knows the brunt of the story, and so, considerately, presses on the eggshells of coal. Shrubs and a puddle is the extent of this boon, scantily enough for a drink and unimpeded defecation.

"You are thirsty. Go on."

Arid sand leads to dirt that is tender underfoot, the water's gleam a welcome change to the inhospitable big city and its squalid puddles. The reflection's lips move, but Melysia's tremble only from dehydration. The water, not the reflection, sneers a mischievous jest at the host. So, rejecting the harpy in a delirious fury, Melysia smites the oasis and its tainted reflection, jabbing her knife in the bed of sand below, submerged in water like a reversed lady of the lake. Having stabbed the manifestation of herself, Melysia explodes, revealing from inside Horace, Hermes, Vulcan, the crab, Scree-ah, Rufus, a half-eaten fish, and Melysia, herself. In response, knowing Katsikoskoni trembles and the remainder of the oasis gradually retreats into the sand revealing two horns, a Fu Manchu, then a goat, and finally a fragmented green gem. "It is time to speak plainly. Yours is the body. Ribs turned fingers uncage the heart. Let guts spill free and water the sands. You are free."

A newly golden Diothor, darkness cast aside, lunges at Melysia.

Vulcan produces a finger — of his own flesh and blood pure as the day Jove left for the Arena, buffeted by the sandstorm that fateful night and healed since then — pointing at the goat, "What have you done to us?"

"What you have done unto yourselves."

"What is your aim?"

The goat crooks its head.

"Do not play coy! You have an angle. Enemies are fine so long as I'm the one making them. If they make me their enemy, that goes to show they have something to gain from me. What do you have to gain at my expense?"

"In place of wisdom, you've tempered bitterness. Do not mistake the two."

"You got something to say to me, punk?"

The goat bleats.

Vulcan rolls up his sleeve and proceeds to tackle his aggressor, "To arms! I will depart you from the mortal realm."

"Yes, you will." He sidesteps the Atlantean Vulcan, leaping from the puddle leftover from the oasis. Vulcan sinks under the weight of his burdens, enveloped in a waist-high sinkhole. "And I am you," the goat resumes. "Have you a name or has it you?" The goat lands on Vulcan's head before the rest. "Thoughts?"

Horace responds, "Oh, dear goat, you are a sight for sore eyes. I will be the one to answer your question. There is to each of us a name. We are Horace, Hermes, Vulcan, Scree-ah, Rufus, and Melysia."

"Only one among you does not, the crab. Step

forth."

A red spec skitters front and center, clacking its claws.

"He needs no name. He does not speak. Others do not speak to him. He simply exists, and is therefore closer to the spirit of the universe, but none closer than a good rock. In simpler times, we'd worship the sun. Now, man creates monkey in his image to worship his vanity, but I digress."

"An intriguing proposition, but we all heard it yell in short, violent aphorisms."

"Nay. Each of you in perfect synchronicity projected what you thought it said. Share a mind and become crab. The masses begrudge their slavers, but what are we if not slaves to ourselves? What we scant do freely for others we do with utmost urgency for ourselves free of charge. Flesh demands obedience and death be the penalty, but this has been circumvented. As of now, you are both like minded and individuals, a pairing often mutually exclusive. Be not fooled by false unions of goodwill. They are unlike yours. Man is for himself even when for others, for it is his will to be selfless, and is therefore selfish. You are truly one. Mazel tov. Scarier than any group, jointed by willful spasms rather than flesh and bone, are like-minded individuals, willful slaves to one another. You feel it, do you not? You have surpassed natural bounds as deviants stabbing yourselves to spiritual death. Here you are, at the precipice of neutrality, the average of all positions — the precise coordinates — at the intersection of Yin and Hedophilia. Double-O zero! The Arena is not the destination of pilgrimage. Perhaps it is a pilgrimage from the desert to the city, that path no one walks, save back, and so the greatest enlightenment is found there the second time. True, man started in the wild, and over generations domesticated himself. Let him take that road anew. No, man will become himself. It is neither Hedophilia, nor a Yin gatehouse where operations are centralized, but a Yin far removed from influence and illusion, the only segment of wall little used by the motley militia and unbattered by Atlanteans for millennia. Look upon it and see a pretense of insecurity! The progenitors have erected this fence well within a forest of terror. To onlookers, it would appear there is no fence at all! They would have no recourse but fear the wolves teeming within, but their cattle are safe. Somewhere, behind the cover of brush, is a fence, just as here there is a wall covered by the expanse of desert. Had it not been fortified, would the Atlanteans have even bothered still? I assure you, they wouldn't have found it, so they wouldn't have known. How else could you make this epiphany here, in this place? That is where an epiphany is made, at the borderline of things, the edge of a knife unknowing whom it strikes. Jove? Horace? Vulcan? Hermes? Crab? Hawk? Greyhound? Golden retriever? Melysia? Fish? It knows not the disowning of yourselves."

Horace recalls the fateful skewering executed by Hermes at the Yin camp, "We had been spliced once before."

"You three had been so driven to stab each other in the little time spent apart from your host. It is only in your conjoining you had tossed all grievances aside and learned to stab yourselves. All of King Monkey's creatures are alike in this regard. I can become this or that. Likewise, I could have been you and you me. All shall band together in time."

Scree-ah caws.

"Yes, even the inhospitable city dwellers, those who call the persecution of like-minded individuals, those who called for the extinction of Jove. As the wolves of Atlantis prey on the cattle of man, so too does your kin turn upon you. All around is forest teeming with predators; to which side of the fence do you belong? Is the city not a forest wherein defiled trunks lie stacked sideways to emulate trees and the shavings of effeminate, beardless men litter the grounds as leaves in winter. Bring spring's sun. May light shed the skin of callousness so our wounds may sew shut the cycle that rips anew anon through time a torturous penance, a sentence to life."

Vulcan interjects, having enough time buried in the sand to observe and contemplate the green shard, "Bah! Enough of your riddles, goat-faced cur! Is that the Egg, the artifact of power in possession of Atlantis, the mover of tides?"

"'Tis but a fragment, dear child, as you are."

Hermes asks, "Why withhold it?"

"Gain favor with friends not by telling secrets, but by withholding even from strangers. If you keep a stranger's secrets, friends also, thus you will be but a humble friend to all; I discriminate equally, so not at all."

"Are the fates of our fallen comrades a secret?"

"No, for you have seen them with your eyes. Some are dead, liquified in a puddle of sorrow. 'Tis better to suffer then relieve, rather than be born with everything and spiral. Life is fundamentally flawed. Die then live as opposed to live then die. The void in between is heavenly, the rest a slaughter. Fret not; this is a grace period; they will perhaps live again. Or not, who knows?"

Vulcan grumbles a worryingly but relatably long period to cook up a retort, "Keeping secrets doesn't make friends, either."

"Friends have enemies and enemies friends, and

all of them can be so fickle. What offends one gratifies another. It's convoluted, especially if your enemies could have easily become your friends. Why have friends when the hospitality of strangers will do?"

"You certainly don't have mine."

The goat, having tormented the host of his throne, leaps aside the fragmented egg. "As I said, why have friends? Go on, take it, friend."

"The least you could have done was hand it over long ago."

"The least I can do is nothing."

***

"Such difficulty."

"I may only resist as much as you press. If I am stubborn, so are you."

A juicy vein bulges from Vulcan's forehead, but the goat's immeasurable tranquility inspires absolute restraint atypical for a temper such as his. "Fine. Why now?"

"When something unimportant breaks, someone unimportant comes to fix it. If this trivial matter is of import, so are you."

"You wish to mend the divide?"

"Here, standing before me, are representatives of the three great philosophies: a stoic, a nihilist, and a racist, altogether an average and unremarkable man. Around them is an irreconcilable war of aliens, barring the peace. Ravines in the ground, too, once held together. The Egg is no different. Did you have a divide in mind?"

Vulcan whispers of "Aeroscorpion."

"So be it. I am merely letting you have it, just as I had it lay here all this time, and just as I had let it conjure waves for Onemsiz, Mon, Calypso, and Hermes. It's almost like it wanted to, the way I was poking it."

Hermes recalls the waves he surfed, "My waves were not a product of willpower?"

"Perhaps. You've spoken neutrally, apathetically, detachedly, and so it may as well heed your fate."

"How can it obey if I do not command with intent?"

"Fate . . . fate. It is your fate to disobey nature and its laws. Had you been someone more impressionable, your lack of foresight would leave you surprised at your own results. That is the source of the exhibitionist half of pride, utter foolishness. Behold, the waves heed fate. And now I leave its tools in your hands. You shall know the reagents of the power that yields you — no surfboards required. Training wheels are off. Swim."

The Egg shimmers of gold-gilded embroidery, the epicenter a calm green hypnotic bubbling within. Melysia runs fingers along yellow lines, reaching the cracked edge.

"Take it." That could have been anyone.

She caresses the gem as if it were a fragile glass, though it causes even the serpentine cracks in the ground to tremble. Highly pressurized water spews from every fissure, every crevice of this dry 'scape, forming anew a wave high enough to scale the wall, sweeping everyone against their wills, or lack thereof; there is no fighting it. The goat executes an elegant backstroke though it will not change the destination. The fish carcass seems unbothered, limp but adrift. Does it yet live? Even Scree-ah, intrepid flier, knows no escape as she and others are swept to a trench, sinking with the water, itself, to a depth so far out of reach of the sun. The hole from which they entered appears no larger than a pin, and the light that did shine grows ever dimmer, supplanted only by the transluminescent shine of mushrooms along the wall, some of which, uprooted by the torrent, make for a welcome addition to an otherwise monotone broth. The torrent assumes the hue of tropical waters, a paradise without all the bloody sand. Not too soon does the ravine twist, turn, and expand into a larger system of caverns. And yet, in spite of that, the way is not lost and there are no stragglers, only strugglers bruising and banging against debris, suffocating all the while; only those of clear mind

mind which rocks they hit and which bubbles they huff, for even in this tumult, opportunities present themselves. But if the universe would have them drown in a pit of ecstasy, so be it. Let there be no recourse; only giggles at King Monkey's pitiful power fantasy in the farcical form of arbitrary lackeys: thermodynamics, motion, relativity, and perhaps the most grounding of them all, gravity.

Even the standoffish Vulcan succumbs to euphoria. It seems not to have any effect on Hermes, however, for he has already attained a similar state. And in this shared tranquility does everyone see, in no uncertain terms, not as they see each other, but as they see themselves. Horace barks like a dog. Hermes screeches the raven. Vulcan forms pincers and inspects them thoroughly before grasping Melysia's knife and amputating his left hand, filling the pool with blood, clouding everyone's vision with frenzied red lit green and mouths with tastes of battle-hardened iron as befits the death of a noble savage.

From a dormant well does erupt a spew of blood-red water and a great many miscreants bleached red like the fetishized demons of hell. All hail before Nusquam, the devastated birthplace of Melysia and her once proud people, home now only to rubble and scavengers: vultures and locusts (even Brahe's palace withered into a formless dune)

— and wash ashore of Abraddon's lawn that bears a mature, nearly blossoming acacia tree before which the stream of blood ends, seeping into the roots.

All rise as if apes learning to stand for the very first time, muddled in excretions not dissimilar to a woman's uteral buggery. Melysia wipes her face, shields her good eye for a moment and gasps; there is nothing before her except perchance the hallucinations that plagued her. "The village is bustling with phantoms of the past. Abraddon's here too, tossing his butcher's axe to throw dice with the priest, Jebediah. How is it I see things?" Melysia consults the goat.

The goat's lip sinks, disappearing into his stained Fu Manchu a mustachioed smile. "It is simple. One blind eye sees what the other cannot. What use are two of either?"

Vulcan raises his stump in affirmation, "Hear hear."

"It may well just be a figment of your psychoactive imagination."

Melysia sits a moment and, unprovoked, trowels barehanded in the perimeter where soil meets the sand. Hands full, she huffs brownish turf. It smells of petrichor, a tang of sweetness. The soil is anomalously healthy in the absence of its caretaker, unless, "Abraddon died here. His blood nourishes the soil long past his death. Vulcan's too.

Big heart, it keeps beating on." Melysia plunges her knife through the bark, bleeding sweet sap, and savors the penultimate memento of her father on the blade's edge. Patches of green litter the ruins of Nusquam, though none quite as vibrant as Abraddon's legacy. Melysia's playing with knives finally catches up to her; she cuts herself, albeit tenuously. "Fuck." The curse is quiet and embarrassing.

Blood drips at the foot of the tree, reclaiming that which was so brutally taken at knifepoint.

The goat feels a sudden, primitive urge to lecture his students one last time. "And so the cycle of reincarnation revolves once more, only this time a draw, a stalemate perhaps? Death, as you may have noticed, has come for us. A question remains: What form do you wish to take before the ultimate subsuming of everything?" The master vaporizes into a totem, at the top of which the skull of a goat lies transfused atop the skull of a man, dying.

Vulcan stares disapprovingly at Melysia's superficial cut, bandaging his own wrist, "Was that not enough for you, you greedy bastard tree?"

"Such is the sanctity of man and woman," Horace butts in.

Hermes lays a palm on the cranium of his old mentor.

Night shrouds the party and, in that short time,

gargantuan cocoons form and weigh on the tree. A ripe humanid hand among them on the stem of a leaf matches the missing hand of Vulcan.

He ascends and harvests the fruit; it fits seamlessly on his stump. "Once again, no consequences for my recklessness. I figured it'd grow back, just not like this."

"Right is he for the wrong reasons not right at all." Hermes puts it this way so Vulcan does not think to fight back — being the type to fight back immediately or else drop a subject if he does not understand something.

Under light of the full moon all pods sprout, revealing within them a gallows of dangling bodies, maybe fifteen in number, protruding from red and pink stigmas. To each, a vine resembling an umbilical cord wraps loosely around the neck, inciting involuntary muscular spasms to the hanged men who dance wildly to their asphyxiation; this and a rustle of wind lets the bodies fall loose on sodden soil with a limp thud, thud, thud. They are perhaps conceived of their own blood, Melysia's and Vulcan's too. A naked, sap-soaked Abraddon and Brahe lie naked in the dirt, the former but a scrawny shadow and the latter devoid of any cybernetic enhancements. Brahe's head is pleasantly round and bald. The nose protrudes slightly.

Melysia runs to cradle the husk of her father who, unblinking, unfeeling, stares emptily that which way his head lies poised. Diothor, beside her, whines longingly for master (or patron, if to be egalitarian of friendship), and puts to use the tool of trade, the dog tongue.

Horace bemoans Brahe's pursed lips a swallow of water. "Here, drink," but to no avail. In Brahe's infantile state do his eyes remain tightly shut. "Get up, damn your eyes!"

Horace attempts to shake his compatriot from the stupor, and in doing so, only shakes him from the mortal coil; his body breaks at the seams like a vegan burger distinctly lacking in structural integrity — a vegan humanid (if you will) gestated quickly from flora — liquifying into a regrettably unsalvageable, inedible slop of gore. Others soon follow, desiccating into a collective puddle until Melysia, kneeling thigh-deep in blood and bile, holds Abraddon tightly, his coincidentally gaping face barely above water, truly dead of brain. The moment persists. It does, until which point Abraddon's unmoving visage dissipates into the pool, piece by bloody piece, leaving but a skull in Melysia's palm. She leans back, the skull outstretched toward the dimly lit cosmos, shivering, and it crumbles as dust.

Hermes stares longingly into the eyes of his

mentor, disregarding the entirety of the debacle. "Better that than to have lived a long and painful life. Who among them after millennia could be just a hermit, soldier, Atlantean, or Hedo? And sane? And if this being experienced an unending stream of consciousness, could they really be just the one? How would they identify themselves? King Monkey? Never mind," he degenerates into a mumble.

Approaching the puddle, Vulcan samples the stew in typical Atlantean fashion and spews it back. "These bones do not carry cohesive memories. Intriguing."

Teary-eyed Melysia rummages through the rubble of her home, uncovering a dusty axe amid the ashes and sets to work on the tree. Timber yells of toppling. Vulcan heaves drywood around the goatly effigy and sets it alight with a glare, alone. Horace skins branches, and Hermes casts each twig into the fire, savoring each one burn alive before tossing another.

Everyone and their stomachs stare at the half-eaten fish that followed them. None a bit squeamish, Scree-ah plucks the eyes, leaving Vulcan to butcher the rest. Melysia sharpens a half dozen branches. Hermes, the great skewerer, skewers cuts of meat and hands them to Horace who sets them to brand. Kebabs point to the epicenter of the pyre, its flames engulfing and intermingling with the totem and through the eye sockets like an angry, all-seeing, powerless god (powerlessness an implausible power privy only to a god who does nothing but watch, and perhaps not even that). The hermit crab crawls on spindly legs upon its branch, mighty pincers shredding somewhat rare meat.

Diothor kneels beside his bounty and lady. Hermes produces a wooden phallus and inspects it against the fire; Horace and Vulcan do the same, balls cupped in hand. Their hands acclimate toward one another, merging the fascinum whole once more. The hands of Horace and Vulcan slip away, leaving the responsibility of safekeeping to Hermes, hands firmly clasped about the girth and brought close to breast. The fascinum of Jove had healed to its rightful orientation.

Horace addresses the cock holder. "We needed but reheat the adhesive to form it whole. It is a most solemn duty we neglected," then turns to Vulcan who speaks also, "As beholder, you will have the final say, just as a housewife must obey her husband."

Wordless Hermes dons the artifact as the new Jove, Jove II, born of Jove.

"Listen up, you shite-eaters," Melissa boisters out from the periphery with Diothor at the hip,

"I've been hankering to read *The Playbook* for a while now so gather round," and opening the book, its leathery binding creases a noise like the refreshing stretch of bones at the crack of dawn. Old papyrus emanates an intriguing stench with the intensity of a library in its entirety, its feeble pages weaved with the density of thousands of works unearthed from a dusty dig site, an archaeology returned to the living in spite of its perceived destruction, rather forgotten and ignored that razed. She processes the fragments of her dharma before reading them aloud, "Let go of Abraddon, keep the dog, open a fortune telling parlor." She then goes off script, "I mean, duh. I was going to do all of that anyway. Figured if the bitch Parmacena could do it, so could I."

"I thought it'd be more profound, cryptic maybe. Seems tame, or obvious?" acclaims Horace.

"Who said it had to be anything other? If Jebediah is to be believed, it's just mushrooms," suggests Hermes.

"The readings are good enough for me. I'd know, I'm an apprentice Gypsy . . . And speaking of knowing things, if it were just mushrooms, then it'd just be mushrooms, which it ain't! That's ignoring the noggin it has to go through. I figure you'd know better, because, thing is, mushrooms don't mean tits by themselves!" Melysia passes *The Playbook* to

Vulcan who seems to struggle to read what little was written on his page, "Become the colonel. Hazy and low resolution like a damned dream, incomprehensible."

"Makes more sense than you seem to think. You might've been an Atlantean but we're not so different, you and I. You'll always be my colonel, Vulcan chap," speaks Horace, snatching the book. He lingers on the page a moment, perhaps making sure he'd read it correctly, "Take an army and march on Yin," he manages before bursting into a chortle, "Huh! Fancy that, direct! No idea where I'll get an army though."

"Hold fast, Horace," says Hermes, "that might mean something has gone awry. Don't you think something is brewing?"

"Lars did suggest we return. Let's hope we're that army."

"Just the four of us? Seven tops," Melysia interjects, eyeing the ravenous crab who'd remained mostly silent on the pilgrimage from Nusquam to Hedophilia and back.

"And why not?"

"We could return with an Atlantean army," salivates Vulcan. Nobody takes him seriously, except maybe Hermes, who, now unmolested in the privacy of his mind, couldn't be bothered to say as much.

It was then his turn on the carousel of prophecy on whose page was written nothing at all, "Nothing."

"No shit. You never really seemed all there," jokes Melysia.

"In good spirits, girl? The way you've been cursing up a storm, I'd think you were trying to invite Atlantis," Vulcan grins.

"Don't even start." Melysia stretches her blind eye with a finger and sticks out her tongue.

Meanwhile, Horace turns his attention to a despondent Hermes and recites from memory, "Hur hur this here feller's a sodomite and a gay."

"Way to tell on yourself, idiot," cackles Vulcan, chomping on a kebab fresh off the spit.

Hermes remains in that bubble of quiet nihilism until Scree-ah flocks to his shoulder with a chunk of eyeball dangling by a thread of nerve clamped between beaks. Hermes looks knowingly, in response to which the bird forcibly inserts her pecker between his lips and spews, feeding Hermes as if he were a clueless newborn whose visage alludes not excitement, only wide-eyed disillusionment with a world so far removed from the void. Pupils expand, then retract, discombobulate and reattach, and, finally, open and close.

Having assimilated millennia of thought, insight,

and experience, Hermes spurts residual black bile on the foreground and glares unknowingly, expectantly, even, at the avian curiosity — Scree-ah — as if demanding an answer, but upon further consideration, realizes he knows as much as she, and she so much as Horace, Hermes, and Vulcan, and they as them and ours, everyone who hath seen and been seen, and with the breathing and passing of air does Hermes know of he whom last breathed it. Specters and fauna, willows and daisies millennia old reveal themselves on the land. And on the passing of air might he know where it shall go; the future reveals itself; tentacles of fire and molten hell upon this world tell perhaps of armageddon, but sooner still the specter of Horace splays from his person and looks around bewilderedly, and little sooner does Horace do the same. Hermes gazes upon the specters of his compatriots that overlay one another like a snapshot of the fourth dimension, each bewildered at Hermes in his own right, but soon to regain composure as the specters foretell. It is only when each person is perfectly still that the specters become momentarily inseparable from host and only then that Hermes may focus on anything other, less nauseated than a second over yonder period of time, a momentary reprieve in between hallucinations he may act at all without distraction.

Does anyone else see this way? No. If they did, they would be somewhat irked by Hermes's imminent disrobing and inconsolable yowling brought on by a fiery pain traversing through his loins. A foreign, yet domestic object can be felt and heard slithering, jerking, conniving through flesh and limb, searching for reentrance, surging for a surface; any one will do. And upon inspection of his member, he is brought to kneel, for embedded neatly into the urethra is an eye not unlike that which was fed to him. Had Jove any foreskin, he might keep the eye from peering into the past and future. The circumcised of King Monkey really hit the nail on the head, burns too.

Is this, then, why Hermes sees things as they were and will be? Why does Melysia, for the most part, see things and their intent as they really are? Why do the cannibal fish people see things as others do? Why do most others see things as they appear, or do they only appear to?

The native Hedoes (back when the lands went by a different name now lost to antiquity) kept a tradition, a rite of passage even lowly Hermes remembers, whereupon juveniles lay their penises on hot coals as a test of endurance, and whatever more. Drawn to the goat effigy like moth to flame, or moth to lamp, or moth to sweater, or moth to merciless applause and execution, Hermes ambles forth on bloody knees and lays his phallus upon the fire and basks, basks in the pain of billions, pain the illusion, pain the drive, coalesced into one being and his burden, the being of all things in one body. The torch aflame resembles that of Melysia's own ball of eye, the world a phantom limb momentarily reconnected by the primordial pyre.

Vulcan bites his lip seductively. The fire whispers sweet nothings, temptations of glory and destruction, a small forest razed beneath his feet. Why stop there? Burn the husks, the houses, the helm. If it's all inevitably lost to entropy, make sure it goes out with a bang like a pretty firework. Bellowing a ferocious warcry, he puts torch to fire and relishes in the heat, the burning away of flesh, destruction his namesake. The small hairs of his bare chest and arms tear violently off and simmer and gleam in the wind as ashen sparks, Vulcan his own fire and forge, and with heavy fist moves to pound his breast, hammering his very bones to the anvil of will. And as fist nears the chest does something hum, and the closer the two forces come does it drone louder, bolder. And moments before contact, a grinding screech gives way to an explosion of sparks. It's too bright to see a damn.

So as the dust settles, a golden silhouette remains a moment more. What is left? Branded per genitalia, glory be her name, Delilah. Her voice is unwieldy and rusty, but not as without practice. "Bloody hell, where's it gone?" The transhumanist prostrates before the logs and scrambles for her member in flightful panic, breasts askew slightly obstructing her view. Newly monkeyed Delilah embarks on a new conquest, a tirade of feminine emotions, neuroticisms, shrills, and megrims. It is slowly drowned by the misogynistic universe, allowing Horace the peace of mind to focus on his transformation:

In the oranges, Horace beholds a welcoming hearth, promises of warm camaraderie, home, apple pies, and other such pleasant nonsense. Without qualm, the agreeable Yin soldier would have certainly followed his compatriots into any danger so long as they made it clear they'd do it both, leaving Horace not so much as a democratic tiebreaker, and produces from his nethers a stalwart chode of noble soul, sturdy and reliable, trim but wooly.

He burns a mellow fire, calm and steady, soothing, comforting, empathetic. Take care, or someone will take for you, and what they'll be taking is advantage — of you — good and honorable Horace. Something is drawn to the body, a growth; at first, it appears as a film enveloping head to toe. A hairy, festering tumor emerges from his face, boiling, bubbling, fabrics tear. In time, two ear-like shapes make themselves known, twitching, forming, feeling, and any clothes rip themselves completely off, revealing a second posterior, glory hallelujah, a gory mula-maker. Horace's hands slink free, and he feels the hands of his other. A rather stoic Horace runs fingers along the contour of the fellow, feeling calluses and sun-scorched scabs in familiar places. Hips link to groin and back to hip and healthy, husky arms brush against the other's ribs and pectorals, sublime vitruvian curvature made manifest. The growth largely separates from Horace's body, and Horace comes face to face with himself, briefly attached by a phallic umbilical cord, head to head, and it severs at the tip, leaving Horace as he was moments before, the self made selfless and creation his dharma.

Hermes stirs upright, visibly lightheaded, and gestures with the whole of his body a single, delirious command. Impassionate, direct, he raises arms outstretched to the heavens, to a blotch on the face of the moon the distant screech of a dragon, to Aeroscorpion.

"Wreeeeee!"

XVII

Book of Leviathan

Thus by the campfire did Delilah spew into Aeroscorpion's mouth the goings on of the past months just as Scree-ah spewed into Hermes the contents of the ancient fish eye. The Atlantean lie gobsmacked on the ground and came to his senses after a moment's recuperation. It is with a gaping maw he thought to speak, then decided against it for lack of knowing where to start.

Delilah initiates the conversation. "How are you holding up?"

"Well enough."

"Why come now?"

"I recognized the stench."

"You couldn't say as much when last we spoke."

"Let us resume from the Arena, not Hedophilia."

"That'll do."

For this time Horace stares into the mirrored depths of his soul, entranced by the infinite recursion between the two mirrors of he and himself. "Who are you?" they echo into each other. "Horace." And that is all the two need to know as they both look to Aeroscorpion. The original raises his palm and the copy obeys, knowing well the structure of order from their time in Yin, or perhaps intuitively from temperament.

"Can we trust the Atlantean?"

"I do," says Vulcan.

Aeroscorpion speaks also, "We have shared a short bond from our time in Atlantis at most a week. It is no different from the previous bonds I had with other riders who, now, so far as I know are dead. I made a commitment to this one and so I shall see it through. Did you not also make bonds with Grimwald, Lars, Brahe, Onemsiz, Mon, Jebediah, Calypso, a goat in no more a length of time? You have spewed into me the knowledge of Yin. So it is I wish to share with you that Yang is nigh, come to reap the fruit of the humanid theater. He has organized all Atlantis to this cause, even the non-militants. It is not a matter of days they march on your wall; I expect to see them over yonder horizon any moment. If nothing else, it will be a battle between two great arms. I wish to see it."

"And what if you are killed in Yin for your ugly mug?"

"I have with me a sack, Horace," says Delilah.

"So you do," laments Aeroscorpion with a tinge of nostalgia in the motoric humming of his voice. "I will not hide. Let them know with whom they deal."

Foreign chimes doth sound their eerie call in the untenable garden of Nusquam. Melysia, having seen some shit, is quite unbothered by the spectacles before her and stands atop the precipice of the tallest dune to proclaim with arms outstretched, "Quit faffing about! There be Herrmans!" And over the hill, bottles of beer suspended from a pole clang together in merry harmony. Beside it, a silver platter of pastries gleam in the sun. Standards of the beer and pastry; troops of Herrmans and Scarabs are comen. At their helm, two oddly proportioned women march meatily, arm in arm. Delilah, formerly Vulcan, steps forward, hands over hips, akimbo.

And in the five minutes the forces of the wall did walk, the Joves stared them down. How dare they travel to the ruins of nowhere, the beginning of somewhere, to inconvenience us? They will speak at us with the neuroticism as if first having seen us the moment our smells come to pass their lips, oblivious they'd had five minutes to better formulate their thoughts. They walk with wanton conviction, the nerve! The women stop ten paces from Delilah.

Upon closer inspection, it is apparent these are no women at all, but vaguely passing renditions of Delilah, herself. The mediocre features of the first Delilah betray him to be the colonel of the Herrmans, so unremarkable his birth name it need not come to mind. The second has the makings of a shaven beard pocked with stray and overlooked hairs, a likely opportunist filling in for the vacancy of his namesake, the Scarabs. Their demeanors are so timid that it is not clear which of them took the initiative to speak or which is the senior. "We are Colonel Delilah. And you are?"

"I am Colonel Delilah."

They are completely unaffected by this revelation. It is perhaps the case they had paid mind to their line of questioning and not the answers they'd receive in return. Perhaps they are not particularly well endowed with the knack for name-remembering. Perhaps they and the whole of Yin are of open mind to coincidences.

"Very good. We've been sent to investigate an anomaly in the region. You wouldn't happen to know about that, would you?"

The Joves look at each other and to their cohort for answers.

"No? Well, truth be told, we don't know what we're looking for either. Some rubbish about blips on a radar and severe gamma radiation. Would you mind if we had a poke around?"

And from the ranks of the many, a third Delilah torpedoes through the arms of the first two, only this one is identical to the Delilah opposite her. "Hold fast, mongrel!"

Delilah points at herself inquisitively.

"Do you have it, the rock? Some call it an egg."

Delilah looks around as the two impersonators boogie hesitantly. No one pays them mind.

Where a lesser shrew might have lost her patience or sought to make an example of dissidents, this one remains calm. "Have it, do you?"

Everyone shrugs, as does Melysia, and not because she has the emerald shard, but because she has no idea what the bloody bugger is going on.

The other Delilah sighs condescendingly.

A valve somewhere on her person releases steam. Her very flesh disintegrates into a fine, red mist, revealing a skeleton, a chassis all metal, no flesh. He has no nose, for he needs no nose. He is the Brahe, bother, bellend, and fiend, or so read his obituary at the foot of Nusquam's oaky tombstone — now fully android, formerly cyborg. The two fakers take heed and tear off their fatigues, hairy bosoms in the wind. The hammer of the boogie strikes down hard without regard for polity.

Face to face with the slayer of her father, Melysia spits at his feet, memories of sloppy joe fresh in mind.

A tense Horace replicates once, as does his clone, and their clones, too. 'Tis strenuous first and easy after, like practicing with a non-dominant hand or nostril. It is after every breath and before every release that a new progeny fills the Arena where once, whence, was naught.

"How do we play this, gentlemen?" Horace and his clones suggest in unison.

Hermes's limb tingles; phantom shapes cloud the sky like floaters and the field aglow with fluids brings hark of the end times — whether in the fashion of Ragnarstein or the chopping of Yang's limbs — to this very place. Speechless Hermes, who sees double of everything, projectile vomits 'tween the forces of good and not good enough.

Horace raises an open palm, a gesture of peace. The fresh green of the troop do not wish to die; it is on their faces. "Return home."

"Not without the egg. Who will die in their stead? There are reports of fish in the region." Brahe seems to confirm Aeroscorpion's account of Atlanteans on a death march.

Horace gives his progeny a once over. "He

without cannot win the game rock-paper-sense, and you'll not have your egg if those damned fish people can help it. I know you as a rogue element, but are we not allies? We go together. Mine will keep the Atlanteans at bay."

Brahe seems to catch on. "Affirmative." But you never could know with Brahe; it could take an entirely new meaning in his mother tongue. Turning to his detachment, he raises a hand disenthusedly and twirls it with a flourish, "Strip. Go on." No sooner do the smallclothes of the two fakers adorn the flag posts. The rest follow, surrendering their equipment to the Horace battalion. They will march home naked as the day of their births.

Brahe removes his desert fatigues and beret and folds them orderly-like, bestowing them respectfully to the last reigning Delilah who dons them with ease, like they'd been hers. Hugging snugly about her figure, it is the same uniform she wore months ago. A direct and mechanical salute leads into a full body rotation free of excess motions, waving of hands, swaying of hips, or whatever other embellishments a humanid might entertain when moving around, and yet executes them with the finesse of a dancer. He turns to face the pasty compatriots who so bravely and faithfully followed into battle two crossdressers, watching them strip before the impending storms of armageddon that would consume the memories of the living live and living dead alike, "This is the Delilah whom you shall follow." The Atlantean Aeroscorpion raises no suspicion, for the men stare dumbfoundedly at Delilah as men might do. Delilah does little but look pretty. As a woman, that is enough. She will be granted entry to the wall, the Seventeenth Regiment's battering ram. The Horace Battalion in Nusquam will cover the Herrmans and their analogues on the march home.

Melysia makes it known she will remain behind in the homeland, the animals to keep her safer than she would have been with just the Horaces. Nobody thinks to question her; it is a strange time, not least of all because this patch of nothing could very well be safer than Yin, itself.

Thus after a day's travel, one hundred score tuchus corralled like cattle migrate hitherto a spot of shade so their backsides might not flush with the colors of spanking and war before long, though long may well come first before the short of it.

Brahe remarks, "An army of Horaces, unstoppable in the right hands. Had we the time or resources, we could sponsor a whole regiment of killing machines, but I am the sole reigning field prototype I know of, which is not to say there are not a number of recreational models among us. It is a shame progress might be cut short with every passing day, a testament to the perseverance of the Atlanteans. Savages."

"All the more should we exercise moderation, caution. Can't say we're me any more than I am with each second that comes to pass. I believe they . . . we will do the right thing."

"'Belief' is a strong word. Times like these, I wonder if anyone believes anything; if you so quickly question your clones, how could you be sure of yourself? And they'll be thinking the same. Too little conviction for belief. It is better to assume, assume as in not take as true but act as if it is until otherwise."

"Say, what happened to the accent?"

"It is lost to antiquity. I have been civilized. I am a machine, and yet I wonder what is lost. Is my programming but an illusion of what was? Am I but a heat guided missile? Behind these vast calculations, who am I really?"

"Intelligence is intelligence, artificial or otherwise. And who's to say we're not walking illusions?" Horace gestures broadly at the passable mirage of naked men. "Chin up, if you're feeling dumb, look around and find babbling, multipurpose machines with little more function and personality than that spigot on your person. We're not so different, you and we."

"But my brethren are cogs."

"Quite, brother Brahe." Horace places a reassuring hand on the shoulder.

"I see. Humanids are machines like machines are machines, laid bare to the threads of fate, programming, call it whatever. Should we not see the future, may we hypothesize fate all we want; in ignorance, free will is illusive. I am free of nothing, but not anything else."

Horace continues the thought on behalf of his comrade. "In our hubris, we think we are like the simulation to the humanid and not a tardigrade zipping through a motherboard. We are but walking abstractions, the manifesting story a byproduct; what the sodding bugger do crabs have to do with it after all?"

"Bugger?"

"Something I picked up on my travels."

"Or a word you forgot you used before?"

"Sure, why not?"

"Hold fast, good Horace. I want to show you something."

On the way back to the wall, ravens scatter about a field of crucifixes. One such crucifix bears the remains of Grimwald, officer. The torso remains largely intact. He is otherwise disemboweled and missing a bottom half, puss streaking down the pole into a lukewarm slop, disrespected and brutalized.

Brahe does not allow his fellow a moment to mourn. "I neglected to tell you, good Horace, there has been a conspiracy. Would you happen to know anything about that?"

Horace squints at him quizzically and, were he a cowardly man, would probe to see where he stands as a friend to truth or a lapdog under the strings of his betters, but Horace does not mince words. "Yes." He gauges the corpse for permission to continue. "There is a dragon."

"Ah, yes. I heard that too, courtesy of our friend before they killed him."

"They?"

"Friends of the warden, unremarkable men — or not. It is a difficult time: There will be a shift in the world order and our brethren are of dissenting opinions to its resolution. My good friend Grimwald sought to awaken Yin, the dragon. Lars told me you'd know. We do not know what transpired in the past. Will it be an ally or an enemy? And in either case, we will lose the wall as Yin takes the fight to Yang, as they call it. And whatever comes, there is a threat on the horizon biding its time. Where do you stand?"

"Who knows? I am but one man."

"Such humility. You are one man many times. Did you not breed an army just now? Who do they follow?"

"Fair enough. I put my trust in Grimwald and Lars."

"Good. I might have killed you otherwise." He pauses and elicits a flat "Haha."

"Did he have to die?"

"The warden, he is paranoid. Even we might not face a warm welcome on our return. And I say this out of earshot of my men, for even I cannot trust all of them. Yes, I told them it was a drill. The egg might aid us in awakening Yin or at the very least hold at bay the fishy hordes. Take heart; Lars yet lives. He will know what to do with it. Pray he is not discovered. Come, we cannot be seen to have tarried overlong with a traitor."

***

Approximately ten days' elapsing from Nusquam to Yin, the internal clock reads the thirtieth of the thirteenth month, the last day of the year.

It is before the wall, a line between the orderly squalor of Hedophilia and the cleanly chaos of the Arena that the accompanying Herms array themselves, their whites turned brown forever more and ne'er to heal. The contagious color of Jove seeps far into the roots of their skin, a kind of metaphysical leprosy from which is born — Lo! — the ashkenigga!

"Time comes, doesn't it? But where might it go? Unsplit the drained sea and tread water as fish 'neath the breathing stars." — Hermes

A lone silhouette stands tall on the parapets, single handedly blocking the crimson sun with a fist; he could make shadow puppets if he wanted to. His dignity alone marks him as the warden, the busybody talker who welcomed Horace into the fold of Yin before disappearing and never seen again until now. And he has something to say: "You shall not pass!" Only walls need not speak. The man is redundant and takes home a sizable wage.

Hermes knows as much, but does Delilah? Don't you hate it when you know someone has something to say, but there is a great distance between the two of you and all the time you're waiting for them to close it you'd fantasize about striking them down instead of hearing whatever cliché and predictable nonsense they might say? She does precisely this to the warden.

"Hey, chauvinist! Open the gates and let flood these lost tushes of yours! And while you're at it, pick on someone your own size!" She karate chops both sides of her pelvis.

Warden Heinrich on high hears nothing (he is too high) of the lamentation of city slumlings and, opposite them, Yins that reek a fishy suspicion. Each man an emperor has no clothes, neither King

Monkey his suit! Should they a purpose serve, 'tisn't his. Perhaps Warden Heinrich might only have recognized them as brothers if they wore uniforms; alas, the cattle brand of allegiance retires to the wardrobe, or the bin. Yin guns are primed at the new line between order and chaos on which stand the naked dispossessed.

Brahe raises an eyebrow to Horace. Horace shakes his head. Hermes taps a foot impatiently because he already saw Horace would do that. Were the crab here, he'd stare 'em down. Aeroscorpion prepares to feed Katsikoskoni. Delilah redacts her uniform and waves it 'round, a new flag and banner. Left leg straight step, right heel into buttock, snip snap those fingers, shimmy and a shammy, then thrust into right foot stomp. Delilah has come down bad like a caveman, a neo revival of pounding the ground with every limb. 'Tis a shame this dance was lost 'till now.

Men on high watch with great interest and damn near forget they've been ordered to shoot. Bah, everyone has chosen a new deity this day. The warden's composure degenerates into some limp-necked semblance of authoritative barking fallen on deaf ears; he is too high for his meager stature. No sooner than his panicky fist unblocks the sun do the nudists amble forth, the sun amply high and large to guide them. Gravity in action is but a coincidence of many things coming together of their own volition.

Every particle is a tourist to a grander attraction. Between here and there, Delilah keeps a massive tush, a dank pitstop on the path to the light. Hedophilia was not built in a day and neither was it sacked in one. So too shall her ass, too voluminous for one sitting, be filled in the fancy of fantasy a-haze in dreams of men and some women who forsooth would dwell on this for days (should they live so long).

Yin soldiers fling themselves off the walls and a number of their cohort die not unlike sperm. Everyone would congratulate the seaman that won, but not one the egg that sat there and did nothing, O cruel and misogynistic universe. There's a goblin running 'round and he's scrambling everyone's eggs in the saucepan of the mind.

A gun shot pierces the soft skull of the man nearest the warden as a show of frontier discipline to keep the rabble in tow. Then came a second, a third, dare I say a fourth? No such luck is had when a man doth dies for the sovereign, and why should any worship a man whence they serve the abstract, a principle? Ass:

Many men go without, save in the fancy of mirage and pleasant delusion. Here, men abstract from behind Delilah's pantaloons an ass, but so far as anyone knows, it does not exist.

The fifth shot — yes, the fifth — kills the warden, he unto himself. Perhaps he could not bear the thought. Who is he if not the sovereign? Nothing, and so he kills himself. (This is conjecture, for he was too far high for anyone to know him well.)

The corpse vanishes as did Abraddon's and Brahe's in the sludge of Nusquam. He is not only dead but properly nothing, having no other characteristics than leadership before today. 'Tis Heinrich's final incarnation. A hawk's caw knells of mourning.

Delilah lingers with the men on the spot of her predecessor's passing. It is her place.

The path is clear; Hermes sees himself where he will be, and so goes there without overmuch hassle. Hermes would find himself before Lars in the infirmary, blood spattering the walls as always, only now unclear whose. "Good morning, friend Horace." Only it isn't morning and Hermes isn't Horace. But to Lars, morning is a state of mind and Horace the most common name this side of the wall. "No more patients." To the untrained eye, it may seem the doctor is in good spirits, but to Hermes, the posthumous image overlaid against his current form emits a slight blur not unlike the flapping of a bug's wings; he's trembling. It's time and he knows it, as with everyone touched by *The Playbook*. A smile makes its way from eyes to lip then freezes, and Lars pats Hermes firmly by the hind-arm. "I misspoke. There is another." The doctor pushes Hermes aside and that same hand brushes against the wall slowly, gently, and with a longing for the bloody good times had, "Adios, krankenhaus."

Hermes's laggards come thither, save Delilah who held back the men of Yin their advance.

His head crooks, embarrassed, as if he'd been engaging in solicitous activity. "No more patients! Feel free to watch, though." His eyes fix on Aeroscorpion for but a moment. "Oh, and aren't you an ugly fucker? You remind me: I had the thought ugly men are just pretty women and vice versa — and I've been waiting all day to share that morsel of wisdom with someone, anyone. Thanks for that. You want my prognosis? Sorry, pal, you've been dealt the wrong chromosome. Ah, but I've seen worse. You'll be fine, legless and armless as you are. Come if you'd like." His eyes drift to the android. "Hello, Brahe." Lars runs a scalpel against the grain of blood on the wall and an opening is made. "Do not fret, I fashioned a hemostat. It'll clamp real nice. Shouldn't be too messy. No one should follow." He closes the door on the way out.

It is a damp yet tolerable cavern. Capillaries spurt on occasion but are otherwise dark and void of matter. It's mostly safe to hold on to them as if rocks on a wall of climbing with the exception of patches of mucussy filament. A torch shines light upon the path.

"Good Horace," and this time it is indeed Horace he addresses, "we travel to the heart of Yin lain dormant for millennia, where I shall make a worthy sacrifice and become one with this big, beautiful thing, whatever it is. It shall have life, my creation!"

Horace replies in kind, "I understand."

"Oh, much obliged. You really needn't have, but thanks. I shall sing your praises for the rest of time, name my first born in your likeness, and found a practice in your honor . . . had I the credentials or a wife. Maybe I can adopt a near-adult? No, no, they'd have a name. And I can't say I have the discipline to keep a habit ad infinitum, bah."

"No issue, really."

"Kind soul!"

The compliment fades into quiet silence and displaces the doctor into the adjacent state, unquiet silence, the kind that grinds.

"Years I and others have bled the wounds of the dying into these walls! Wet rags wrung, the lot of them. We took donations, too, of course, small samples, nothing too moving. I suppose it saved a few hundred lives, saved them from becoming this thing, more specifically. Or are the civilian donors damned anyway, however little a piece they gave? Bah, what does it matter, they're all here anyway, watching, remembering. Sweet limbs of mine. I like to think they're grabbing at me like a vortex of mandibles."

"..."

"Don't mind me. I'm not obsessed, only curious. Aren't you? Any of you? Why come otherwise? Well, I need Brahe for something. But all of you?"

Would, or even could Hermes answer, he might say something asinine and esoteric about the arbitrariness of any and all things, and that his being there was strictly a force of nature. Aeroscorpion might have thought to stay with Delilah, but a girl needs her space to jeze-some-bellends. Brahe follows Horace for whom a sliver of sentimentality survived his organic death, for when he was even half alive, his will shone bright as the light that razed Nusquam that now simmers for Horace who answers, "The Atlanteans are coming. I'd like to put an end to the chaos that threatens us all."

Lars interrupts Horace as if he didn't say anything, "Wait, don't say answer. I did tell you to come back after I figured the solution for this Yang fellow. Oh, if you say so, my champion of the people." A hand waves off the answer to a question that was nothing more than performative and polite, "Now, more importantly, we're here to learn, to create, or perhaps revive an artifact lost to time, a purely scholarly endeavor unmolested by the restrictions of academia and ethics. Nothing too complicated, I assure you. What do you think they got me in for, after all? Malpractice? Yes. Larceny? Yes. But not fraud! 'Tis my line in the sand!" Only Yin isn't his line. And it wasn't Horace's. And it may not have been Yin's own for whom death may have come unwelcomely.

"Say, Brahe, did you fetch that egg?"

"It is in the hands of our compatriots."

"Ah! So you are here for a reason! You may very well be a good kicker, seeing how funny things work out. Don't mind me, I used to gamble. Lot of ancient artifacts from a lost time floating about. Makes you wonder if we were the first to try our hand at civilization. Malarkey we might not even get farther than the last guys! I wonder what ate their asses, ahem." Lars stops and ganders with satisfaction, "This is the place," before him a chamber with a bulbous growth at the center vaguely the shape of a bean the size of many men. "Now we wait." His bottom plummets to the ground, where he twiddles thumbs with intent.

"What for?" asks Horace.

Lars produces a cautionary finger, then a flute. He plays long and hard many seductive tunes to rile from slumber the many spirits he bled into the walls of Yin. It is an affair of half an hour until such a point he stops, "Well that didn't work."

"What?"

"I was hoping I could wake up sleepy the same way you might talk to someone in a coma. Maybe they'll hear you, maybe not. Well, I do have a plan B; the only reason it's not plan A is it's a tad extreme, and dangerous, might I add."

And from the shadows comes a snakelike hissing that jolts Lars from the ground. At times, the hissing would stop; perhaps the snake had a thought before hissing again. Vulcan, in particular, readies himself to kill and murder the evil that dwells in the shadows, the very same that fills the room with anxiety and dread. Lars does not falter and seems pleased, much the same maniacal way he cuts someone open. Thus, a hooded figure emerges on the opposite side of the room dragging with him a coil and a wire that produced the slithery noise. Dropping the equipment, he unveils the hood to reveal himself as Grimwald, officer of Yin.

"Grim, you old goat! Took you bloody long enough," Lars commends him, approaching with a masculine swagger.

They embrace their arms strongly. "I have been vaiting to give you an earful for zhis errand you set me. Vhat is zhe plan?" Grimwald looks to the entourage. "Ah! Brahe, Horace, fellows, good of you to come. I see zhere is an Atlantean vizh you, but I shall assume he is good company. I alvays vanted to meet your people in zhe flesh under neutral terms. I hope you are zhe first and last emissary of your people."

Aeroscorpion thunders a hiss, "Gratitude."

"Hold on. I figured you for dead. I saw your body," poses Horace to Grimwald.

"Eh, zhat poor man, how do I put zhis? He is not me."

Lars fills in, "Come on, it's the twentieth century. Everybody loves a scapegoat. Nobody actually has to get the guy that did it anymore. I figured the warden and his goons were hoping Grim would disappear, and that he did. I might have sent him around the wall for a jog. Besides that, quiet as a whistle. Honest."

Brahe glares silently.

"Oh, don't tell me they duped you too. Could be I switched out too much of your noggin. My apologies. Don't look at me like that. Really, stop it."

Brahe does not look away, but his expression calms about the eyes.

"'If by don't you mean do, I don't think I will' — that's what you're thinking. Anyhow, allow me to inform you we have come to the heart of things. If it wasn't, I would be terribly embarrassed and we'd all die. Speaking of which, we might also die if we used Brahe's full arsenal. Mixed results and such could blow up the whole place, so don't try anything funny." He stops. "Lost my train of thought. Grim, remind me what we're meant to be doing."

Grimwald coughs and looks to the Joves, determining perhaps that they were uninformed. "I had my men, for vhat vould have been a year long journey circumnavigating zhe world, run high and low routing power lines from Yin's plants to zhis very place. It has been a veek." He smiles at the efficiency of things. "On my command, ve vill restart zhis beating machine. Is zhat correct, Doctor?"

"Indeed!" recalls Lars. "The men who died at the walls, the patients I've bled in my hospice — and I figured I'd stop calling it a hospital because, really, that was a consequence of ego to begin with — everyone who spilled blood will now play a role. Brahe?"

"I have observed every Atlantean incursion reads high with gamma radiation. Intel has discovered the source to likely be a rock of sorts. Independent Atlanteans outside the pack do not present the same readings, for instance. I ran simulations with the data and most outcomes suggest it might use any number of advanced techniques to facilitate their logistics network, commanding their ocean. The most likely scenario of less than five percent is a miniature reactor that induces thermal convection. If so, how has it lasted for millennia? How can it work if fractured? If it uses water for a coolant, how come the fish do not burn alive? We are fortunate the Atlanteans for all their ingenuity are intelligent enough only to use it as a mode of transportation."

Aeroscorpion has no response.

"If it was ours," Brahe continues, "we would have figured out a better use. An egg! It is a shame we are too primitive to understand it, or else we might have had a better name for it. We are cavemen huddled in the damp cave carcass of our betters."

Lars, of all people, cuts Brahe edgewise. "Thank you, Brahe. Did I ever tell you he has a supercomputer built in? It's handy when you don't use it to glare people to death." He flicks the tolerant android's nose. "If we didn't have the egg, I reckon we'd spend the evening scraping blood off the walls with towels and straining them onto the damn thing. Now be so kind as to fill up this engine before we kick-start it."

"So the egg commands the tide? This confirms what the goat told us," says Horace to his fellows.

"A goat? Grimwald?" Lars flummoxes.

"I said no such thing."

"No, a literal, tangible goat," Horace responds. "Never mind."

Producing from his person the egg, Horace waves it about with intent; his expert demeanor does not betray his cluelessness, which soon dissipates as he learns on the job the machinations of this curious artifact. Siphoning liquid mortality like a shepherd of souls from the walls of Yin, blood swirls about the heart and seeps into its pallid chambers flushed red from brown.

"Can you hold it?" Lars asks with a gleam of enthused mania.

"Aye."

"Brahe! Telegram!" and Lars set immediately about attaching electrodes about the heart, rigging the whole contraption together with the coil brought from afar through the caverns of Yin.

A mechanical clink sounds from his stomach to which Grimwald approaches. "I vill send zhis to my contact in zhe power plant. Zhat is, if zhey did not kill her. On my vord five hundred zhousand joules of Herrman villpower vill surge through zhe vire and deliver a mighty zap. The line may fail and Yin vill experience a short circuit zhat vill leave it vulnerable, but zhat is a necessary sacrifice. I do recommend everyone stand back."

As everyone moves aside, Grimwald seems to compute a calculation or else a value judgment and motions, "Furzher back," to which everyone heeds. "Good enough."

Grimwald forwards the message and marches with Brahe to the spot everyone had gathered, Lars the last to arrive.

"Vhat do ve zhink vill happen on zhis momentous occasion?" inflects Grimwald with what few moments remained before the reckoning.

Pensive Aeroscorpion let loose the ruminations of the mind. "I was struck a dumb silence upon my mien, for in these walls I smell many men and fish alike, comrades and enemies. The late Goatman lingers here as pungent in death as in life among the latent whispers of my riders of centuries past. There too are hints of loyalists to the cause of Yin. Whatever comes of this amalgamation of many psyches may not serve you as you think. It is antithetical to some who follow the teachings of Yang, mainly the idealists who strive for the perfect union. In my old age I have tried time and time again to maintain the order of my bonds; even mine to Vulcan is no more as it was between I and him so much as it is now I and Delilah, not unlike you to Horace and Hermes what once was Jove unto himself. This she has spewed into me, and I ate of her in the tradition of Atlantis. This Yin will be more inconceivable than this Jove who existed for moments before collapsing into constituent parts. Never mind the war, I only wish to see what chaos transpires; I am too old to own a racehorse. I have outlived them all."

Were Delilah there, she would have nodded in muted appreciation in exchange for these thoughts.

"Zhank you. Aeroscorpion, vas it? I vonder vhat might have been if . . ." A crackle of thunder deafens standers-by from the resolution of Grimwald's reprise, which stalls into silent awe as the heart resumes with a great thud, thud, thud. Blood seeps from the ground and sloshes at the ankles of men like a sea ebbing at the foot of a beach, hankering to begin its pilgrimage from whence it came. Horace relinquishes his grip on the egg.

"Lars, vhat now?"

"Hehe, I do not know."

"Vhat vas I expecting?"

"You know me. I reckon we can hold hands as we're whisked away wherever we're called, the unmentionables if we're unlucky — but at least we'll be together. We're not outrunning this flood."

"Oi vey."

"Hey! I nearly threw myself into the heart before we zapped it so I could become one with my creation, but I wanted to see it through with you people. I didn't spare myself a romantic and heroic death to hear you 'oi vey' at me!"

So there they stood, all seven of them, staring at one another knowingly. In time, the flood swept away every man and woman to their posts. By chance or fate, Grimwald went with Lars, Aeroscorpion by himself, and Horace with Hermes and Brahe through the humid caverns of Yin run hot with life. In the small hours of their travels, they did not suffocate, and inevitably came to the apex of their journey beyond a portcullis of gnashing teeth atop which sat a command center of sorts, whose slits peered out to slithering plates that stretched for thousands of snakelike kilometers, though maybe more tapeworm in proportion. It was here these four were spat out the larger of all the rooms the Joves have seen.

XVIII

Bescrupled Psyche Shadow Autosex

"O numinous tapeworm, you are thin, emaciated, and shriveled, but very much alive in the same way an echo of legacy survives generations of forefathers, brought alive by archivists and their dastardly technologies," prospects Hermes in that sentimental and profound way.

The sensory orifices of android Brahe perk up at the mention of dastardliness. "I, myself, have struggled with feelings of inadequacy. For all the advancements that course through my person, I pale in a shadow. Once a humanid, no longer. I am the better tool between the four of us. To Yin, I am the nothing beneath perception. The future is not humanid nor android. Should I then replace these parts with the likeness of Yin? My, so much work," he chuckles. "What is this hubris?"

"Friend Brahe," speaks Horace, "You are stronger than you know. I only fear that you want to be the strongest at the expense of all others."

"True enough; there is no other way of it. Were I in your position, I would have multiplied without restraint and swarmed every corner. No doubt, my victorious progeny and I would inevitably turn on one another and destroy all the world Katsikoskoni. I suppose that is why every nation needs an enemy with whom to spar, even to the point of bullying, or else dissolve into themselves like the salivating sons of an emperor undoing decades of good work, the ungrateful bastards."

"If I could be bothered to check, I'd say you came upon some axiom of anthropology," guesses Hermes.

"So what if I reinvent the gear? It cannot be helped, this futile exercise. As Lars said, there is something that came before us. We reinvent it anyway. It is hard enough to be original with eight billion of you simians dragging your knuckles all over the place."

"Having a crisis, comrade?" asks Horace.

"Never mind. What are we meant to do here, fellows mine?"

"We are but loyal sailors at the helm. I can't say

why. It's an aesthetic, maybe an intuition."

"Isn't everything?" asks Hermes.

"Maybe to you. To me, it is a matter of heart." Horace bumps it with a proud thud.

"Rightly."

It is at this juncture a soaked Delilah marches into HQ, a shrewish fury sloshing with every step. "What bloody now?"

Horace lets loose a cackle, the bastard. Delilah strikes him down; he didn't expect it from a woman. The old Jove turns to face her from the ground: "What was that for?"

"I was getting it on and the would-be fucker got tossed over starboard." Her disappointment is palatable. "He wasn't even fully erect!"

"So what if he wasn't?"

"Doh, it's not the same!"

"For shame! How'd you figure to come here, anyhow?"

"I fell through a pothole and got swept away by a flood. All Yin is shaking up something mighty fierce. But never mind that, I was getting it on!"

So for a bid of quiet, brave and selfless Horace summons a clone that drags Delilah away by the collar for some autosexual R&R. The clone shuddered as he went.

"I did not think you had it in you," smirks Brahe

a more humanid smile that had ever touched his lips alive.

"Don't even start, comrade."

"I commend your taste, nancy boy; transhumanism is the future."

"I do what I must," Horace sighs. "We can't get this wrong, not when this Yang fellow looms death over our necks. The quiet should help the flow of thoughts."

Hermes adds his piece, "If anything, Delilah is the gut."

Brahe speaks forthwith, "The beast awakens, this I know. In the manner of any living thing, it must be thrown from bed. I suggest that I attach myself to its body from the outside and propel it to the air."

"And if you destroy everything and yourself like at Nusquam?"

"This beast can handle it. Nusquam could not."

"Don't you feel shame, regret?"

"No, a detached sympathy, but not regret. That is aside the point."

"Will you survive?"

"If not, know I am always rebuilt stronger. I may yet fuse with Yin and transcend this lowly form."

"You are never rebuilt but, in fact, consumed by such stronger an entity — and think yourself it," jousts Hermes at the truth of things.

"No difference; I go. It has been an honor, comrade."

"Can you make him stop this foolishness?" petitions Horace to Hermes.

"I will not. I have seen him leave the room before he did. This is the nature of my transformation, of course. I see also that he will succeed in his endeavors."

And Horace turns about to see only himself and Hermes in a room filled with a gassy medium of that dreadful premonition. "Will we win the war?"

Hermes pauses at the poising of this tedious question. "We won't lose, not that I speak for myself. I am the impartial bystander in this, my mind a repository of sequences that play on a loop involuntarily."

"But do we win? Is Yin strong enough to fight Yang? He's had two months to recuperate and organize. Drop in the bucket compared to the millennia they've been asleep, but what if it matters?"

"You shall see. I need time to sift through the visions. Do your best, you will. Delilah played her part; the rest is up to you, friend Horace. I barely managed the trek here; the visions leave me dizzy and disoriented. It is best I stand still."

Further aback the spine of the primordial giant

radiates an oppressive heat cuing its launch; Horace and Hermes do little to nothing at the moment but watch from the slits the gradual rising of a giant. Debris dusts itself off, its shockwave heard throughout Katsikoskoni; Yin shudders at the thought, but whose? And what thought? Any of them: Hermes, Horace, Delilah, Aeroscorpion, Lars, Grimwald, and the thousands others inside and barely out, parasites on a carcass. In the grand scheme of millennia however, this is but a rude awakening to a late hibernation. Those on the parapets fly like fleas. Splatter splatter on the ground and stay there, thank you.

The gate from Hedophilia to the Arena lifts slowly, just not as intended; the whole bloody thing goes, even the cement foundation, a horseshoe to a horse gone rogue. For the first time, a breach bids welcome to fish and societally frustrated Gypsy alike, and the only thing in their way now is the time it takes to get there, which is incidentally the same amount of time Yin has for whatever it is she decides to do in the fight against primordial evil before hell sics its demons, one on the other, treacherous Hedophile and violent Atlantean alike. This is no armageddon, rather a grand reaction. Man will enter such a change of state that they will become one with the Atlanteans, and their blood shall water the clouds. And like a train abed a track of its own — apparently vertical design — rising Yin meets one such cloud, a white one whose innocence is violated, eviscerated, and dispersed. She wasn't even fully erect. And as Yin, dragon that she is, leers down at the state of the union. A haboob is unleashed upon the world, a shroud of darkness swept up in her haste. Hermes neither sees below the dust; Katsikoskoni may well not be there.

A deep grumbling emanates from the void of sand. It is not obvious at first, but it is indeed a voice. "Hither, thou thither. I have scrounged ye at last." A face emerges, teeth and body green with gleam. The voice is clearer now, unmuddied by the sedimentary browns of unlife. "Sometime ago I had asked thy name, antemonkey." Yang flies to meet the challenger.

The room shifts askew ever so slightly and with intent, like machinery running diagnostics. In time, the dragon answers for herself, "Yin."

"The individual hath been subsumed, woe. Come, then, old adversary. Let us make merry the recreation of our conflict. Dost thou remember the old song and dance?" replies Yang.

Groggy Yin speaks at the maximum length patience allows, gears churning from within a dreadful machinery. "I struck thee down as thee thought it best strike the humanids. I had chosen sacrifice and in mine shadow they lived anew anon 'til now, thou dastardly fellow." Perhaps she heard the word from Hermes. Yin continues, "'Twas thy folly thine theater lie barren, spilled of thy common ambrosia meant to flood all the world. If not for mine sacrifice that cushioned thy blast, all the world — hark these words mine — whence dead be dying instead. I prithee ask thee, why?"

"'Tis so. Calamity did spill in every direction, and I did take great pride in squandering the oceans as they once were. 'Twas a foul and scrumptious revelry of my Atlantis from whose height I delighted. But I shan't justify it to thee. Come, then. Let us not tarry. I am weary of thy mug."

The gears screech, furious that they thought to reason with their petty sibling nemesis. "Have at thee, thou common peddler, thou purveyor of loathsome oils, thou whoreson cur!"

The grey Yin cries for war and lunges as a headless chicken running on half a gram of stem, little better than a zombie or a shrew. Her opponent is wizened by the decrepitude of years, the difference being a rude awakening or a restful slumber.

Their bodies crash against each other; the emerald one is limber, the grey deathly and sick with fleas. After initial contact, they batter against each other repeatedly like the necks of two giraffes. A sizable chunk of Yin's neck flies into the cosmos, leaving the head on its hinges. A dreadful draft fills the room. Horace meditates in place, bracing and cloning in the hopes it will accomplish something. To hell with moderation. Even some of his clones clone, and it seems the agreed-upon number of cloning clones is a tentative five broodmasters, or else be flooded in an endless sea of Horaces. This agreement will not last; all will deviate in time.

Hermes comments on the state of the hull to Horace, "It seems we are full of holes." Some are preordained, others newly formed, but Horace is vaguely hole shaped. One such line of Horaces chain together, comrades in arms in arms and legs of sorts; some will die from trauma in the chain link armor. Dumb Yin will hold together, however bleak the odds. Yang perpetually lacerates at Yin, who keeps afloat by the patchwork Horaces that, with their bodies, plug the holes.

"Where is Brahe?" shouts the original Horace through the sonic booms of battle.

"Fused with Yin, his guns will not aid us. He is using all his strength to keep us upright," replies Hermes by his side.

"We have no offensive capabilities whatsoever. Don't we have artillery along the whole bloody shaft? What are we meant to do up here!?"

"Hope, pray, wait. Does it matter? Yin's soldiers will have taken the hint to use them or not. Not like we can see under the dust. Well, I can, but I'm not going to tell you; this I have foreseen."

"Scree-ah!" A hawk flies through the larger of Yin's eye sockets. She brings two fingers, cleanly cut, red and fresh. By one finger Hermes is fed an echo of Melysia from under the dust shrouding Katsikoskoni: Sewage and saltwater do not mix. Vagrants and predators perform a dance and act out their basedness, a performance theater of panic and violence. Melysia lies in a puddle of her own blood, dying beside her dog who puts up a respectable fight. Close by also, tireless Pelvis-Crusher fells a great many foes under the weight of her great club where she stands atop a mass of corpses, her quarry. Blubbery Atlanteans devour the bones of the starving living. King Monkey, the de facto king of men, rains his fire on friend and foe alike, and they on him, shaking indignant fists.

Horace is offered the other finger and smokes it like a fag; and upon completion, Melysia is reformed to the best of his memory. Melysia gasps for air as she condemns her killer: "Ha, I figured you could bring me back with your powers. Parmacena's Gypsy magic rubbed off on me to boot. But never mind that, your people have gone rogue and everyone's clamberin' amok!"

Hermes chimes his horn. "Not even yours could resist the allure of entropy, aye friend Horace? It really does take one, hm-hm. It was the humanids' first and last mistake to form more than one tribe of any more than, say, thirty." He is thoughtful and decisive in this calculation. "So much as one divergence and any ten thousand years later, sociopaths from different countries near and far aim to outbid catastrophe. If I was a more sentimental person, I would say I am glad to be up here." Hermes gestures vaguely to the bloody shitfire sandstorm below, browns intermixing with reds, a murderer's souffle.

"It's great you can ruminate at a time like this, but we need a plan or else everyone's shit'll freeze over and die!" barks Horace.

Melysia beckons with a proud confidence. "Diothor is stacking bodies down there. Don't count him out."

Seemingly at the sound of her voice emerges a reply from the depths, a reverberating "WOOF!" to break the stalemate. Canines flash from beneath the sandstorm like the maw of a shapeless space maggot. A third contender to the way of things makes himself known, and he is a petty god, a good but rueful one. Let rip the skins of green from the great chew toy; Yin looks too shriveled for consideration. A gush of Yang's blood and shit are let poured upon the world of thoughtless, sandy locusts — humanids, the lot of them. Yang is brought low.

Doubt disperses from the minds of the Horaces. They break the trance of hopelessness with a unified chant: "Let's wrap this up!" Only their utterances are not completely homogeneous and a few clones may have been silent. This command, however unremarkable its significance, seems to coincide with the torpedoing of witless Yin — and her wits live inside her the way Jove hath lived inside himself — threefold and chaotic, unaccomplished until late, i.e., the orderly split. Now, he is the above-most. This lasts a moment before Yin descends upon the hazy maelstrom unto a pinned Yang who from the torso down is rendered incapacitated, wriggling desperately a sequence of thuds that would knock the unstable foundations of Hedophilia out from under its undeserved gilded domes. From within the visor of Yin does Horace see a helpless gleam in the red peepers of Yang that watch helplessly at the impending torpedo, his nemesis. Yang bares his teeth, and try as he may to keep them trained on his adversary, the good dog Diothor rattles his body; Yang's neck wrings and presents itself to Yin, who'd remained just out of reach until this very point. Sickly Yin lays its maw upon that enticing flesh, vitals pulsing under its grasp out from whose side stuck out limply the head of Yang. Yin remains clamped until the pulsing ceases, felt by Horace, Hermes, Melysia, and perhaps the rest. He dies a mangled puppet of a snakey tapeworm, Yang at the lap of Diothor (who sizes down and rejoins his mistress in Yin, completing his transformation).

Yin gorges upon the tail of Yang and continues up the length like a streetlight-lit midnight bullet train, and the vagabonds Hermes, Horace, and Melysia watch until the whole of the beast is zipped across and consumed. Each throttle and gulp sends shockwaves across the land. Yin ends where she started, a detached ouroboros not so much consuming herself as her better half. Yin's blubbery tongue restores to its former glory along with clean white mandibles and slender white skin where once had been jagged teeth and patchy skin not unlike the common, undernourished Hedo. This is Yin, and Yin becomes it: healthy, healthy insofar as she might live a long life, should she not kill herself.

The numerous Horaces lax along all the spine and the original, having been entranced by the slithering of Yin along the shaft of Yang and since broken from the spell, speaks, "Is it over?"

"Is it ever?" says Hermes, seemingly not consulting his visions.

"Metaphors might've been Brahe's schtick, but I reckon we should tether her to port and coil up the rope."

"Are you anxious, friend Horace?"

"Among other things. We might have eaten Yang, but he was the stronger. I felt it as we tussled. And if not for good Diothor, we would have lost. I worry this victory is a hollow one on loan. What will happen when the next evil rears its nasty neck?"

"You are right to fear the union. The Atlanteans were onto something with that creed they've made covenant. The incarnation of this conflict will be neither Yin nor Yang."

Melysia rises from petting her dog, "I heard you were talkin' shop about Diothor, ya twats."

"It is so," replies Hermes. "These joinings are cumulative so, while Yang is stronger than Yin at the moment, Yin and dog are stronger than Yang. How does famished Brahe factor into this? And the lot of us? It is curious; the result I see in the periphery of my visions."

"What do you see?" asks Horace. "And do you know the way off this thing? I was thinking we could throw a shindig at Schlub, Yeoman, and Finkle's. See if Jebediah ever left."

"There is no time. Have a gander."

Yin bloats and changes again, pocked with

freckles of green. Twice the size means twice the stomach, and what's this beneath us, nutrients? Nothing is stopping anyone now. Stretching her maw to accommodate the ground beneath, Yin eats through the lamentations of life, men and mer. They sound as animals and little different, delicious and enticing. Children screaming in the yard and pearl clutchers gasping nonsense sound as foxes and monkeys, both. If they scream like animals, how do they expect to not be eaten? Buildings lift from their foundations and fly a bothersome debris, the crumb of a sandwich to be scraped from the corner of an eye. The Joves squeeze in their compartment as everything passes the gullet. The world Katsikoskoni is consumed in the ticking of a minute. Say, what's that bothersome blotch in the sky? Let us sit a while and digest the angle of attack.

From behind silent Horace and Hermes appears Lars; a single tear streams from the face of the doctor, solemnly, suddenly, encore! "Mein Gott! It is beautiful!"

Gaping-mouthed Horace stands dumbfounded at the cosmic phenomena. He comes to weep for the same reason as Lars, only with tears drunk on fear, "All those people . . . dead? Generations of humanid culture, what for?"

"Not quite dead," says Hermes. "They may be no

longer, but they always were. They will always be stored in the archives of time. For all their toils in innovation, these abstracts will survive all catastrophe independent of us. And there's the reincarnation angle too."

"Stow your rubbish thoughts in the hogwash bin, you feckless do-nothing! Is it not our duty to right the wrongs and do justice the sacred institutions of man and nature?"

"What we do to nature, nature does unto itself." Hermes did not look to peer into the future for his next move.

Horace throttles him by the torso. "But can't we do something about this now? After what improbable nonsense we've been through, is it beyond us?" And as he look to Hermes, he sees the phantom quivering of a lip under the snorting of a nostril, or so it seems. The eyes almost blink just as the fingers nearly fidget. He figures if he laid a finger for a pulse, he should not find it. Hermes stands so utterly still that, if Horace did not know him personally, he would have thought him dead, killed of shock or whatever normative cause. All of this to say: nothing — Hermes says nothing, if perhaps a bit dazed. Unless an illusion, Hermes's sphincter is momentarily free from the puppetry of King Monkey. Or else the hand is limp.

Horace looks to his equally useless and

panicked copies. He has no answer for himself, nor him for he. And so he looks past the snake's head to the wheezing corridors of the neck from which heaved a reckoning.

It is a wall of writhing, tortured faces fused to immaculately pink, fresh flesh. The patchwork Horaces stare at the likely original. When Yin had healed, it seems every Horace had fused to the regenerated flesh in their bid to keep the snake from disintegrating apart. A single naked Delilah stands before her fornicator, stomach round with autosex. "Why, hello there."

"What is this place?"

"Do you have a name?"

Horace points dismissively at the stomach. "For that thing?"

The woman waves him off and finishes with an open palm as an appeasing gesture to her surroundings. "That thing, this place, anything." Her every word is calculated, careful not to incite the ire of the unknown. Best be safe.

"We'll have time to think, then." Shoulders relax, maybe slump.

"Quite some time, maybe all of it." A smile is mournful and sweet. The same hand is asking to be held. "Walk with me."

No shame, no change. The thin neck of vulgar Jebediah dangles from a wall, and his body is not seen again until the cockle reemerging a few paces above the seething face glaring vitriol at the physical prime of his upright, uptight past self that stands proud in the center of the hall. If it interests you, the legs of vulgar Jebediah return to the flesh in the proper form of a swimmer, somewhere at the knees. Glistening, muscular Jebediah offers greeting and a smile, a genuine one; it always was.

To the skies return Aquabus and Washington, Hydromothra and Goatman, Waterboard and MacDiver, Flying Dutchman and Davy Jones, and Aeroscorpion who sit in a circle, celebrating their progenitor Yang. MacDiver had not simply burned himself alive; he'd reached the end state before quite a few others, perhaps before changing into something he'd not like. And from the wall bursts out Pelvis-Crusher stained utterly in blood; she never died, nor did she ever stop fighting, Sea Horsepower grunting haughtily by her side. The great wise man Gastrodomwiz sits also among them with a pleased expression at the outcome of events. The tips of his tentacles swish like a cat's tail.

Calypso is seen wearing an outfit unlike the one she died with — like she didn't much jive with the postmortem dress code and did her own thing. She acknowledges Horace and Delilah with a kill-me-now smirk as Turkey argues at her from over a table.

A door in the flesh leads to the interior of their cottage; Onemsiz and Mon have been busy setting up shop. They were always the type to keep harmony no matter the venue. Mounted as a trophy, the Goatmeister was spared his gnarly Fu Manchu and dreads. In truth, he was built around. He doesn't seem to mind. Judging by the tone of his voice, he's flattered, "Never mind if you replace the parts, is it the same ship if you change the name? Beautiful vessel, how's about Bessy this time around?"

Lars approaches from behind to meet Grimwald and Brahe, the latter naked as the day and nose intact. Clouds are unwelcome weather. Today is for clarity. A chandelier hangs above; in the grains, metallic Brahe looks down on the humanids, but he is here. If he didn't exist, he wouldn't be.

Meaty on the shoulders and a little sparse at the shins, Abraddon the butcher keeps one hand on his daughter and the other on his dog. Both arrived some time ago while Yin had consumed Yang and the world. Turban-wearing Parmacena glares from a distance with vampiric teeth that snarl, averting her gaze from beggar Joshua as he compares notes, his beggarish insights to hers.

And in the maws of the fish, the face of Jove comes face to face with Horace and Delilah. In consuming the carcass, a part of him had been lost and in turn, or, at the very least, pushed aside to share a body — or else fractured. Who knows if man eats the fish or is subsumed and changed in his eating it? Humble, quiet Jove slacks at the jaw just as the fish around him, clueless to the answer of the question that hangs in the air before them.

This is as much a reunion as it is the afterlife: the life after, more so than what comes after life. Or maybe not. Who knows, really? The entirety of this thought exercise could have been gibberish.

"We've hit a dead end."

"Where's that daft-lookin' sod?"

"At the helm, methinks. 'Tisn't farther than the way we came."

On their return, where once were men now stands something other, something humanoid? These stem cells wear black skin suits like kuroko, a sort of background actor. It seemed King Monkey had relinquished the grip on their sphincters. They gather around Delilah and Horace and, producing bashing slabs, go out with a thud, thud, thud, thud, thud.

Alone, Hermes has come from his stupor of overlaying images having seen the rest of time. He still bothers to look from the shutters of Yin's sockets straight into the sun, or perhaps off center. Because that's what eyes do. "Come aboard my spaceship, O post-cognitive castrati, and sing your monkey nonsense. And pray your life lasts so long as the singing midget is tall. Bah, don't ask. You won't anyway . . . No, I can't stop it."

"Wh . . ." In fact, this is the most pathetic-sounding "Wh . . ." one can imagine.

Can Delilah really be interrupted if she was never to finish her thought? Or was it Delilah who interrupted Hermes who *was* to say something by the machinations of fate? "Why not?" He says it as though he'd already heard the question and is mulling it over. "It may seem abrupt, but it was obvious to MacDiver who threw himself into the fire. This is the combined will of everyone aboard, the greatest differential and worst democracy."

"Not unlike the three of us at one point. Heh. Okay, rude. It wasn't a tough question to guess, but do you really know what I'm thinking?"

Hermes accuses Horace, "Do you know what you're thinking? I've seen things down to the basest unit. That means thoughts, too. I can see where every neuron fires and how fast it moves; and I would sooner die than live a moron — if ever I became so slow as I once was, the way you are now. How do I know what you'll think, you think to ask? I possess the whisper of a spirit whose inception I place at the beginning of time itself, the primordial fish. Big leagues, son. And even if that wasn't the case, I'm basically you one cousin removed."

"But we . . ."

"All partook of the fish, yes. But I ate him twice, and that sufficed — an acquired taste, if you will. Hm!" he pauses with a chortle, perhaps amused at his next line. So, by then having recovered his wits, he continues, "Eat your cake and eat it too, as Brahe might put it. It was incest of the self. You did it too, in a way, however late." An eyebrow furls.

The corner of Delilah's lip curls smugly and Horace is only mildly embarrassed — only.

"It seems Jove was a narcissist; and so the one-dimensional consciousness that is Delilah congregates with the one-dimensional consciousness that is Horace. You are wed; kiss the bride or some bother. In each other's eyes ye see the stars no differently than were ye to look therefore out the glass. Yes, there was such a time we three were one, a three-dimensional consciousness at least one order more than most, though nary productive in the least. Why do you think that is, two-dimensional creature? Do not think: I will tell you as much, you bidimensional slug . . . I have been harsh, for two is more than one, and one is that which shoots straight and true at its goal in spite of the obstacles. And as man fights another, so too does the union of cosmic

Yang fight against himself. O, once multidimensional Jove, an unaccomplished loser in your own right, were split asunder and ascended the ranks threefold, only to fight amongst himselves and achieve an equalized nothing anyway, no different than if they three had done nothing at all, which is what he, the one, had done once upon a time, cunning bugger — to intuit a multidimensional motivational vector equals zero, whether a model of us three or all the world in a Yinnite blender. It all goes to zero."

Horace asks anon, "That makes about as much sense as it does, but I suppose some of those who claim you can say a lot without meaning anything themselves go long without understanding a thing, and I reckon that's me. At the very least, I think I've gathered it's better to start a loser than end one." He breathes. "How does it feel knowing you're the most conscious person 'alive', if you can call it that, aye?"

Hermes has the good sense to let the poor man finish his question. "Do you think it chance we happened upon these powers, coincidence that a post-natal giraffe is bequeathed the 'power' to run? It is the way of things, and things are decided by an even higher power. As a conscious being, I but pay witness. We are all as good as slaves to King Monkey. It would take a pure act of randomness . . .

no, unlogic to break free, a continuous string of un-logics, in fact, but then we'd be at the whims and rules of a regent — and we were, for a time. They don't see each other very often, if ever, you see. Do you think our breakage of selves coincidence? Everything coincides, I suppose. No matter. It's as if we were a logical exercise of the present Regent Chaos or absent King Monkey. Can we but rise from the confines of nature and defy by will what no man has done before, if even we are the first of this world and order? That is what I thought until we found all Atlantis seemed to possess a similar power of incarnation." He pauses a moment despite knowing what he is going to say. "You've seen what our compatriots have become. At such a moment King Monkey decides to stop puppeteering sphincters, these slates lose themselves, their personae; these are the machinations of King Monkey the Deterministic, personification of nature itself deified by the lesser conscious. Are my words even my own? That asshole makes us blabber such nonsense. And who's to say King Monkey has it any better, that he isn't subject to the whims of Emperor Spineless Sleazebag, the One Who Smiles at You? The Great Organized Book Club has been preaching this for years, the yokels. Well, they did before they got co-opted by the very same. Bah, the wheel will be reinvented, reincarnated, with the mindstream reincarnating itself and its very idea, like it or not, reinvented by even me, just as we will be reincarnated into something not entirely dissimilar to ourselves. It only takes time, patience, and extreme prejudice. Why should we break the wheel of anti-will? Let it be someone else: why us? Let it be Jove III for whom will be granted divine intervention from whatever such pantheon rules King Monkey . . . Do rules follow rules? And their rules? So fucking meta, this nesting of rules in which we've come to roost. It's sodding recursion, a buggered jackanapery."

"Pick that up from Melysia?" prods Delilah before being cut off by Horace who asks his last of Hermes, "That's all well and good, but what's the meaning of life?"

He ponders a moment and shrugs. Delilah of all people answers, "Life is when you're the bottom monkey high on cortisol waiting for the top of your troupe to show a hint of weakness so you and your buddies get together and tear his balls off. Well, it's not the worst thing, not having balls."

Horace peers into the sun that approaches ever nearer and disregards the woman, "But never mind that. I've had a thought on the Atlantean's reincarnation schtick: I figure it's either reincarnation — that's the narrative — or everyone is so similar that we might as well be talking to the same person; it only seems like they're reincarnating. And one more thing to get off my mind before we burn up: I'd've thought we'd be replaced by something more interesting like a hive mind that merges across time, or perhaps it's no less as base as Turkey's, Goatman's, and Abraddon's multi-chronological consciousness integration if even they can do it. Or, if an entity in the future already merged all consciousnesses across all time, maybe we've been joined forever along in a feedback system that goes one way where King Monkey talks to us and not the other way round. Or maybe an intelligence so far removed from its base instincts will cease to exist at all; why would it want to? Could that be why we're broken down into parts; the metaphysical is made physical and the metaphysical physical, which is to say Hedophilia is both and neither the crown jewel and a slummy sprawl? And that any one person is a mix of single-dimensional, polytheistic personalities — who for simplicity tend to champion one — instead of a single, omnipotent being. Can you imagine if every five seconds you were possessed of a different demon from the pantheon that sways you off course. Couldn't get anything done, I reckon. So who, really, is Yin and where can we find King Monkey? Now that everyone shares a body, where can Autismos run from Neurotypicles, two eternal nemeses that react violently at both the emergent and molecular levels? Does trailblazing Autismos escape into the borders of outer space forever expanding away from the normative establishments that build in the wake of his exodus? And what will become of us?"

Delilah offers a closing statement characteristic of a closeted romantic come to bear: "I damn well hope I get a laser sword for my troubles. Or do I turn into a baroque green-thing? Will we make like Autismos and surrender our belongings and with due haste begone, mass for energy? Torture one's bloodline long enough and these diasporous people will want nothing but to schlep for schlepping's sake! Skedaddle, then, cowardly Ashkenigga! Bah!" But these were just as much the words of engorged Yin, muttering unto herself.

A disembodied, booming voice shouts not through space, but as a vibration through all living things of adequate consciousness, "THE GREAT FILTER!" And it repeats as though it had been shouting for all eternity. Only now do we hear it; you, me, everyone. For all intents and purposes, God is speaking to you among the other things you hear and have heard: The thoughts in the palace overflow with rabble battering at the gates. Before this, you were not conscious enough for this particular revelation. Redundant, yes, but it bears repeating lest it slips from thy mind, lost to eternity. But that's why I wrote it down. For you see, writing this was an ordeal of multidimensional consciousness, several years on and off. Only once the dimensions aligned like planets was I able to sit down and write for a month, one year at a time. Yes, I am a narcissist and think highly of myself; I am very cognitive, yes I am — I hear you think I think, and that may be true, but I considered it only after I thought you thinking it; it was a good idea. I thank you kindly for that idea.

— These were the last mangled thoughts of Yin in the fashion of a spurt of intuition, an unwelcome intrusion on the psyche that thought to invite itself to the palace. If she had the time or means, she might jot it down to later write in a journal. Should Bessy? Meh and a thud, thud, thud!

Epilogue

Tired Eschatology of a 9–5; Push Your Buttons While I Have Gone

The emergence of this happenstance would lead the cumulative reincarnation of critters and dirt to merge with something greater still, though it is not known to us how conscious the sun might be. And yet, as the foodthing enters the gullet, so too might it join with man and plant its likeness fully in the mind. A lesser-dimensional consciousness might eat a pretzel and think it tastes of salt, but a higher consciousness might assimilate it, and as he eats it, realizes he gives consciousness unto it, and it may think: Lo, I have become one with you and here is what I think: "salt." Yes, taste is but a thought of the thing within you translated for convenience.

Just as we are most conscious of the things before us, so too do we, in a way, give consciousness unto it — the flickering of an ego in the attic lit by a dusty light bulb. For shame:

Through the millennia, man eats ham and grows a consciousness little by little until he wakes. By far, the lot of us have waken but once upon a toddle, but nary at all later — you know what I mean. It is the moment you snap into reality and everything becomes a continuous stream of consciousness. And after the fact, the nutrients are wasted on the arms and legs, which will twiddle thumbs and sit dispatiently on a leash led by another led by another led by another to whom you willfully yet begrudgingly submit, coward. Woe! The stars are stolen away by smog sickly grey and we have devolved into conscientiousness, nary a dream and lesser of conscience, only suits of black and drab, unembroidered napkins draped from the white collars of lap dogs. Perhaps rubbish in the palm of a polymath is worth more than all the world in the hands of a common Hedo who would make a circus out of it. In the usual case of proverbs, there is no guarantee this one will take root.

It was from Brahe Melysia borrowed the sun to see past the infernal smog of Hedophilia, impure crown jewel of King Monkey's domain. Who need be impressed? Pearls before swine and all that, only these swine roll contently in the muck of sin within the confines of their purview, clouded from the stars and imaginings of preindustrial men and their flamboyant thrifts. The fall of the last bastion and frontier, Nusquam, under whose sun simple truths were most clear, damned the fate of the rest of the world already teetering on the edge, pushed up by the dormant evils of spinelessness and insincerity, lurking in the smog like lanky vampires pale with the skin of slovenly maggots. These vampires are not cool, and whatever is the point of an uncool vampire, a lesser asshole? Let the greater asshole galvanize you to the good, O destitute conmen and middling sociopaths who might this read, provided you are not too busy hustling and making fools of yourselves to be decent, consistent folk. Or, at the very least, renounce attachment and become the neutrality that stands at the helm and watches purification dispassionately from afar or within. Or why even this? Bah! Dick around then, with your dicks that are small.

A cosmic serpent neither flies nor glides but flows through space and gazes on a star through slits that shine white brighter than scales aglimmer — a mirror unto sender never longer swooning over Hedophilic smog, semper squalor razed 'neath fiery gaze ephemeral — impregnating the sun.